Callisto Lodwick

THE
DROWNED SIREN

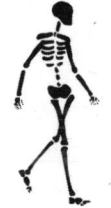

DATURA BOOKS
An imprint of Watkins Media Ltd

Unit 11, Shepperton House
89-93 Shepperton Road
London N1 3DF
UK

daturabooks.com
No Three Rules

A Datura Books paperback original, 2026

Copyright © Callisto Lodwick 2026

Edited by Gemma Creffield
Cover by Sarah O'Flaherty
Set in Meridien

All rights reserved. Callisto Lodwick asserts the moral right to be identified as the author of this work. A catalogue record for this book is available from the British Library.

This novel is entirely a work of fiction. Names, characters, places, and incidents are the products of the author's imagination or are used fictitiously. Any resemblance to actual events, locales, organizations or persons, living or dead, is entirely coincidental.

Sales of this book without a front cover may be unauthorized. If this book is coverless, it may have been reported to the publisher as "unsold and destroyed" and neither the author nor the publisher may have received payment for it.

Datura Books and the Datura Books icon are registered trademarks of Watkins Media Ltd.

ISBN 978 1 91741 518 7
Ebook ISBN 978 1 91741 519 4

Printed and bound in the United Kingdom by CPI Group (UK) Ltd, Croydon CR0 4YY

The manufacturer's authorised representative in the EU for product safety is eucomply OÜ – Pärnu mnt 139b-14, 11317 Tallinn, Estonia,
hello@eucompliancepartner.com; www.eucompliancepartner.com

9 8 7 6 5 4 3 2 1

To the students of St Andrews

7th May, 7:30.

12.5 hours after the party.

The reporters arrive a few hours after the police. They swarm onto the streets of the town like cockroaches, rushing around with their shining, shell-like cameras. From every window, students peek out, watchful. These are the lucky ones, who either have not or will not be questioned by the police. They are simply poised to take in the spectacle: the watchers watching watchers.

All eyes, cameras and flashes are trained on one lonely figure, sitting on a set of granite steps. Above her towers the Victorian Gothic hotel, grandiose in the height of its windows and the details carved into its facade. The girl looks terribly small against it, and her torn dress and puffy eyes only add to the sense of pity the crowd feels. As the cameras snap photo after photo, she becomes less of a person and more of a painting: something you would gawp at in a museum. And indeed, in the weeks and months to come, this will be the image attached to the case: the iconic photo of a young woman in the prime of her life, weeping on the steps of a hotel with muddy fingers and a gown stained – even if only metaphorically – in blood.

It has all gone very well, the girl thinks. She has chosen her pose perfectly and artfully stained her face so her makeup runs just so. She looks at the cameras just enough so that every glimpse causes a frenzy of flashes. Her mind may still be cloudy with alcohol, exhausted from the endless police questioning, but she has kept her wits about her. She remembers how to present herself.

And all will go well. All must go well. She planned it – no, she didn't plan it – it was all an accident – wasn't it? She told the police all the correct things, the truth – not the whole truth perhaps, but whoever says that?

Her mind is spinning. Her composure slips – not much, but enough for her pose to falter and her legs to lose their grip and send her slipping down the staircase. This is unacceptable. To lose composure – to be made to look too vulnerable, in a way that ceases to be beautiful, that renders her merely human – that she cannot afford.

She steels her mind and staggers to her feet. She allows one last look back at the cameras – a tearful shot for them to remember her by – before she strides back into the ruined hotel, ready to sort through her mind and figure out what happened last night.

6th May, 00.00.

Nineteen hours before the party.

A young woman sits at her desk, staring out her bay windows at the expanse of sea. It has long since faded to darkness, marked by an empty expanse of blackness instead of the twinkling lights of her surroundings. She will miss this view, she thinks. She'll never be able to come back and visit. After tonight, she will never show her face in this town again.

The sixth of May. Finally midnight. On the morning of the seventh she will pack her bags and leave, step onto the half-four train, arrive at the airport by six. Her plane takes off at eight-thirty, then she will be ferried into a brand-new world where a glorious life awaits. But for now, it is the sixth, her last day in this university town, and she is turning twenty-two.

Everyone will come tonight. Everyone must. No invitations have explicitly been sent, but the word has been spread; Eleanor Sanders is renting out the Radcliffe Hotel for her twenty-second birthday. *The* Radcliffe Hotel, with its sweeping sea views and the mysterious penthouse apartment, the one Eleanor started renting last year and which no one else is known to have been in. *The* Eleanor Sanders, who returned after one summer with a book deal and hundreds of thousands of Instagram followers and Hollywood blowing up her phone. To miss this would be insanity. So, hundreds of students cancelled their flights home, postponed their summer jobs and stayed in town a few days more after exams – waiting to see what Eleanor Sanders would put on.

6th May, 8.34 AM.

Eleven hours until the party.

The sea is wonderful in the morning. It is lovely at any time of day, but in the hours after dawn, when the air is still clean and fresh and carries the scent of promise – that is the time when something truly magical occurs in the water. That is the moment that Eleanor is truly allowed to be free.

She dives, somersaults, spins, and paddles backward with glee. In the ocean, she is sleek, seal-like, strong and fast enough to swim for hours and miles on end. In another life, she would like to have pursued swimming as a career. But the world can only fulfil so many impossible dreams, and Eleanor has already had her share of luck. No, not luck – hard work. Anyway, she doesn't have it in her to strive towards a world-class swimming goal after the last few years.

She has already been in the water for an hour: swimming makeshift lengths, creating her own sets, and just paddling about during her rests. She used to train with the university swim team, but she hasn't visited in the past year. Not since LA. She has time, but it would distract from her work. Ruin her image. One becomes alluring through seclusion from people, not socialisation.

Memories of California slip into her mind, carried on the waves all the way from the Pacific. It was so warm there, so lovely. The waves were larger and more challenging to swim around, but brilliant to body surf on. She learnt to surf there – though 'learnt' was a strong word, as she was still terrible. Jack had taken her, and he'd held her gently as he tried to teach her how to balance – but she can't think of Jack now, not after everything that happened. He still confuses her: she can't work out if she misses him or not. Perhaps it was the idea of him, the same thing that had driven her into his arms in the first place. Or more accurately, driven him into hers.

The water suddenly turns chilly: it is colder without Jack to keep her warm, she thinks. She swims back to the beach, taking care not to step on the shells as she gets out. Spread out to dry, they look like tiny butterflies. Odd, how something can become so beautiful only after it is dead.

She should tell George that. If only he could be bothered to talk to her. This evening, if she has her way, he will be forced to.

The Radcliffe is only steps from the beach: close enough that Eleanor didn't bother to bring shoes. She slips through a side door, a route she knows well, and patters up the plush stairs to her penthouse, dripping salt water in her wake. Over the past year, she's created a well-worn path of bleached white carpet, the salinity too ingrained for the staff to remove. It is comforting to know she's left her mark.

Tonight, she hopes, she will leave an even bigger one.

3rd September.

Three years and eight months before the party.

Her mother left St Andrews a few hours after dropping her daughter off at her student hall, once her room was arranged to look slightly less clinical. They stood in the doorway, at an impasse: for the first time in her life, there was nothing left for her mother to do. She didn't belong in her daughter's new life.

Eleanor watched her drive away but forced herself to turn before her mother's car faded into a dot on the horizon. She wasn't a toddler, and she wouldn't be attached like one. Besides, some students had travelled halfway across the globe to come here. She was four hundred miles away from home, a village two hours from London that she had lived in for eighteen years and had seen every corner of. Her summer had been spent counting down the days until escape, yet now that it was here a strange melancholy hung over her.

The girls in the next room along invited her in for drinks, but Eleanor slipped away after half an hour. She told herself it was because it was all too overwhelming – the room too stuffy, the strangers acting too familiar – but really there was a strange emptiness at the heart of their interaction. A lack of authenticity or grandeur. It was just part of making friends, Eleanor told herself, the 'awkward' stage, but making friends had never been her forte – she had spent life as the awkward girl in the corner, the one who never quite understood people the way those around her did, whose words never came out quite right. She had put this down to size – there had been hardly anyone in her village, let alone a group of like-minded young women. Here, she had decided, everything would change; at long last she would meet someone worldly, someone important, someone who would see her for what she really was and embrace it.

So to settle down already – to buddy up with the first group of people she found – seemed impossibly benign. Eleanor had been dreaming of escape, of adventure, of the sort of epic friendships you read about in fantasy novels, and she wasn't getting that in her dorm.

She'd travelled all morning, and she was alone for the first time in her life. So, as darkness fell, and a stream of people rushed out the students' halls towards the clubs, Eleanor walked out by herself.

It was cold and a light drizzle had begun to fall. Eleanor took one look at the queue outside the student union's club and walked on, wandering past the shops she'd strolled by with her mother just hours earlier. It all looked so different in the dark, so imposing.

Then the buildings petered out, and Eleanor heard what she was looking for.

A great expanse of darkness lay before her: terrifying, perhaps, but thrilling also. Eleanor rushed forward, down the steps and onto the sand, pulling off her shoes as she raced towards the waves. The frigid water enveloped her toes, and she gave an involuntary shudder: relief and thrill, mixed in one. This was what she'd come here for, this was why she'd chosen this small Scottish town over livelier universities in behemoths of cities. So much water. And it was all hers.

Without thinking, she pulled off the rest of her clothes and tossed them behind her. The water sent more shocks through her body as she waded in, but she didn't care. Instead, she splashed towards the depths and dived expectantly. The cold was gleeful, her sudden freedom of movement thrilling; she laughed manically as she crested the waves and broke the surface. There were no bored acquaintances with glazed-over expressions here, no endless petty politics in an attempt score an invite to the hottest party. This was adventure. This was grandeur. This great, open expanse waiting to be filled: this was what awaited her. Eleanor opened her mouth and screamed with glee.

She shrugged her clothes on and stumbled back, shivering, down side streets she'd never seen before. A few drunks looked at her curiously, but she waved them off: she was too high on life to bother with those who'd dulled their senses to it. Yet, as she approached her hall, her feet twisted in another direction.

The old library was still open, even at this hour. It was much smaller than the main library and was housed in what used to be an old stone church. The heating was ineffectual and intermittent, but it was quiet and isolated without being Eleanor's prison of a room. Best of all, it was full of books.

The titles were all from the first half of the last century or older: Eleanor's eyes brushed over them greedily. Here a Virginia Woolf, there a first edition Dickens. A textbook on archaeology from the 1880s, a treatise on the history of the Church in Scotland.

What would it be like, Eleanor wondered, to be remembered like that? To have your name in gilded letters for thousands of pairs of hands to hold. To have your words devoured by eyes across the world? She thought of her own attempts at writing, lying half-finished at home, and grimaced.

Eleanor slipped through empty corridors: the fluorescent lights were too slow for her, flicking on a second after she scurried past. She rifled through the printer and returned to the library's centre with stacks of paper, piled in haphazard haste. Eleanor rammed a pen she stole from the front desk so hard into the paper the ink splattered, and she did not look up for the rest of the night.

She wrote for hours. The rain fled, the moon sank and the sun peered over the horizon. Eleanor's head ached and her hand throbbed, but she refused to stop: it wasn't worth it, would never be worth it, until she had something that could rival the classics before her. Something that would forge her name into iron, chisel it into stone, make it something that would rest with weight upon others' tongues.

It wasn't right. There was something off with everything she'd put on the page. In the harsh light of day, her writing was revealed as nothing more than the raving squiggles of a mad woman. All of it was trite and useless and completely and utterly forgettable.

The door to the library creaked open. Eleanor spun in her seat: how dare someone intrude her sanctuary? In a few short hours, she had forgotten the notion that anyone else could be so enlightened as to seek refuge among the shelves. Deep within her, a serpent raised its tail in ire: it would spit on this stranger, drag them down and make them forget they had ever seen her.

The intruder was a bespectacled man, around thirty, holding a coffee cup to try and bring some life to his eyes. His gaze roved over Eleanor with bemusement – the thought that a drunk undergrad had ended up here was comical. That look was worse than any other reaction: he hadn't worried for her, hadn't glanced at her papers. She was something to chuckle over, something to mock.

That evening, Eleanor's hall held a bonfire: a friend-finding exercise. Except, everyone else already seemed to have friends. Eleanor arrived late, once the shadows had descended and faces had turned formless, carrying a shoulder bag. She didn't reach for its contents until the flames were close enough to lick her boots. In once swift movement, she pulled out her papers, blotted and ink stained, and cast them into the fire. The tongues licked greedily at her work, devouring it within seconds. Eleanor stayed watching, eyes locked to the fire until every last sheet turned to ash.

She didn't need that work. It was petty, repulsive, boring. It would be different here. She was born again, baptised by the North Sea. She would forge something new, something better: a book, a friendship, a life. There was something inside her, coiled and ready to unleash. She would not deny it. It held the promise of adulthood, of freedom and she refused to let it slip away.

6th May, 9:53.

Nine hours until the party.

Eleanor keeps a leisurely pace as she strolls down the high street. Her hair is neatly styled; her trench coat unbuttoned so it flaps just so. No one who sees her would know she's been walking up and down this road for the past half-hour, giving each coffee shop window unbothered glances as she goes.

There – a promising bow perches upon a woman's head in the window of one of the chains St Andrews' town council has begrudgingly allowed to blot their main tourist road (just not too many, and only in buildings with enough character, whatever that means). Cheyenne would never frequent such an establishment – she's too economically conscious to support large corporations that exploit their workers. She prefers small tea shops that are forced to exploit their workers due to rising energy bills.

Sure enough, there they are at the counter: Raquelle at the head of the pack, her list of everyone's orders as overwhelming as the massive pink bow perched above her ponytail; Sam behind, casually cool in his khaki shorts, one arm wrapped around Gina, who, clad head to toe in tweed, looks like a caricature of a Brit drawn by an American. But Cheyenne likes that sort of thing, so who is Gina to argue?

"Henry, Gina!" Eleanor calls as she steps into the tea shop. "Raquelle," she adds when the girl fumes at almost being forgotten. Her parents own around half of Gloucestershire; she isn't used to being ignored. Eleanor gives them all a broad smile as she asks, "Are you coming to the party tonight?"

Raquelle shrugs. "Not sure."

"Well, you'd better make up your mind soon!" Eleanor raises her voice, starts garnering looks from the tables nearby. "I'd so hate for you to miss it, our last big event together."

"There's still graduation," Raquelle mutters, her faced flushed from the nearby scrutiny. A first-year leans in to whisper to her friend. This will be all over the town in an hour.

"You know graduation won't be nearly as fun." Eleanor has no plan to be in the country, let alone the town, for graduation, but Raquelle has no need to know that. "There's a seat in the Radcliffe's bar with your name on it."

"We'll be there," Sam assures her – always nice, Sam, far too good for the sharks that swirl around him – and Eleanor flashes him a smile. "Wonderful!"

She doesn't give them the pleasure of her leaving: instead, she leans closer and asks what they're getting. "The almond hot chocolate is delicious. Oh, but I forgot: Gina can't have nuts, can she?" She makes a sympathetic face. "Such a shame to live like that."

"I cope," Gina replies in monotone. Beautiful hair, Gina – perfect ringlets cascading in an artfully framed twist around her face. She claims it's natural, but everyone around her has eyes – and Eleanor, at the very least, has a brain.

Eleanor smiles, flips her hair. She learnt the move from Cheyenne, though she'd never admit it. "I'll let the caterers know tonight. I think there were some dishes that might have to be changed – wouldn't want you getting hurt. And one more thing–" her voice drops to a stage whisper, and the entire café falls into a hush to hear her words "– make sure George and Cheyenne come around. I've got something I need to say to them, and it really can't wait."

She beams one last grin and steps back into the morning sunlight, acutely aware of the eyes fixed on her back: Raquelle and Gina staring daggers; Sam perplexed; the rest of the customers wide-eyed and awestruck.

Isn't it wonderful, Eleanor thinks, to have power?

10th September.

Three years and eight months before the party.

Eleanor fidgeted uneasily outside the lecture hall, one finger playing with the straps of her bag. She felt copiously alone in a sea of people: everyone else was already buddied up, happily chatting to some person they met at dinner or at coffee or in their last lecture. It all seemed mysteriously simple, like they all had the key to a sect of knowledge forbidden to Eleanor. How exceptionally unfair.

She should talk to someone. Walk over, chat them up, work the crowd. But she'd been at that all week, and her mind was numb with the swirl of names and faces she'd attempted to memorise and then promptly forgotten. Today, just for an hour or two, she could use a rest. So, when she slipped down the aisle of the lecture hall to the front row, she was prepared for an hour of solitude.

And then someone sat next to her.

Technically there were two people, but it was forgivable that Eleanor's attention was drawn to the first. She was tall, blonde, tanned: the sort of girl you expected to step from the pages of a magazine. Her teeth were white, her eyes were blue and when she opened her mouth to introduce herself, her accent was American.

"Cheyenne," she said. Even her smile was perfect. "From Los Angeles." She tilted her head quizzically. "I haven't seen you around."

"I haven't been out all that much." Not quite true: Eleanor had forced herself out every night this week, tottering to the nearest nightclub with whoever she'd met at dinner that day. But the bars spooked her: she disliked the crush, the smell of sweat, didn't trust the people around her enough to drink the alcohol that would numb her mind to all of that. Meanwhile this girl, she was sure, was out all night, partying at the trendiest underground clubs before being whisked into some exclusive afterparty fuelled by young couples taking endless lines of cocaine. She wondered what Cheyenne looked like with her clothes off, then instantly banished the thought.

Cheyenne tossed her head, sending her ruler-straight hair into a fashionable cascade of volume and layers. "You have to get away from the main streets," she said, confirming Eleanor's suspicions. "You should come with us sometime. This is George," she added, pointing at the mousy-looking boy next to her. He looked very proper in his green turtleneck, rendered forgettable by Cheyenne in her blouse and trench coat. "Lives a few doors down from me. We're both doing history and economics. Got all the same classes together."

"I'm doing history too," Eleanor said. "And thinking about adding economics." She would never have been allowed to combine the two in England – but up in Scotland, students could pick and choose whatever they liked, even after they arrived at university.

Eleanor had never considered taking economics in her life, but Cheyenne was so suave and cool, and pretty, and she had talked to Eleanor first. No one had done that in the entire week since she'd been at uni.

"Excellent!" Cheyenne's eyes shone. "Definitely do it! George, our gang's got a third member!"

Because it was Cheyenne, what she said went. As soon as the lecture ended – some dull drivel about the global significance of social anthropology – Cheyenne linked her arms with Eleanor and George and dragged the pair outside. "You're from England, yes?" she asked Eleanor, though it was less of a question and more of a command for Eleanor to fulfil.

"Of course. Not far from London."

"Oh, that's gorgeous. Perfect. I love England. Love Scotland, too. Have you seen much of the country?"

"Barely," Eleanor admitted. "We always go to Europe for holidays. Too rainy up here."

"But it's sunny now!" Cheyenne gestured around them with a broad grin. "And the perfect temperature – it's always too hot back in LA. I'm sure the beach is perfect!"

"I swim there often," Eleanor admitted. She had returned to the ocean almost mechanically, whenever the chattering crowds in the dining hall or the shifting faces in the club became too much. The ocean was gentle, all-encompassing, relentless. It would protect her – or if it didn't, she could master it with her own strength, cutting through the water and relishing the sensation of it parting before her. Above all, she was completely invisible, completely untethered, completely and utterly free.

To say all of this to a strange girl – no matter how beautiful she was, or how the glow of her smile warmed Eleanor from the inside out – was impossible. "It's beautiful," was all Eleanor could say. "And exhilarating. And liberating." Now she just sounded like a dictionary. Idiot.

But Cheyenne couldn't hear Eleanor's deprecating thoughts. She only smiled and wrapped an arm around Eleanor's shoulder. "Poetic," she said. "And so brave – surely it must be freezing?"

"That's half the point." Eleanor tried a casual smile, like she was used to speaking to strange girls about swimming.

"Awesome. And it must be so good for you!" Cheyenne was already moving in the direction of the sea, chatting all the while about how the closest she'd come to the beach here was the top of the local cliffs, how fresh the sea air seemed, how even the seagulls snatching snacks were endearing. Every so often, she turned to ask a question of Eleanor or George – sometimes about the country, sometimes about their personal lives. Where had Eleanor gone to school? What were George's thoughts on beach holidays? Was the latest scandal about the Prime Minister true? She spoke as if Eleanor or George knew him personally. Had either of them ever been to California and would they be interested in visiting? Eleanor paused, unsure what the right answer was. She settled on: "Only if you show me around". Cheyenne beamed, and Eleanor heaved an inward sigh of relief.

George sidled up next to Eleanor and bent down to whisper in her ear; Cheyenne was too lost in her own world to notice. "Don't mind her. She's just enthusiastic. But she's lovely, really."

Eleanor didn't need to be told: she had eyes to see. But she thanked him anyway and gave him a genuine smile. Poor George was so perpetually on-edge, he needed something to soothe him. Even the sudden squawk of a seagull threatened to send him jumping into the sea.

Cheyenne squealed with excitement the moment they stepped foot on the sand. "Take your shoes off, George," she commanded as she stepped out of her shiny leather boots; Eleanor's own trainers felt suddenly inadequate.

"Do you have to wear a wetsuit when you go in?" Cheyenne asked as they approached the water, and the fine sand began to harden beneath their feet. "That's what surfers have to do at home, unless it's the hottest day of the year."

"If I go at night, I swim naked," Eleanor admitted.

Cheyenne's eyes lit up. "Fantastic. Isn't that amazing, George?"

"If I say yes, you'll think I want to look at naked women," he retorted. George was hanging back, reluctant to get his feet wet. Cheyenne just rolled her eyes at him.

"He's trying to be proper," she stage-whispered to Eleanor: there was no doubt George was able to hear. "But you should see him after three glasses of wine. He's actually a huge lightweight."

"Be nice, or I'll push you in," George retorted.

Cheyenne only tossed her hair and raised an eyebrow at Eleanor. "See? He does have some spirit when he wants to."

Eleanor was spared from thinking of a witty retort as a wave came in, submerging her and Cheyenne's ankles in the chill. Cheyenne gasped and clutched Eleanor's arm for balance. "You swim in this?"

"It's not so bad, once you start moving." She took Cheyenne's elbow in turn, steadying her. "Just take another step in – look, you're already used to it."

Cheyenne kept making noises somewhere between horror and delight as they grew deeper. They rolled up their trousers – Cheyenne didn't seem to care that her fine linen might wrinkle, and Eleanor's jeans were too battered for her to care. Eleanor was careful not to lead them in too deep, on the off chance a freak wave came up and drenched them.

"I could do a minute," Cheyenne declared, chewing her lip as she stared across the waves. "As long as I was moving the entire time. Then I'd have to get out."

Eleanor tsked. "As long as you keep swimming, you'd be fine."

"I don't believe you."

"Oh, I am very confident in your abilities."

It was true. Cheyenne has such confidence and verve it seemed possible that any obstacle would simply melt away at her touch. The water itself would warm up by the fire of her own ambition.

Cheyenne giggled: it was too hot for Eleanor to tell whether her cheeks were red from the sun or a blush. "We'll just have to try it one day." She glanced back to call to George, but stopped short when she saw the distance between them and the shore. "Look how far we've come!" she cried with glee.

"Should we head back? We probably shouldn't leave George waiting."

"Oh, George will be fine – let's stay a little more. Just a minute."

The sun beat down on them as Cheyenne dipped her fingers into the water. She placed them in her mouth and sucked hard. "Salty." She cocked her head. "Tastes like Los Angeles – only without the asphalt."

"Were you expecting it to be candy-flavoured?"

Cheyenne shook her head and fixed her eyes on the horizon. "No. But it's easy to forget that all the seas are connected – that I might have swum in this same water back home. This place feels like another world."

"It might as well be." How could she say that it was Cheyenne who made Eleanor feel otherworldly?

Cheyenne smiled. "I'm glad I came."

A sudden wave lapped dangerously close to their trousers; both girls squealed. "I think that might have been our cue," Eleanor remarked, glancing back at George. He was staring out at them, but she was too far away to read the expression on his face.

"Don't mind George; he's just precious," Cheyenne muttered as they strolled back to shore. Yet, as soon as they reached him, Cheyenne practically jumped into his arms. She garbled on about how beautiful it was, and how chilling, and how Eleanor was almost superhuman for swimming in there without clothes.

"You'll come next time," she commanded, staring George right in the eye. She was a few inches shorter than him, but her presence was such that they seemed to be the same height.

"If you say so," George replied, and winked at Eleanor over Cheyenne's head.

The sand stuck to their feet as they walked back, but Cheyenne didn't seem to mind. When she strolled barefoot onto the pavement without blinking an eye, she seemed every inch the California surfer chick: if only she had denim shorts and sunglasses.

"I have those at home," Cheyenne admitted when Eleanor said as much. "I left them though – didn't think they'd match the style here."

"And what style is that?" Eleanor asked.

"George's, of course." She gave him a good-natured shove. "You know he went to Eton?"

George went bright red. "You don't have to mention that every five minutes."

"Half your wardrobe is tweed." Cheyenne leaned in and gave him a flirty kiss on the cheek. Eleanor winced even as he pushed her away. "Don't be ashamed – I think it's very romantic."

A devilish twinkle sparked in George's eyes. "What would you do if I said I was moving to the US?"

"Call your parents and have them disown you."

"You're so cruel."

Cheyenne turned on her heel to grin at Eleanor. "You are coming for lunch, aren't you? We've missed the catered one in halls, but the food's so bad it's no real tragedy – and I know the *nicest* restaurant. It's got pictures of the Queen and everything."

Eleanor was meant to be on a budget, but Cheyenne's arm was wrapped around her own, her laugh was in her ear, and her palm was warm against her skin, still sticky from the salt spray. Half an hour later, when Eleanor was sitting on a plush restaurant seat with Cheyenne grinning across from her, she felt like the luckiest girl in the world.

The next day, Eleanor was enrolled in history and economics, and within a week, she, Cheyenne and George were inseparable. Cheyenne took her out, as promised. Each night, Eleanor watched her twine her slender body around a boy until she had to look away, her cheeks burning. She waited for Cheyenne and George outside their dorm building in the mornings and they'd walk to class together. They got lunch side-by-side as Cheyenne grilled the other two about their lives in the UK. "It's so quaint!" she'd say as she heard about Eleanor's village or George's boarding school. "Just like out of a movie!" Neither corrected her. After all, Cheyenne was from Los Angeles and what could be more exciting than that? This, Eleanor was certain, was the grandeur that was promised to her.

She talked to George less, and never without Cheyenne. Cheyenne was the Sun and they were planets, passing each other intermittently in their orbits. But he was a nice man – quiet and thoughtful. He went along with anything and preferred to watch drama rather than create it. Exactly, Eleanor thought, what Cheyenne would want in a friend. She often wondered what they talked about, late at night, once Eleanor had gone back to her own halls. There was nothing romantic, she was certain of that, but who did they talk about? What secrets passed between their lips during the witching hour? What friendship did they share that Eleanor, somehow, despite her proximity, could not access?

She told herself it didn't matter. Cheyenne was hers. She only chatted to George because they lived in the same halls. Sometimes, in her wildest dreams, she liked to imagine they were talking about her. Cheyenne saying how wonderful Eleanor was, how much she wanted to kiss her, to take her back to LA and spend days lounging on the sand...

No. Those were dangerous thoughts. A friendship, Eleanor told herself, a magical friendship right out of a book – that was all she could hope for. More than hope for, she had it. She was filling the expanse of her own empty sea, day by day, moment by moment. Yet late at night, when she should have been asleep, she still typed out stories about two girls lying together, one from London, one from LA. The glee she felt was sickening, but she loved it all the same.

16th September.

Three years and eight months before the party.

"Try that on," Cheyenne ordered with a smile. She stood next to Eleanor in a vintage boutique, the kind that took old women's throwaways or charity shop dregs and charged eye-wateringly high prices for them. Her hands held a dark red vest, checkered with tweed. It was the sort of thing socialites wore back in the eighties, the kind Eleanor would never have touched if Cheyenne's fingers weren't holding it. "I really think it'll suit you."

"Are you sure?" Eleanor had never stepped into this kind of shop in her life. The dim lighting, the wood panelling and the smell of mothballs lurking amongst oversize coats was all disconcertingly new to her. Only Cheyenne's perfume, already recognisable after only a week together, was familiar.

"Certain," she replied, with all the confidence of a woman who spent her life watching film stars parade down the red carpet. Eleanor had never grilled Cheyenne about life in LA, but this was the sort of thing she could easily imagine occurring. In her fantasies, the paparazzi confused Cheyenne for an A-lister; they swarmed her, desperate for a flash of her body to plaster in magazines, and it was Eleanor who batted them away…

Cheyenne lifted the jacket onto her and leaned around her body to do up the buttons. She pressed her head onto Eleanor's shoulder to gaze upon her in the mirror. "There," she said in that gorgeous accent. "Don't you look beautiful?"

Beautiful wasn't quite the right word for it. Cheyenne was beautiful: she glowed with a magnetic field that drew eyes to her. Eleanor was shapely, elegant, stoic: her eyes glowered out from a face highlighted by the smart lapels around her neck. It wasn't unease in her eyes, or fear, it was a steely determination. A complete confidence in herself and her place in the world.

By herself, stranded alone as the world turned around her, Eleanor had never been sure of herself. Next to Cheyenne, everything suddenly seemed possible.

"I didn't know a jacket could do that," Eleanor admitted.

Cheyenne nodded thoughtfully, as if she hadn't heard. "You could do with more highlighter. Nothing much though – that would be tacky. Just enough to make you a little more worldly."

"I am worldly."

She chuckled. "In a different way. Normally you look like a girl, Eleanor. Dress like this and you can look like a queen."

Her face turned as red as the jacket. "That might be a bit much."

"I don't think so." Cheyenne grinned and smoothed Eleanor's coat down. The pressure of her fingers against Eleanor's chest sent fissions of heat through her core and into her heart. "You're just the type to marry some Lord. There must be someone with a title around here."

"They don't want me. My kind's ten a penny. You're more unique."

Cheyenne shrugged. "In the last century, nobility only married Americans because they needed money. They'll stay away from me out of fear of their image – or so my mother told me."

"Fuck your mother."

Cheyenne blinked: for half a second, she seemed almost taken aback. But that was impossible; Cheyenne was too suave and cool and put-together to display so base an emotion. At last, a smile sneaked up the side of her face. "Yeah. Fuck her. She wanted to keep me at home, you know. Working with her and Dad."

"Doing what?"

"Movie production." She made a face as she turned to sift through racks of pastel-coloured dresses, but to Eleanor it seemed impossibly glamourous. Her mother was an accountant. "I can't stand that shit," Cheyenne went on. "Everything about it is so fake."

Yet, when Cheyenne eventually found a frock she liked, one that clung to her curves and set her standing sultrily out amongst the mass of dreary-eyed shoppers milling around her, it seemed to Eleanor like she had on her own kind of costume. Cheyenne was more of a lady than Eleanor would ever manage – or better yet, some kind of jazz age flapper who smoked cigarettes and rouged her knees and drove her own motorcar.

When Cheyenne threw a trench coat over her new purchase and slumped against the window, still dappled with sunlight, she seemed every bit the bright young society girl, posing for her portrait.

"It's such a beautiful day," Eleanor remarked as they strolled down the street, bags misleadingly light: both had worn their new purchases out of the shop. She couldn't be sure, but Eleanor was convinced that every half-glance in their direction was so down to Cheyenne's beauty. "I don't want to go home."

If she was alone, she would have swum: rushed headlong into the sea and floated under the hot sun. But now she had Cheyenne, and Cheyenne couldn't go to the beach again. Something within Eleanor knew Cheyenne craved variety; that to take her to the same place twice would scream of a restricted mind. So Eleanor suggested they climb the hill above town, and Cheyenne, flashing her broad, white smile, agreed.

The world was gorgeous: hot, dry, and golden. Like a reveller at the end of a party, tipping the bottle up to guzzle the last dregs of summer. Everything was gentle and lazy. Leaves just hinting at turning brown decorated canopies that dappled the soft, forest floor with puzzle pieces of light. Birds performed a symphony just for Cheyenne and Eleanor – tiny jewels in the trees, visible only through the titillating flash of plumage.

"It's still so green," Cheyenne breathed as they climbed through the strip of forest, hewed neatly between farmers' fields. The wheat hadn't been cut yet, and it stretched out in an endless windblown carpet. "Back in LA, this would all have dried up by now."

"You should see it in the spring," Eleanor replied. "It's all drying up now."

"But I will, won't I? I'll be here, with you. And I'll never, ever have to go back to California, not if I don't want to." There was a cold determination in her voice, the one Eleanor wouldn't have understood had she not dived into the water and gazed with fury at the library books. There was the urge for freedom, for power, for a life that burnt so brightly no one else could ever extinguish it.

"I won't go either," Eleanor admitted. Her voice was softer than Cheyenne's, but she hoped it conveyed the same deep emotion. "Not ever."

And just like that, Cheyenne was smiling again, even if her smile was meaner than the innocent expression she'd worn when they first suggested venturing out into the wilds. "Isn't it wonderful I found you?" she asked, perhaps to Eleanor, perhaps to herself, perhaps to the world around her. "Someone that *understands*!"

And just like that, they were at the summit – gazing over the town and the sea and the mountains far across the bay. Bathed in the afternoon sunlight, the streets almost seemed to be paved with gold.

Cheyenne only spent a moment surveying her domain. She gave it one look, smiled with the easy confidence of one who has it all, and collapsed onto the grass – a dry spot, of course, without any burs or bracken that would threaten to pull at her trousers. She gestured excitedly for Eleanor to sit down next to her.

It was calmer up here than Eleanor could have predicted. Lying still, her face to the sky, with no sound but the rush of the wind and the caw of the crows and the panting of Cheyenne's breath, it was something like what she imagined heaven to be like. Only floating in the sea could send her to a greater state of ecstasy – and the sea didn't have Cheyenne in it.

"Aren't the clouds beautiful?" Cheyenne murmured. "I swear they aren't as puffy back home."

"Surely clouds are the same everywhere?"

"You're wrong. They're whiter here, and softer, and so close you feel you could reach out and grab one – and the sky is this perfect shade of blue."

"I thought California was famous for its skies."

"It is. But you can get bored of anything. This sky is so beautiful because it's new – if you could see it differently, I think you would appreciate it."

"I do appreciate it," Eleanor assured her. She knew Cheyenne couldn't see her smile, but she beamed up at the sky all the same. "Especially when you show it to me."

A teasing tone snuck into Cheyenne's voice. "Has anyone else showed you the sky like this?"

"Never," Eleanor admitted.

"You never sat with a boyfriend and stared at the clouds?"

"I've never had a boyfriend." She'd never even had a proper friend before.

"You haven't been up here with girls from your hall?"

"Of course not," she declared. "None of them understand me. There's only you." Though she couldn't see it, Eleanor could feel Cheyenne's smile.

Something cool brushed against Eleanor's hand. She extended a finger to find Cheyenne's there in return, poking her, playing with her skin. Her nails ran smooth against Eleanor's skin.

Eleanor was too hot and lazy for games. She seized Cheyenne's hand in her, intertwined their fingers. Cheyenne made a satisfied noise deep in the back of her throat; Eleanor sighed alongside her.

"It's so wonderful," Cheyenne said, quietly enough that Eleanor wasn't sure she was meant to hear. Then, louder, "You're so wonderful. I'm so wonderful. Everything's just perfect."

And when Cheyenne lifted their linked hands and lay them on her chest, Eleanor couldn't help but agree.

* * *

They left the summit only when the sun sank behind the hills and the air began to chill. Cheyenne 'oohed' and 'ahhed' at the sunset, and pointed out every different shade of purple. "In California, the sun sets over the sea," she explained – keeping up a constant babble as they walked down the hill. "It's so strange to see it dip under the mountains instead – and the colours are completely different."

"I'd like to see it someday," Eleanor remarked.

Cheyenne's reply was snappish, and Eleanor immediately knew she'd said something wrong. "No, you don't. It's so ugly over there."

Eleanor had never seen pictures of California looking anything but beautiful, but she didn't dare say it. "I suppose it is pretty here, isn't it?"

"So gorgeous," Cheyenne agreed. "And so clean. Even the night air smells different – fresher, somehow." She was in such a state of ecstasy that even passing a group of drunk students vomiting in the streets couldn't wipe the smile off her face. After a while, Eleanor threw caution to the wind, forgot the importance of not overstepping, and grinned along with her.

It was only when they returned to Cheyenne's hall of residence that the energy began to ebb. Cheyenne didn't hesitate before dragging Eleanor over the threshold, nor escorting her up the stairs. It was only when she passed a particular corridor that she stilled. Her face slipped into something stony and stoic.

"When did you last see George?" Eleanor asked.

"This morning. He didn't want to come shopping for blouses."

"That's fair enough. But… such a shame he never saw the top of the hill." It shouldn't have been such a struggle to get the words out. Yet the truth of the matter was that Eleanor hadn't missed him – she'd been too delighted that she got to bask in Cheyenne's uninterrupted presence.

Eleanor shook her head, trying to physically shoo the dark thoughts away. George was their friend – *her* friend. It was her job to take care of him. And when Cheyenne rapped abruptly on the door and a bleary-eyed George shuffled out, she was truly glad to see him.

"Oh," he said with a smile. "It's you."

"Who else?" replied Cheyenne breezily, and burst into his room with the ease of someone who spent half her time there. Eleanor followed, but couldn't hide her wince as she stepped through the door. The entire place stank of acrylic paint. An easel faced the window, as if George was opening a gallery for birds.

"What are you working on?" Cheyenne asked.

"The beach." A shy smile flashed across his face. "It's not finished though: I can't get the waves right. And I can't decide...'

"On what?" Cheyenne was getting impatient.

"No, it's stupid... actually, probably better not to–'

"Spit it out, George." That was Cheyenne again: Eleanor could imagine her parents saying those same words across the table of a Hollywood boardroom.

"Well... I might add human figures. Not very detailed – just enough to add a centre to the composition. And the two of you looked so beautiful the other day...'

"Oh!" Now he had Cheyenne's attention. "You mean we'd be in an actual painting?"

"Not your faces."

"We're painters' models, Eleanor!" From her perch on the bed, Cheyenne grabbed a throw pillow and tossed it at Eleanor as she squawked with delight. "We can be like those artists' muses from the nineteenth century – shall I pose for you in the light, my dear monsieur benefactor?"

"I think it's lovely, George," Eleanor murmured. She wasn't quite sure if he could hear her. Cheyenne hopping around the room, glistening in her new dress, would take up anyone's attention. But he must have heard her, as after a few moments he whispered a quiet 'thank you' in return.

"Oh," said Cheyenne at last, once she'd finished giggling. "You should have seen where Eleanor and I went today – the hill above town, you'd love it! You could do a lovely painting of the view at sunset – it's better than anything in California, or so I was telling Eleanor."

George's eyes gleamed. "Is that so?" He looked to Eleanor for confirmation, but she went pale under his gaze. He had to be told – of course they couldn't keep their trip a secret, and really, there was no secret to keep at all. She and Cheyenne had gone on a nice walk and admired the view: nothing scandalous about that. And yet somehow, telling anyone else about their moment on the hilltop seemed to spoil it. It had all been so perfect, and so perfect because it was only them.

But Eleanor liked George. She cared for George. He was her friend. So she smiled and nodded and said she was surprised he hadn't noticed how sunburnt they must look. George laughed and took her hand to sit her down. The first thing Eleanor noticed was how bony it felt, how unlike the warm security of Cheyenne's. When he escorted them down to dinner, she grinned at everything he said and came to his defence when Cheyenne ribbed him. Afterwards, when they had retired to the common room and Cheyenne had disappeared off to talk to one of her myriad acquaintances in the corridor – Eleanor trying to suppress a stab of jealousy – she leaned over to talk to him.

"You don't mind, do you? That Cheyenne and I walked the hill without you?"

He cocked his head. "Why would I mind? You two were out together – you're allowed to have fun."

"But I feel horrible. Us having fun, and you locked in your room all day, working."

"I like working. And besides, we don't have to be joined at the hip."

The conversation flowed on to lighter topics – the weather, classes, the poor quality of dining hall food – but Eleanor's mind lingered on George's words. Was it really possible for him not to mind? She would have been seething had their positions been reversed. She liked writing songs and poems and stories, yes, but she liked Cheyenne more. Was George truly unbothered, or was he inwardly seething?

"You will tell me, won't you?" Eleanor asked when it drew late. It was the slow, sleepy moment when eyes began to droop and everyone collectively realises – and collectively denies – that it's time to head home. "If there's something wrong – or you're upset, or feel left out, or–"

"Eleanor." He placed a hand on her shoulder. "You fret too much. Doesn't she, Cheyenne?"

"Let her care about you, George," dismissed Cheyenne with a wave of her hand. "Isn't it nice to have real friends?"

The barb was carefully concealed, but even Eleanor could tell it stung. She *had* seen George with others – he had a pack of boys from school that he sometimes hung around with – but he seemed painfully gangly and awkward next to them as they flashed their watches and bragged about expensive ski holidays. George might have worn well-tailored clothes and spoke in the right accent, but he was never quite macho enough to fit in with that group. He only really smiled with Cheyenne and Eleanor – and far more with the former than the latter.

It was all, Eleanor realised, surprisingly familiar. She had lived that same dynamic time and time again, with the boys in the village and the girls on the swimming team. The endless attempt, the subtle rejections and the terrible, creeping realisation that these people all understood some intangible secret that you would never be privy to. That must be why Cheyenne had attracted them – she had a talent for breaking down walls, reaching into your mind and teasing out the words you'd always imagined yourself saying, the ones that would make people love you.

Almost unconsciously, Eleanor reached out and squeezed George's arm. She understood.

"It is lovely, isn't it?" George said merrily. Yet when he turned around to speak to Eleanor, his expression was genuine and his fingers lingered on her hand against his jacket. "Thank you, Eleanor. You're very sweet."

Sweet. She could be sweet. There was nothing better to be than sweet, Eleanor decided, for that endeared people to you and showed you could be caring. And she did care, surprisingly fiercely, about the abandonment of George. For if he and Cheyenne were both so casual about it, did that mean that they were leaving *her* out of just as much?

The worry ate into her long into the night. No matter how much she tried to focus on her readings on regicide and rebellions, insecurity seemed to have crept into every shadow of her room, jumping out at her whenever her eyes wandered. Even Napoleon, banished to Elba, only served to remind her how desperately alone she suddenly felt.

Yet Napoleon had returned. Even if Eleanor was right – and it was a big if – hadn't today proven how much Cheyenne loved her? How much George valued her as a friend. This was nothing, Eleanor decided, nothing more than the sleep-deprived worries of the mind at two am.

Even so, she struggled to fall asleep.

6th May, 10:37.

Eight hours until the party.

The lane Eleanor snakes her way down is familiar: a cobblestone path off one of the main thoroughfares, charming if you ignore the scents of piss and vomit that linger perpetually in the corners. The main door is still unlocked, and when she climbs the stairs to knock on the door of the upper flat, the scent of stale chlorine still lingers in the air.

The girl who opens the door is blurry-eyed and still in her pyjamas. She nearly drops her coffee cup when she sees who's standing before her. "Eleanor?"

"Hello Molly," Eleanor says, and steps in without being invited. The moth-eaten sofa that sags in the middle, and has a stack of paper wedged under one leg to stop the wobbling, is still in the same spot by the window. The damp patch in the corner still hasn't been fixed. The kettle is boiling in the kitchen; Liz's houseplants are blooming. A cosy old place, despite it all.

"No training this morning?" she asks as Molly spoons more sugar into her coffee.

She nods. "Weights at one though, and then pool time this evening. You remember the schedule." Her voice isn't accusing, just weary.

Eleanor nods. She doesn't miss the early mornings, the freezing walk to the pool, the grogginess of the changing rooms, but she found she did miss the gasps as they slipped into the water, the jokes they made, the camaraderie they gained. That she could go back to. If she lived a completely different life.

"Well, you're not going to training tonight," she declares. "You're coming to my party instead."

"Oh!" Molly fumbles with her phone to confirm the date. "Happy birthday! How does twenty-two feel?"

"At the moment? The same as twenty-one." Eleanor lets her gaze cross over to the street, watches the little people going about their little lives below. "But with time, I think it will be different."

Molly nods, but her eyes have glazed over. This is clearly too much for her in her half-conscious state. "I suppose if I ask coach what the set is I can do it earlier in the afternoon…'

Fuck the set! Eleanor wants to cry, but she stops herself. She has never been able to do what Molly does, put the swimming team above all else. Swimming itself, of course, but arranging her life around the training group has never been her strong suit. Even when she was still on the team, she'd always make up her own sets and do them by herself. "As long as you come," she says instead. "Liz too. And Avery – how's living with her?"

"Well, we've had two years of practice," Molly says. *More time than we lived with you* is the silent subtext. She follows up with an equally banal question – 'Any news from LA?" Eleanor flinches.

"Not much," she lies.

"Still keep in touch with Jack Flannigan?"

"Of course." This could be true, if you looked at it a certain way. She gets his texts: the memes he sends, the pictures from California, the occasional reassurances that she will be okay. She rarely responds.

"Well, he hasn't gone out with another girl." This makes Eleanor pause. She hadn't thought of Molly as the kind of girl who read the tabloids. "I check for you," she explains, like it's a friendly gesture, even though two years have gone by with she and Eleanor barely talking. No, Molly checks, like everyone else in this town, for the celebrity gossip. To have some insight into the slightly-famous Eleanor Sanders' life, and to learn about her somewhat-more-famous possibly-ex-boyfriend.

They're only on a break, the tabloids reported, words spoon-fed to them by Jack's publicist. Her heart aches every time she thinks of him, that open, smiling face, still waiting for her. Too open; too trusting. She never did deserve him. After tonight, perhaps, she never will.

"As long as he's happy," Eleanor says at last, and Molly gives a noncommittal nod. She busies herself with tidying the flat as Eleanor watches. It was not so long ago that Eleanor used to do this. Wash the dishes, wipe the countertops, empty the bin. Odd, her memories of living here are all bad, but that had nothing to do with the flat itself, nor the people in it. It was the things going on outside that tainted it, and Eleanor had the foolishness to let them in.

"Well," Eleanor says at last, awkwardly. She stands and wipes an imaginary speck of dust off the sofa. "I have to be off – more people to invite, you know. Though really it's an open invitation. The whole town will show up."

"They'd have to be mad not to," Molly replies. She chews her lip thoughtfully. "You know that film Jack's in?" she says at last. "The one that's coming out next month, the western?"

"You mean *Silver Lining*? I was there when he filmed it." Much of it had been shot in California, despite it being set in Utah. Cheaper for the film crew to stay near LA, and California in the summer was certainly hot enough to emulate the wild west. The script was simple but hard-hitting, and Eleanor had hummed appreciatively as she marked some of the lines in his script.

"Not as good as yours," Jack had said when he saw her admiring it.

She laughed. "I'm allowed to like other people's work."

"As long as it's not so good it makes you think it's pointless to write anymore because you'll never reach its heights, which sends you into a depressive spiral, which sends me into an equally deep spiral because I can't bear to see you hurting, which..."

She tossed a sock at him. "You didn't do that when you saw Martin Hughes win his Oscar in *Lighthouse*."

"How do you know? Maybe I'm just excellent at hiding my depressive episodes."

"Or maybe it fostered a deep appreciation within you for art in all its forms and expressions." She laughed, and kissed him, and that night they chattered excitedly about the project over the shrimp Jack had cooked for them.

"Exactly," Molly says, bringing Eleanor back to the present. "The point is, that's total Oscar-bait. And he *is* the lead."

"Co-lead. Kieran Phillips plays his father and his role is just as, if not more, heavy."

Molly makes a dismissive gesture. "They have lots of separate categories. The point is, I wouldn't be surprised if he was going next year."

"Well, the Oscars are pretty far in the future. The other studios have quite a lot coming out, and some of the streaming companies–"

"Forget the other studios." Molly's smile is one of barely-restrained giddiness. "The point is, even a nomination will catapult him up the ladder. And if you're on his arm–"

"My script's just finishing filming as we speak." Eleanor has even been invited in to watch the wrap. "Hopefully out in November, if post-production goes well. So you never know – maybe I'll be at the Oscars by myself."

Molly's wistful look turns strangely sad. "Don't you forget about us, Eleanor Sanders," she says.

She shuts the door, and with that the final connection to a life Eleanor could have had vanishes.

October.

Three years and seven months before the party.

Everyone wanted Cheyenne. Who wouldn't? She was cheerful, friendly, beautiful, a social butterfly. People swarmed around her when they went out, all desperate to get a piece of Eleanor's friend. It would have made Eleanor seethe, but Cheyenne's popularity made Eleanor more popular by extension, so she tolerated it – even if the most she ever exchanged with these hangers-on were a few friendly words. That old awkwardness slipped in every time she tried to start a conversation, as if there were an invisible wall between herself and the person she was talking to, preventing any real connection. As soon as they turned away, their eyes misted over and Eleanor could tell they had already forgotten all about her.

But Cheyenne enjoyed them. She was often off with Raquelle, another English girl from a private school in the south, or Gina, whose Edinburgh accent was so posh she might as well have been from London.

"Are you sure you're Scottish?" Eleanor teased one night.

Gina shrugged. "I can dance a ceilidh." Eleanor couldn't tell if there was a hint of indignation lurking on the underside of her tongue.

Gina and Raquelle brought boys with them, too. Sam, whose sun-kissed Australian skin was made less exciting by Cheyenne and her American accent – and Henry, whose parents were in a high enough tax bracket he wore tweed. Cheyenne liked to throw them sultry glances – especially Henry. It made Eleanor want to vomit.

"Honestly," she complained to George after an evening being driven mad by dead-end conversations and getting ignored by Gina and Raquelle. "You're a boy and she doesn't do that to you."

He shrugged. "It's different with them."

"Well, it doesn't make sense," Eleanor pouted. "They're not even that attractive."

George's tone was carefully cool. "She clearly thinks they are."

"No, she doesn't," Eleanor muttered. "She only likes them because they're rich and foreign. The same reason all these people like Cheyenne."

George flashed her a glance, and Eleanor instantly realised she'd said the wrong thing.

"Not us of course," she said quickly. "*We* understand her. But everyone else – they couldn't care less about Cheyenne as a person. They just like the way she makes them feel." She knocked her drink – some fruity alcohol that Cheyenne adored – back and skirted around the room towards the bar. Gina looked up and cast her a cold look, and Eleanor considered that she might not have been as quiet as she thought.

What does it matter? she told herself as she mixed drinks with abandon. *Cheyenne loves us, not them. We're a team.*

And what a team they were. In between lectures they frequented Cheyenne's favourite spots in town. There was the university art gallery, which Cheyenne claimed would be so romantic to smoke outside of. "I don't, of course," Cheyenne said with a shudder when George pointed out a tobacco shop. "Awful for you. But doesn't it just look so beautiful? Everyone vapes in LA – fucking disgusting. No allure whatsoever."

Then came the library. They ran their fingers up and down the spines, racing to find the most ancient tome they could, desperately trying to stifle their giggles and duck behind shelves at the first sight of the ever-watchful librarians. If a student looked up from their work with a glare, Cheyenne would simply roll her eyes and strut past.

Finally, there was their favourite book shop: Topping and Company, an expansive, high-ceilinged place, packed wall to wall with bookshelves interspersed with photos of the great and good who had come to speak there. They could never stay too long, for the sight of the newly-printed authors, names emblazoned proudly next to the awards they'd been nominated for, aroused a fierce, primal jealousy in Eleanor that made her heart burn and her toes twitch.

Cheyenne would stroll around the local shops, running her hands up and down cashmere jumpers and purchasing trench coats and berets because they made her look mysterious. They leaned over the balustrade at the top of the clock tower and imagined they were flying. Even ordering coffee made Eleanor feel like a sage. Cheyenne wanted only the prettiest, quaintest tea shops, and would whisper to Eleanor to ask what type of scone was best. "How do you drink afternoon tea? Is it jam or butter first? How do you pronounce it again?"

"The town is a postcard," Cheyenne declared one evening, as they lounged under the shade of an oak tree near Cheyenne and George's halls. Eleanor had just come from swimming practice, her hair was damp with chlorine and she wore a tracksuit and oversized sweatshirt from her home club. Cheyenne could have stepped out of the pages of *Country Life*.

"George, you should paint it," Cheyenne said.

"I could write about it," Eleanor cut in. George didn't need all of Cheyenne's adoration.

Cheyenne blinked through long blonde eyelashes. "Of course. After you did so well in history."

The class she was referring to was a history tutorial Eleanor had only just managed to squeeze into. The tutor, who specialised in an area of European history Cheyenne was particularly interested in, held court at the top of a rickety old staircase in a building that hadn't updated its insulation since the 19th century. Students would pull off their jumpers as they slogged up the stairs, then rush to get them back on as the autumn winds cut through the draughty windows. Once, when Cheyenne tugged her jumper over her arms, her top snagged and revealed her entire midriff, all the way to her bra. It was the same skin Eleanor had seen at the beach, but the sight of flesh in a dark, narrow stairwell seemed tantalising and illicit.

In their tutorial that morning, the tutor had asked for a creative response to the Crimean War – 'something to liven up the class'. Cheyenne fretted over hers, but Eleanor typed out a script for a play and submitted it without a second thought. She only remembered its existence when the tutor cut through her daydreams of golden skies and golden hair to commend: "Eleanor's excellent script".

She twisted her head away from the window. "My script?"

"The play you wrote." For once, the tutor – an old man with a moustache so bushy it threatened to leap off his face – was staring at Eleanor with rapt interest. She was no longer a faceless drone in a sea of unwashed students: she was someone of note. Someone worth listening to. Someone important.

"About the soldiers?" he went on. "I liked it. Very moving. Do you take classes?"

"Classes?"

"In the English department. They've got a module about writing for performance – I assumed you'd be on it."

"Oh. No." She looked around – Cheyenne was staring at her, head cocked. "Perhaps I'll take one next semester."

The tutor nodded and moved on to the rest of the class – some long drone about trade and empire and imperialism. Eleanor couldn't listen. Her eyes were locked on Cheyenne. As the tutor praised Eleanor, Cheyenne's eyes lit up like suns. Hunger lurked within her – hunger and ambitious delight.

"I can't believe he praised you!" Cheyenne exclaimed as they made the long descent back down to the ground. "He's so crotchety. But you must listen to him – he thinks you're great!"

"He's a history professor, not a theatre critic."

Cheyenne waved a hand dismissively. "Well, *I* think you're great. And now you match with George – two *artistes*!" She said it as if she were French, beret, onions and all.

In the quad, Cheyenne went back to Eleanor's suggestion of eulogising the autumnal afternoon. "Some pretty poem would be nice. Very nineteenth century. I love Lord Byron and Wordsworth. America's got nothing like them."

"Walt Whitman?" Eleanor suggested coyly.

Cheyenne threw her head back and scoffed. The sunlight caught her profile, accentuating the curves of her cheek and making her eyes sparkle. "Too much of a focus on America. I want the Old Country." She said it with reverence, as if it should be capitalised. The country that Eleanor had spent all her life in and thought of as little more than a reasonably pleasant – if damp – island. In Cheyenne's mouth, it became a mythical, romantic place, where the echelon of high society slipped from country gardens to chafe against the raw wilderness of majestic moors and the open sea.

"Oh, to be in England," George muttered from under the tree.

"Don't you know any Robert Burns?" Eleanor snapped from her side of the trunk. "It's sacrilege to quote that here."

He shrugged. "It would be more offensive to try and do a Scottish accent."

"We could ask Gina," Cheyenne suggested.

Eleanor blinked. "You realise she sounds English?"

"I'm sure she could manage something lower-class if we put her up to it. You know," she went on before the others could protest, "she learnt how to dance ceilidhs at school? That's so romantic. We didn't do anything like that in America!"

"I didn't do country dancing in England, either," piped in George.

Cheyenne let out a wistful sigh as if he hadn't spoken "Can you imagine? Spinning around to the music in a flouncy skirt as the wind whistles by outside, knowing a thin wall, a candlestick and your community is the only thing keeping you from a cold and frigid death?"

"Or you could go to the one the Celtic society puts on every week," suggested Eleanor drily. "They even heat the building and use electric light."

The inconvenience the seventeenth century didn't appear to deter Cheyenne, so she escorted George and Eleanor to the local dance hall that weekend. Though not exactly antique, the hardwood floor had been installed before the Second World War, which thrilled Cheyenne's American sensibilities enough that she leapt into learning the steps with vigour. George was her first partner. "You don't mind finding someone else, do you?" she asked Eleanor. "Only it's much more traditional to do it with a man."

Eleanor ended up with a short, quiet girl she knew vaguely from her halls. Dancing with her was all wrong. Her hands were too small, her waist too soft, her demeanour too meek and her steps too hesitating. Cheyenne, Eleanor was sure, would dance nothing like this. She was too electric for the plodding, stammering George; she seemed to light up the room when she spun. If Eleanor looked over, she could see the light in her eyes, twisting around in a skirt as all eyes were drawn to her effervescence.

Maybe Cheyenne hadn't danced with her because she was scared of the possibilities. Maybe she was terrified that if she touched Eleanor's hand, the sparks would be too bright to ignore.

When the band stopped for an intermission, Eleanor dropped her partner's hand without saying goodbye and rushed into the crowd. Cheyenne was somehow nowhere to be seen; neither was George. Instead, there was only the horrible crush of people, the heat and sweat of the dancers made worse by the blinding lights. Eleanor swayed, dizzy.

There, from the corner of the room, a cool breeze, tainted with the aphrodisiac smell of salt. Eleanor stumbled over desperately, losing all qualms about shoving people as she made it to the door. It had started to rain: a thin, weak drizzle that appeared to cover everything in a coating of dew before the damp properly settled. Eleanor slumped down on the step without a care for her clothes and began rubbing the moisture into her skin, desperate to scrub herself clean of the sweat.

Laughter echoed from the street. Eleanor's ears pricked at a familiar voice. "It's through here, see – mind your step! Don't be shy Gina; you said you knew how to do this!"

Sure enough, a group materialized from the fog. Raquelle's bow was ridiculously large as always, almost enough to draw attention away from Cheyenne's glistening blonde hair. It was harder to see now, as half of Cheyenne's ponytail was covered by Henry's arm, making a vain attempt to shelter her with his coat.

Eleanor shoved down her disappointment, and waved to them from the steps. Cheyenne grinned when she saw her. "Eleanor! What are you doing out here?"

"I was hot," she explained when they got closer. "Did you invite them?"

"I might have let the word slip." Cheyenne glanced back and giggled at her entourage. "It's perfect. Gina can teach us anything we don't pick up!"

"And I get a dance partner," Eleanor agreed.

Even better, the next set involved the dancers organizing into groups of six. George was to one side of Eleanor, and, at long last, Cheyenne was to the other.

It was strange, holding Cheyenne. Their hands were sweaty, the proportions awkward, Cheyenne's body either too hard or too soft. In Eleanor's mind their bodies should fit together perfectly, in real life their mechanisms ground and squeaked.

Maybe it was Henry's presence, Eleanor assured herself. If they ditched him – and Gina and Raquelle, and maybe even George while they were at it – everything would be alright. The dance would be perfect, harmonious, and they would spin forever.

6th May: 11:04.

Eight hours until the party.

Eleanor keeps her head down as she leaves Crail's Lane. Her mind is swirling, half sick with what Molly said.

It shouldn't hurt so much. It's not as if she hasn't gone through it all in her head a thousand times over, examined every facet of her motivations, every angle to her character. If she were a handful of words in her script, Eleanor would have cracked the psychoanalysis long ago. She would have a full profile of the character; her wants, her needs, her deepest, most repressed desires. It infuriates her that she can't do the same to herself. After all, what is she if not a creation of her own mind?

Maybe it is knowing the ending that allows you to know people so well.

She doesn't need to be at Jack's side. She's got enough success from that already. And ultimately, that desire for success was what drove her away.

The thought makes her feel slightly sick, so she banishes it.

Without thinking, her feet have carried her to the old castle. A crumbling ruin overlooking the North Sea. The ocean looks different up here, crueller, more menacing. But the grass in what was once the main courtyard is soft and welcoming, and Eleanor collapses on the ground gratefully.

The sky is an alarmingly bright blue; the sun is warm. Eleanor is weary – perhaps she hasn't eaten enough, her logical brain tells her – but deep inside she knows it is the stress of the day: both what has passed and what is to come. Her mind is wrestling over a dilemma: should she do it? She only has the one chance. But what if it goes wrong? How would she cope? What would people say? Her life would be over – or at least, her relationship with Jack, which is the longest time she's ever been happy. And what about her career? She only has her book deal because she's Jack Flannigan's girlfriend, not because she's Eleanor Sanders, successful screenwriter.

But wasn't that the point? To become Eleanor Sanders, successful screenwriter, through being Eleanor Sanders, Jack Flannigan's girlfriend? Isn't that the crux of the problem?

A sickening pit opens deep within her, and Eleanor closes her eyes and bites down on the inside of her cheek. She can't think of Jack. Not now, with tonight looming, and Cheyenne a blazing torch inside her brain.

A chill breeze cuts through the castle, jolting Eleanor back to life. That's too cold for Los Angeles: it's a San Francisco thing, as she'd discovered when Jack took her there for a week. They'd battled their way against the winds on the piers; screamed in delight as the gales sucked their breath away as they crossed the Golden Gate; leaned against each other to battle the cold as they strolled down the beach.

"Now you see," Jack told her as they drove back south and the temperature grew warmer, "why I can't stand the heat?"

No, no, no! She isn't to think of Jack.

This castle isn't good for her. It brings back too many memories.

She stumbles to her feet and rushes to the exit, almost forgetting her coat. A seagull caws as she passes: a fat one, perched on the gate out, refusing to move. She gives it the finger and it miraculously flies away.

"Quoth the seagull, nevermore," she mutters, and laughs to herself as she strolls back home.

December.

Three years and five months before the party.

Cheyenne's birthday was the fourteenth of December.

"An awful time," she complained. "Just before Christmas. People always forget about it." It was made even worse that it fell right before exam week, when students were deep into their revision.

It made Cheyenne stew. "We should do something fun," she declared as December began. "We can't just sit around all night and read in the dark." She glowered out the window. The Scottish winters were taxing on everyone, but the darkness especially affected Cheyenne. Even back in October she'd complained about the chill: "It's like the sun doesn't work here. It shines, but it doesn't heat."

"We *are* supposed to be studying," George cautioned, looking up from his readings on the Franco-Prussian war. "I'd prefer not to fail in our first semester."

"We won't fail. We're smart: we got in here, didn't we?"

Eleanor made a noncommittal sound as a reply: she didn't want to risk angering Cheyenne even more.

"So," Cheyenne went on, "I was thinking: Nice."

Eleanor blanched. "You mean in France?"

"Why not?" She shrugged. "It's warm; it's sunny; it's

Mediterranean. Just think how magical it'll be to stroll those streets. How romantic it'll be to see the ocean…"

"We live by the ocean."

"A real one! Something warm, something swimmable – I mean for normal people, Eleanor. And it's so beautiful there…" She gave a dreary sigh and sank back into her seat, luxuriating in her imaginary pool.

It was a nice thought, but Eleanor's logical mind was voiced by George's mutterings. "We can't go. We just can't."

But what Cheyenne wanted Cheyenne got, and so, ten days later, they were standing blurry-eyed by their front doors at five in the morning, waiting for a taxi to take them to the airport. Eleanor was so tired she felt nauseous, but Cheyenne's presence next to her was steadying. Cheyenne seemed to have rejuvenated at the prospect of travel: she chattered non-stop around the terminal, made small talk with the passengers next to her on the plane and charmed the taxi driver into giving them a discount when they arrived in France. Eleanor kept her head down and tried to work on her story.

"I've been brushing up on my French," Cheyenne told Eleanor and George for the sixth time that day as they arrived at their hotel. One suite for the lot of them, with separate bedrooms adjoining a living area. A balcony next to the sofa offered a distant view of the sea – and close-up view of several other buildings – but they took what they could get. Eleanor wasn't quite sure what it all cost: Cheyenne had arranged it and changed the subject whenever any of them mentioned price.

"Europe is so cheap anyway," she said when she was really pushed. "It's because people here have such tiny salaries."

That first day, they raced down to the beach to watch the sunset. The west-facing spots were all crowded with spectators, but when Cheyenne pushed them to the front no one objected. "You have to be aggressive with the French," she whispered. "Such a pushy culture: nothing like the Brits."

"Pushier than Americans?" Eleanor quipped.

Cheyenne smirked. "Americans pretend to be polite. The French don't bother."

Eleanor didn't want to think too hard about what Cheyenne had said: she was here, in France, at the beach, by the sea, and she was dying to get in. She pulled her clothes off, exposing her bikini, and rushed into the waves. It was so warm – at least compared to Scotland – and within moments she was cutting through the water. She surfaced ten metres from shore and waved an arm at Cheyenne and George. "Come in!"

Cheyenne was taking her time to undress, letting people see her, while George looked painfully awkward as he shivered with embarrassment in his shorts. Eleanor paddled back towards the beach to see them in and then, when Cheyenne was looking back towards the beach, snatched out an arm and pulled her in.

Cheyenne shrieked while Eleanor laughed, and for a second she thought she'd made a horrible mistake, but then Cheyenne's grimace turned to a smile. They were two girls, giggling together and relishing their sunset swim. It was just as Eleanor pictured when she took Cheyenne to the beach in Scotland but even better, because this was so warm that they didn't need to keep moving. Instead they could float and intertwine their legs: Eleanor's entire body shivered every time Cheyenne's bare calves brushed her knees.

"Do you go in the ocean a lot at home?" Eleanor asked.

Cheyenne rarely spoke about LA, unless it was to say how much better things were in Scotland. Her life was a series of blanks, occasionally half-filled in by a tantalisingly vague brushstroke.

"Sometimes." Cheyenne frowned, as if she hated to be reminded of it. "I surfed sometimes."

"I'd love to surf." Eleanor sighed wistfully. "The waves are rubbish in Britain though."

"There's a surf club," Cheyenne said. "I hear they throw good parties."

"That's why I don't go. They're too intimidating." Eleanor furrowed her brow as a thought occurred to her. "If their parties are so great, why aren't you a member?"

"I could join a surf club at home," Cheyenne's look was pensive. "I want to do something different here. Something British." Her face faded back to a smile as she ruffled Eleanor's hair. "Like you and George."

"We're really not that interesting."

"You're interesting to me. George!" she called, changing the subject. "Come join us!"

George's swimming was mediocre at best, so they splashed around in the shallows until it got too cold. The streets teemed with people, out drinking and dining. That night, showered and changed, they went out on the town: Cheyenne knew a girl from clay pigeon shooting who had a house in Nice and had told her all the best clubs. She still attracted wayward dancers to their circle, still ended up with her lipstick smudged all over some man's face at the end of every song. But come the end of the night, she was still at George and Eleanor's sides, ready to stumble home together.

Eleanor woke up early the next morning. She hadn't drunk very much, too wary of losing Cheyenne in the crowd. With George still snoring and Cheyenne lightly breathing, she slipped out the door and down the few blocks to the seaside.

It was much quieter now. Only a few dishevelled souls who had spent the night on the beach and some dedicated early morning joggers. No one bothered Eleanor as she slipped into the water, nor during the entire hour she spent cutting back and forth. She churned out a rough approximation of one of the swim team workouts she was missing, then lay on her back, watching the pink of the sky fade to a gentle blue. Even the sunrise seemed more beautiful here.

She was drying off when a familiar voice made her freeze. "You really love the sea, don't you?"

Cheyenne was sitting on a nearby bench, a coffee in hand. Her hair was artfully dishevelled, as if it had been styled in her sleep.

Eleanor smiled as she dried her hair. "I thought I'd made that obvious."

"It's just different to see it in action." Cheyenne smiled softly: a private expression, not meant for the hordes of crowds that had surrounded them last night. Something real at last; something just between them. "You would like California."

"I thought it was hell on earth, according to you." Eleanor flopped next to her on the bench with a cheeky smirk.

"It is. To me." There was a strangely pensive look on Cheyenne's face. "But you would like it. Especially one of the little beach towns. Full of surfers."

"And swimmers?"

"And swimmers." She smiled again, then pulled Elanor to her feet. "Shall we get breakfast? The French all eat *pain au chocolat* here, but I'm not sure that's very healthy. Still, when in Rome..."

Cheyenne could have made her eat dirt for all Elanor cared. Cheyenne's hand was on her arm, Eleanor's skin was tight with salt, and the streets were coming alive around them. There was, as far as she was concerned, no greater paradise on earth.

6th May, 11:52.

Seven hours until the party.

Eleanor cuts a line above the harsh linoleum, breathing in the scents of vegetables as she strolls down the aisle. She spies herself on the security camera, a dark shape amid the common hoards. Does she stick out? Will a bored security guard suddenly start and spit out his coffee when he sees her, *the* Eleanor Sanders, on his screen? Will the footage be pulled up by journalists later, ruthlessly scrutinised, shared to thousands of people desperate for a glimpse of Eleanor's day-to-day life?

Probably not. She is not very famous, and even then, she's a writer. Being Jack's girlfriend seems to get her more staying power.

She picks up a nectarine wrapped in plastic. Why plastic? So artificial, this country. She misses California, where the fruit is fresh, where biting into it makes you think you're in paradise instead of the smoke-filled pit Los Angeles lies in (unless you live up in the mountains, like Jack). Even the nuts are sadder here: they almost look to be wilting in their shells. Eleanor buys a bag anyway. They *are* delicious. Such a shame Gina can't eat them – for a moment, Eleanor imagines watching her choke. Then she snags a packet of almond flour as well. Perhaps a guest will ape California and ask for a gluten-free option.

There were so many people at the check-out, their faces interchangeable and blurring into one. Eleanor suddenly hates them all. Each individual figure thinking they're so special, that they'll live a life worth the pain and hassle of existing. How many of them still dream of grandeur, still clutch the childhood hope that they are the ones who'll be remembered?

What fools they are. There is room for one person, the one who fights for it, and no one fights harder than Eleanor. Not even Cheyenne, despite her nepotism. What good is birthright if you don't seize it?

That was the difference between Eleanor and the rest. Eleanor takes.

She steals half her basket from the supermarket, stuffing goods into her bag when the attendant isn't looking. See how easy things are when you want them? The law-abiding hoards suddenly sicken her.

No one she cares about appears on the walk home. Eleanor is glad. She isn't sure she could handle a Cheyenne sighting. Not yet. Not until tonight.

As she tries to slip up the back stairs, a cough sounds behind her. It's one of the maids – a new one; Eleanor doesn't know the face. Young, fresh, a student on their first job. At least Eleanor hopes it's their first.

"Is something wrong?" Eleanor asks. She tries to be kind to the staff, but the difference in their positions always creeps into the pauses in their conversations. Eleanor and this girl could attend the exact same lectures, get the exact same grades, eat in the exact same canteen for lunch, and yet here is Eleanor – heads and shoulders above this other girl. But that's what comes from being vicious, ambitious and taking the initiative. It's what Cheyenne's parents did, what Jack is doing, and what Eleanor must do.

The maid shakes her head. "It's only that management wanted to see you. About the event tonight."

"Oh yes. I need to let the catering know: no nuts downstairs." She pushes the sack of peanuts further into the recesses of her bag.

"They would prefer you told them yourself, miss."

When Eleanor announces her arrival at the front desk, she is ushered to one of the plush sofas in the corner of the Radcliffe's lobby. She eyes the drinks and cakes they ply her with suspicion – she'll have to check they don't add this to the bill for the night. Not that the amount matters – Jack's chequebook is thick – but it's the principal of the thing. She can't have the hotel sneaking charges past her.

"We just wanted to run over some of the details of the nature of tonight's gathering," says the manager, a thin, balding man with a bad habit of nibbling his lower lip. Eleanor can never remember his name. When she moved in, she was too emotionally frayed to care, and now it feels a bit late for all that. His assistant, though, is easy to remember. A black-haired, blue-eyed woman called Natalie who has lived in St Andrews since birth and likes to make small talk with guests. Eleanor always wonders what she thinks of all the students.

"As you know," the manager says, "the Radcliffe is a high-end establishment, and we wish to preserve that atmosphere for the safety and comfort of all our guests. I need to ensure that this event won't become...'

"A drunken washout?" Eleanor suggests. She taps her fingers on her legs in irritation. "I've been to plenty of

Hollywood blowouts. This will be nothing like that." She cannot guarantee this, of course, but it is easier to ask for forgiveness than permission.

The nervous lip-nibble is making an appearance. "If you could go so far as to simply provide us a guest list, it would greatly reduce our worries…'

"You want a guest list? Stick every student in the town on it." Eleanor waves a hand in dismissal. "We've been over this before. All other guests will use the side door and makeshift check in. I've paid the rental bill, a deposit and will cover any damages. What more could you possibly want?"

"We allowed your purchase of the penthouse, Miss Sanders," the manager warns, "but we will not tolerate any negative press, even by association."

"I haven't given you any bad press!" It's a struggle to keep her voice down. "My boyfriend – Jack Flannigan – and I paid a fortune to allow me to live here, and in that time, I've been the perfect house guest. If anything, you should be upset I haven't managed to get your name in the papers. You keep quiet, and play your cards right, and you could have a pair of Oscar-winners holidaying here. All I'm asking is one night."

"Eleanor," Natalie warns, her face a well of sympathy that even her flattering smile – pasted on for only the most difficult and important of clients – can't hide. "Just don't do anything you – or we – will regret."

"I won't," Eleanor promises. "Don't worry. Everything will be fine."

At that moment, she really means it. Yet, as soon as Eleanor disappears upstairs and the pair of frowning faces fades away, she isn't so sure she believes herself.

January.

Three years and four months before the party.

Eleanor spent the last few days of the winter holiday humming with anticipation. She couldn't help it. Her life in the village was small, her parents overpowering, even her trips into London were uninspiring. By contrast, Cheyenne lurked on her phone, an endless stream of pictures of beaches and sunsets and palm trees. LA was not too dissimilar from Nice, though Cheyenne would never admit it.

Eleanor wondered what the Pacific Ocean felt like.

That was the other thing she missed – the ocean. She had the local swimming pool, of course, but it wasn't the same. She wanted the open expanse, the freedom of being unrestrained by walls, the unpredictability of the waves and current. She wanted to feel that she had conquered something, not just paced endless laps of some uninspiring concrete cut-out.

She even called St Andrews "home" a few times, the phrase artfully slipped in when it seemed casual. Eleanor pretended not to notice her mother flinch or see her father's downcast eyes. Instead, she stared out the window, as if, if she tried hard enough, she could see all the way back to Scotland. Failing that, she would pick up her phone and scroll, living vicariously through Cheyenne.

"Why not go out and see someone?" her mother suggested one morning. "What about your old friends from swimming? Or Hettie Grange – you were ever so close to her back when you were children!"

Eleanor hadn't been close to Hettie since she was ten, when the other girl had grown out of playing pretend in the woods and vanished into the popular group that gossiped about grown-up topics like makeup and school uniform violations. Eleanor's social life had never quite recovered from that. Once, when she was particularly furious after another night spent watching parties through blurry mobile videos, she tried to blame it on Jackie spreading rumours. But in reality, Eleanor had simply stopped seeing the point in friendships. People were only going to leave you in the end. By the time she tired of isolation, she was sixteen, and everyone in the village had been joined at the hip for too long for them to dream of inviting anyone else into their club. Her last few years were lonely – a karmic punishment, she decided, for forgetting the value of other people.

That left her with Cheyenne – her sole true friend in the world, and her only hope of redemption. *You are so lucky*, she reminded herself during another lonely walk past the village green and the crowded pubs with fogged-up windows. *So very lucky, that you've found anyone at all.*

She took the train back north because it was something that Cheyenne would do – sit and stare moodily out the window, twisting a lock of hair around her finger as she worked on her novel. Well, maybe not worked on her novel, Cheyenne wasn't one for writing as far as Eleanor was aware. She *was* decent enough at acting. "Mom and Dad could have got me some bit part in one of their films if I wanted", she liked to claim, "but I'd never have been star material. The arts are your area," she said to Eleanor once. "One day, you can write something brilliant, and I'll get some studio to adapt it." Eleanor had glowed with pride for days.

Cheyenne said the same things to George (it irked Eleanor, though she told herself she didn't mind). After only a semester, the desk in his room was covered with canvases– all of them remarkable, as far as Eleanor's untrained eye could observe. He would often mention, in his quiet way, about submitting them somewhere. "Send them to a gallery in London!" Cheyenne would say. Her eyes glazed over with the excitement and romance of it all, and she started gushing over the London fashions. George met Eleanor's eyes and they shared a fond smile.

Eleanor hadn't talked to George much over the holiday: Cheyenne dominated her thoughts and time. She hoped he was all right. The Nice sun had done him good, but leaving him by the shore as she and Cheyenne splashed around had become far too commonplace. As soon as they returned to Scotland, he had retreated back into a shell of himself to prepare for exams. The most Eleanor saw him smile was when she or Cheyenne praised his artwork.

It was snowing in Scotland. So different to the dismal rain that lurked south of the border. The station was abuzz with activity: a crush of warm bodies in one steaming rush towards their homes. Eleanor clutched her case and imagined the shock Cheyenne would have when she returned from California. Or maybe not. Cheyenne had been skiing. Eleanor had seen the pictures of her in her fur-lined ski jacket, lifting a glass of champagne at some mountaintop restaurant. She was underage in the US, but it didn't matter. Eleanor could just picture Cheyenne fluttering her lashes and getting served anything she wanted.

A message flashed on her phone just as she made it through her door and collapsed on her bed. It was from Cheyenne: *Plane delayed. Too snowy. See you tomorrow xx.*

Eleanor's first thought was how odd it was, that the weather wouldn't pause for Cheyenne. One of the few things in life that girl couldn't control.

The disappointment came after, hard and bitter. They had arrangements for dinner: a reservation with George, Henry, Sam, Gina, and Raquelle. A sudden burst of anger pulsed through Eleanor. How dare Cheyenne condemn Eleanor to a meal with those people, when the only person she really wanted was Cheyenne?

She reluctantly dragged herself to the restaurant. Maybe it wouldn't be so bad? she told herself. It was a new year, a new chance with the others. And if all failed, there was always George to talk to.

The others were already sitting down when she arrived as Eleanor had taken several minutes to coax herself out of the door. "Evening," she said as she slid in next to George. "Good holiday?"

Sam laughed. "I miss Australian summer already," he said, draping one arm around Gina, who giggled coquettishly.

"It was alright." George let out a sigh and rolled his eyes. "Parents, you know?"

"And brothers," Raquelle piped in. "I couldn't cope."

"Did boarding school make Hugo worse?" Henry teased.

"You can't imagine what it's been like." She gave a theatrical groan. "You see a lot of Cheyenne then?"

Eleanor jolted and started to speak, but Henry beat her too it. "Quite a bit, yeah," he replied casually. "She calls a lot. Says she misses us."

Eleanor bristled silently. Out of all the people, Cheyenne had been talking to Henry? And everyone knew? What about the way Cheyenne had looked at her in Nice? Had that meant nothing? The thought was too horrible to entertain.

Even George being the favourite, she decided, would have been better than this.

"Are you going out again?" Gina piped up with a sickeningly sweet smile. Eleanor's stomach sunk in horror.

"Maybe for drinks," Henry said. "Nothing too serious."

"She likes you a lot," Gina remarked, and Eleanor's ears became overwhelmed with an anger-fuelled buzzing. She clutched her glass so tightly it flexed under her grip.

Either George didn't notice her anger, or he didn't care. Eleanor wasn't sure what was worse: that she'd hid her heartbreak so well no one could tell, or that they all knew but couldn't be bothered to acknowledge it. Maybe George was just upset about his parents; maybe he couldn't see what lay in front of him while the emotions of home lingered in his mind. It was an odd feeling – now that Cheyenne wasn't there for Eleanor to cling to, her place in the group was even more precipitous than before. In most ways, she was a stranger. It was terrifyingly reminiscent of the village, or even her first few days at university, where she'd scraped out an existence filled with little more than ambition.

They headed to a club after dinner: it was packed with groups of friends overjoyed to be reunited. Eleanor tried, she really did – she sank shot after shot, jumped around on the dance floor – but without fail the others would gravitate away from her, drawn into their own smaller circles of two or three.

Sam went off to snog Gina, Raquelle pulled George into a corner where she furiously lectured him about something, and dancing with Henry felt terribly wrong. For a second, Eleanor was struck with a strange fury. She considered kissing him there and then, making him fall in love with her, letting him forget about Cheyenne. But she was too shy, and Henry, despite everything, was too nice. So she wandered home at eleven, where she collapsed straight into bed without even unpacking.

When Cheyenne comes back, she told herself, *things will be better.*

A vision of Henry danced before her eyes, and she struggled to believe her own thoughts.

February.

Three years and three months before the party.

The town theatre was a small place, lucky to boast both a full auditorium and a black box that could hold, at a stretch, twenty people. Cheyenne adored it. "Live theatre is just better than movies," she declared one evening, as she sat with George, Eleanor and Henry watching yet another play by Oscar Wilde. "There's a spontaneity in it you don't get in cinema; a tacit agreement between the audience and the performers to create a sacred space."

George looked at her blankly. "Are you quoting something?"

She blushed. "I may have been procrastinating on my essays. But it's academic, so it counts!"

"You should audition for something," Eleanor suggested. "If you love it so much."

Cheyenne made a face. "If I wanted to be an actress I'd have stayed in LA. It wouldn't have been difficult: Mom and Dad would have found some part for me. But I hate actors. They're all so *superficial*."

"Isn't that the point?" asked Eleanor.

She shook her head. "People in LA are another type of artificial. Nothing like you get here, where people are genuinely nice. Anyway, no one in Hollywood is making anything as good as what Oscar Wilde wrote."

Eleanor hated Oscar Wilde: she found his farces of London high society ridiculous and out of touch to the average modern-day viewer. Most of all, she hated how he was remembered for being so mediocre. Maybe she should get into playwrighting: it seemed the bar was lower.

When she was lucky, Cheyenne would take her to a cinema broadcast of a professional show, saving Eleanor from the train wrecks that were local student productions. They saw Shakespeare, Euripides, Brecht, Miller and some godawful artsy thing that only solidified Eleanor's view that the playwright industry was stagnating (all the decent script writers had probably gone to Hollywood to work for Cheyenne's parents).

"It's nothing like seeing them in person, of course," Cheyenne said. "When I lived in California, I used to go on trips to New York every year and we'd always see a whole slew of shows. Once, my parents even tried to adapt one, but it was a total train wreck! Don't tell them I said that, though. One of these days we should get down to London: I need to go to the National Theatre. Is it really that ugly in person?"

The next play on their agenda was Chekhov. *The Seagull* was playing with a lauded actress from some hit TV programme as the lead. Eleanor was coming home to St Andrews from a swim meet early to see it.

"You sure you don't want to stay for afters?" Molly asked in the changing room as she towelled down her hair.

"I'm sure," Eleanor replied, wrestling with her sock. It was determined not to slide onto her foot, and her hastiness was only making it worse. "I agreed to go ages ago."

"And you'll get home safe?"

With a final tug, the sock was pulled on, but it caught on her heel and tore a hole as it went. Eleanor cursed as she shoved her shoe on anyway. "I've got my train route all sorted. Don't you worry."

"But it's late..."

It was, in fact, half-dark already, and only growing gloomier. But none of that mattered when it came to Cheyenne and her plays. "I'll be fine."

"Text me when you get back."

Her only reply was a brisk nod as Eleanor stepped out the door.

Edinburgh was a grey city at the best of times, and the twilight haze only made it more so. Eleanor traipsed past shop windows shuttered for the night, bars and nightclubs just opening up, and the great edifices of stone buildings, looming large above her. They were like canyons, funnelling people down to lakes or waterfalls, caves or oceans. Yet even in the downtown, things were quiet, sad, dull compared to London. How odd to be Edinburgh, a city always playing catch up.

There was the Scottish National Gallery, full of paintings and sculptures by people long dead. How many people were enshrined within those walls? So many, and yet so few at the same time. There were far more artists down in London, even more around the world. And yet if you took a sample of the people on the street, how many of them would ever be placed in a public space to be venerated? How great the swathe of people that had crossed the earth and been completely forgotten.

Her hair was still wet when she boarded the train. She let the water drip onto the seat as she watched the lights go by, relishing the moment when the whole cabin went silent as they glided over the Forth Bridge and the landscape went dark.

Somewhere further down the carriage, a woman started screaming about government plots. A pair of tourists chattered excitedly about their plans for tomorrow. A young couple leaned against each other in one corner; across from them were a pair of girls (Eleanor couldn't tell if they were friends or dating). A student furiously pored over her books while an elderly gentleman tapped his cane.

So many people. So many lives. How many of them memorable? Who would live on past their death?

Almost no one, Eleanor decided. Almost no one.

Cheyenne would. That was inevitable. And perhaps Eleanor herself, if she wrote her books and rode Cheyenne's coattails.

It was much easier, being Cheyenne. She was beautiful, yes, but her parents had done most of the work for her. She could have been an actress – an actress! – and she turned it down. What choice that girl had. What freedom! What a life she could know, and what opportunities she could snatch from other people.

The whole nepotism lark really was quite unfair.

It wasn't late, but the town was quiet: winter drew everyone inside, to their lights and the hearths and the glow of their laptop screens. Eleanor passed the beginnings of a handful of house parties, but for the most part encountered almost no one. She liked it that way: it lent her a uniqueness of experience.

She paused at the threshold of the theatre, where the blasts of warm air from within cooled her frostbitten cheeks. Her stiff hair started to drip chlorine again. Her stiff fingers rummaged in her pockets to pull out her phone. *At Chekhov. Where are u?*

There was no response until dangerously close to curtain. *We thought you weren't coming, made other plans. Sorry!*

Eleanor had told them she would make it. Surely she had told them she would make it? But the memory was fuzzy. Maybe Eleanor had merely said she'd been at a swim meet, and when she mentioned she'd be cutting it close, Cheyenne had presumed it was too much hassle for her to turn up.

For a second, Eleanor considered asking where they were, rushing out to join them. But the usher – a dusty-smelling old man with a kind smile – was already gesturing for her to take her seat. She'd bought her ticket months ago, she might as well use it.

The play was about a writer. A famous one. So star-studded that the young woman played by the glamorous actress was so overwhelmed to be in his presence she couldn't speak properly. *"He's so famous!"* she gushed. *"And he's right here, fishing by the lake!"*

Eleanor could do that. Eleanor could write well enough to make her the famous one, the one other people would fawn over. Even Cheyenne wouldn't pass up an opportunity to be around her, to let her stardom rub off. What a life Eleanor could know, if she only applied herself.

As the author exited and the dialogue droned on, Eleanor stood up and slipped from her seat. There was no one in her row – hardly anyone in the audience at all – and she thought her exit went unnoticed until she had left the auditorium and was almost out the theatre's doors.

'Excuse me miss?" a soft voice said. "Will you be going back in?"

It was the old usher, smiling politely as he leaned on his stick. There was something tender in his eyes: genuine concern, perhaps, that a young lady didn't like the work of Chekhov.

"No, sorry," Eleanor said breathlessly. "Something just came up, something that I had to do." She took one more step, then turned around to add, "the play: it touched me. Inspired me. But it made me remember something – I have to go."

And she was off, sprinting through the dark streets like a tortured Cinderella. Though come to think of it, Cinderella had been tortured plenty as well. Perhaps Eleanor was luckier, to have her fate in her own hands: no need to rely on benevolent fairies or nameless princes. A good theme, she decided, for a story.

She rushed to her room without dinner, even though her stomach was growling. An artist, she decided, could subsist on nothing but the strength of their imagination. Instead, she flung open her laptop screen and worked all night, typing long into the early hours of morning. Her hands ached, her mind grew numb, but she forced herself to keep at it. If ever she began to tire and fray, she forced the images of Chekhov and his writer into her brain. When that didn't work, she thought of the artists in the National Gallery, the authors on the shelves of the university library, the poets, the painters, the dancers, the actors, the stars. And Cheyenne, blazing bright above them all.

"You look tired," Cheyenne observed two days later. Eleanor squinted up at Cheyenne, who now appeared to be wreathed in a literal halo. Eleanor's eyes focused and revealed it was only the electric light of the library behind Cheyenne.

Eleanor shrugged. "I've been working a lot."

"Getting a head start on the essays?"

"No. Creative stuff."

Cheyenne smiled banally. "Well, tell me when it's published."

"We'll see," Eleanor replied quietly. In the light of day, everything that had seemed genius in the witching hour suddenly appeared pale and uninspired.

It was a grey February afternoon, the kind that sucked energy and banished lifeblood with its tepid glow. They'd just had two back-to-back lectures, and were now sitting in the library cafe with their coffees, pretending to work. Cheyenne had taken one sip of her drink then spat it out, declaring she'd get a better one later. Eleanor tried to focus on her laptop screen, then her book, but the words only blurred before her eyes, and she soon found herself sinking into oblivion.

Footsteps sounded to their side. Eleanor ignored them until the seat to her left sank down and a sickening familiar voice filled her ears. "Coffee for you?"

It was Raquelle, fresh from the coffee shop with a box of paper cups. Her perfume was overpoweringly strong in Eleanor's exhausted state, and she was wearing what Eleanor immediately decided was too much makeup. Completely unsuitable for the occasion, but Cheyenne didn't seem to mind.

"You're an angel," Cheyenne declared. "How was your lecture?"

"Awful. I *hate* French."

"Why do you take it then?" Eleanor demanded. It came out snappier than she intended – or perhaps it was just as abrasive as she was feeling.

"It's a love-hate relationship."

Was Eleanor imagining it, or was that the tinge of a sneer?

"I wouldn't expect you to understand; not when you don't do a language."

"Of course; economics is *much* easier."

"Don't mind her; she's exhausted," Cheyenne broke in. "Do you want some of my coffee, Eleanor?"

Eleanor hated coffee, but she took a sip without hesitating. Anything from Cheyenne was not to be declined.

"Anyway." Raquelle leaned over the table towards Cheyenne, so close their foreheads were almost touching. "Did you hear the news?"

Eleanor had to strain to hear.

"What news?" Cheyenne asked.

"Penelope Hale is coming to play in Edinburgh!"

Even Eleanor knew who Penelope Hale was. She was a star of the moment, one of those celebrities who suddenly burst onto the A-List out of nowhere. Her brand of pop was less musical and more lyrical: her voice was low and she couldn't hit any kind of belt, but the words were punchy and the sing-song repetition was addicting.

Cheyenne seemed to deflate as the words came out of Raquelle's mouth. "Oh. Her."

Raquelle seemed puzzled. "Is something wrong?"

"She's just a bit…" Cheyenne leaned back and fiddled with her hair in an attempt to look disinterested. "…American."

"F Scott Fitzgerald was American, and you like *The Great Gatsby*," Eleanor pointed out, only to immediately regret it. She must truly be tired to be siding with Raquelle.

"That's different. He knew how to critique his country." Cheyenne broke their gaze and stared across the table, out past the quad and into the distance. "Also, I went to school with her."

"You went to school with Penelope Hale?" Eleanor and Raquelle gasped as one. It was hard to tell who was more shocked.

Cheyenne shrugged. "It was a fancy high school in LA: what's there to be surprised about? Plus, Penelope's mother is an American daytime TV star and her father became very wealthy through tech investment. She already had her foot in the door. That's the only reason she's got any fame at all. Just listen to her and you can tell she can't sing." Her voice was the most detached Eleanor had ever heard.

"She can write though," Eleanor said, more forcefully than she had intended.

"Anyone can write. It's getting onstage that matters." Cheyenne must have seen Eleanor flush, because she leaned over and made a sympathetic face. "Not for novels, Eleanor." It wasn't very convincing. "Honestly, I'd do a better job with those songs than Penelope."

"Jealousy isn't a good look, Cheyenne."

"Eleanor, I know you're tired, but kindly shut up." Cheyenne's tone was more agitated than Eleanor had ever heard. "I don't want to see Penelope Hale because I think she's a bitch, and at the moment Eleanor, you're acting an awful lot like her." She grabbed her book and slammed it down on the table so loudly that the tables around them turned to look over. "And her nails look like shit," she muttered under her breath.

For the first time in their lives, Eleanor and Raquelle exchanged a concerned look. It was a strange sensation: for a moment, Eleanor felt a giddy thrill at the sudden connection. Then Cheyenne glared at them, and Eleanor remembered where her loyalties lay.

Trying to focus with Cheyenne in a bad mood was like attempting to enjoy your last meal before execution. Eleanor couldn't take another fifteen minutes. She left with only the curtest of goodbyes, finding for once that she didn't care if Raquelle and Cheyenne were left alone together. Let Raquelle get devoured by the lion for bringing up Penelope.

"Have you heard?" said one of the girls at swimming that evening. "Penelope Hale is coming to Edinburgh!"

"Penelope Hale!" said someone that weekend at the club in the queue for the toilets. "The tickets will be insane, but I can't not try."

"I just love her music!" cooed a young woman to her boyfriend over coffee. "Something in it speaks to me!"

"You were right," Eleanor admitted to Cheyenne as she sat down next to her at a lecture. "It really is tiresome to keep hearing about Penelope Hale."

Cheyenne clucked her tongue appreciatively. "At least someone has taste." Eleanor rode the glow of the compliment for the rest of the day.

March.

Three years and two months before the party.

"There's been a development," Cheyenne said one afternoon while stirring her coffee.

Eleanor looked up from her book and frowned. "With what?"

They were sitting in one of the common rooms, ostensibly studying – though Eleanor had read about one page in the last hour thanks to their semi-constant levels of chatter. She was just getting into a passage of her book when Cheyenne's phone had pinged. Eleanor looked up to see her frown at it.

"I can't live with you next year." Cheyenne tossed her head airily, as if this were the most casual thing in the world.

"What?" Eleanor nearly dropped her book. "But we've been looking for a flat for weeks!"

Cheyenne shrugged. "Henry's found a place with a few of his mates, and they're looking for an extra." She dropped the British slang like it was natural in her American mouth.

"And you just took it?"

She pouted. "You know how much of a nightmare it is to find a flat. And besides, what'll it look like if I say no to Henry?"

Eleanor was indignant. "Who even are these friends?"

"Some of them are girls, don't worry. Gina, Raquelle, Sam – you know that lot."

"This is ridiculous. George, back me up."

He avoided her gaze. "Sorry Eleanor, but I've got another flat lined up too."

Her voice went very quiet. "What did you say?"

"I've got another flat lined up." He took a deep breath and rocked back and forth, like he was working up the courage. "When Cheyenne mentioned they'd been asking her, I asked some of the boys if I could live with them, and they offered me a place."

Eleanor's anger had been replaced with a sinking pit in her chest. "When did Cheyenne tell you this?"

He shrugged. "A few nights ago. We were up talking."

A braver Eleanor would have yelled, would have stood up and slapped them, would have given them a piece of her mind. But these were her friends – and Cheyenne was perched on the sofa with an expectant expression.

"I should have told you earlier," Cheyenne said, "but I didn't think they'd have a place until now and it didn't seem important. If we'd have found one first, I'd have gone with you lot." She cocked her head. "You'll find someone to live with, won't you? Don't be upset."

Eleanor forced a breath down. "I'm not upset," she said, and forced a smile. "Just a bit shocked, that's all."

Cheyenne flashed her perfect teeth. "I'm so glad." But when she went back to reading, the silence was thick enough to be cut with a knife.

At last, George cleared his throat. "I submitted to the gallery."

"Really?" Cheyenne shot up in excitement, the tension forgotten. "That's amazing George! It'll be wonderful for your career."

"I might not get it," he said shyly.

"You will. It's the one we went to in Edinburgh, right? They loved me when we visited – maybe if I drop them a line..."

"When did you do that?" Eleanor broke in. She hadn't even known George had been thinking about submitting any of his paintings, let alone narrowing down galleries.

Cheyenne waved a hand. "A few days ago. That was when I told George about the flat. It was a very spur-of-the-moment thing. You were at swimming."

Eleanor had already been made a fool of once today, she was determined not to have it happen again. Cheyenne was trying to play it so casually now, when she purposefully – for Eleanor was sure this was purposeful – hadn't mentioned the trip earlier. She knew she had done wrong.

Eleanor wasn't in a mood to fight, so she simply smiled brightly and said, "Did you like it?"

"It was amazing," George gushed. "All the art was so good though – I'm not sure I can compare."

Cheyenne snorted. "I promise you, it'll be fine. Besides," she added, "didn't you say the owner went to your school? That just about seals the deal."

"Maybe," said George, but he didn't sound convinced.

"You'll be grand," reassured Eleanor, but she wasn't sure she meant it. The mood remained uneasy, and when it came time for Eleanor's swim session, her stomach dropped when she saw the look George and Cheyenne gave each other as she left the room.

6th May. 14:23.

Four hours until the party.

The rain starts again: a fine mist that condenses into droplets on coats and hats, then solidifies into steady, plonking drops. Eleanor can't stand Scottish rain. What does it bring to the country? It doesn't render everything lush and green, like England, nor does it result in a sudden explosion of colour as it does in California. It just rains, and dampens, and moulds – and even those moulds are an ugly shade of grey.

In California, the land and sea are a contrast: dry air, cool water. Here in Scotland, standing on her balcony, Eleanor cannot tell where the rain ends and the ocean begins. Just one endless slab of grey, stretching out into oblivion like the sad lives of the people trapped here.

In the corner of her eye, a shape flounders. A rowing boat, crewed by a group desperately trying to return to port. They look doomed: already their bow is dangerously low and taking on more water with every wave. If they have any sense, they'll change course and paddle to the sand, but university rowers aren't known for their brains.

A stupid idea, really, seafaring. Why not just swim if you're that desperate to touch the water? The dock in town has been there five hundred years, and claimed many lives.

Endless dreary lives, snatched away by the depths. Perhaps it's better to go like that than to plod on relentlessly.

If she squints, she can pretend she sees an ocean liner passing by. Distress signals on the Titanic were ignored by nearby ships, who thought they were signals of celebration. Now, the drowned dance in the depths every night. A cold, violent death, but a peaceful afterlife.

No, she decides, it would not be so bad.

The damp seems to have made the room stiflingly hot. Eleanor paces around it like a captive shark, the sort that go mad and die after being held in a soulless aquarium for too long. Sometimes the orcas would even kill their handler. A train of revenge before their eventual death, for they can't survive in the wild after all their years in a cage. A cruel way to go, kept apart from the sea.

She's cleaned everything: plumped the cushions, poured out the nuts, adjusted the furniture in an inviting manner. The first bunches of catering has arrived – gougères for the indulgent, celery sticks for the weight watchers, and almond-flour cakes for the celiacs. She has arranged the paintings just so – involuntarily her eyes flick to a seaside image of two girls wading (anticipation curls in her stomach; she shakes it off). She has pictured her visitors arriving so many times, gone over every possible situation in her head over and over, so now that the moment is almost here it feels like nothing more than the fabric of another fantasy.

She cannot fuck this up. Not when she is so close.

Staying here is driving her insane. Eleanor throws on her coat in the spur of the moment and rushes out the door. She doesn't head in the direction of the sea – it feels too dangerous, somehow, to go in there now. There is too much of a risk of sinking in and never emerging. Instead, she walks the other way through town, past where the Victorian grey stone fades to dreary brown pebble dash, where what passes as a town ends and suburbia begins. There, cutting through a damp alley that hasn't been cleaned for at least two and a half generations, she finally makes it to the forest.

Forest is perhaps a generous term. The woods are a thin swatch of greenery cutting along an ancient stream. It's got a Scottish name that Cheyenne thought sounded romantic but turned out, when translated, just to mean "old brook". She walks past mud and stinging nettles to the top of a dingy hill – again, a generous term for something that is, at most, fifty feet above sea level.

Today, it is a peaceful park: the sort of place families picnic, dogs run and students gather to drink as they watch the sunset. Yet years ago, this was a hallowed place: a cemetery, a cremation site, a place to lay the village dead to rest. If you stand on the top and look in the right direction, you can still see the outlines of shallow graves.

Cheyenne once told her they burnt witches out here. Eleanor wonders what it would have been like, to be so hated by the people you spent your life with that you were killed. Not a spur-of-the-moment, inadvertent killing either: something planned, meditated and acted upon. Or was it more sudden: a group frenzy, driven by hate?

Eleanor wasn't sure which would be worse.

So many who lived, even in just this little town. So many who died. Were any of them poets? Or singers, or metalworkers, or any who could work magic with a loom? So proud they must have been, of their work, their fame, the lives they had built for themselves. All that, and yet it had been snatched away by time and death all the same.

From one of the graves, a corner of stone is still visible. Eleanor crouches down next to it, hovering on her tiptoes to keep her haunches out of the mud, and presses her fingers to it. Cold, and damp, with no memory of the people who had touched it, worked it, loved it. Of course there isn't, it is only a rock. But a tragic one, all the same.

A sudden desperation takes her, burning as fierce as the pain in her calves from the awkward crouch. She digs her fingers into the dirt and tears wildly, not caring as her nails break and thistles tears at her skin. She shovels dirt to the side like a mad dog, unrelenting in her hunt for the dead. It is not flesh or bones she cares about though, but names, memory. She has to know if anything of their lives remains.

The rain turns the soil to mud around her, washing what she has removed back over Eleanor's arms and legs. The cycle continues relentlessly even as she cries out in frustration, her yell growing to a ceaseless, never-ending wail. There is grief in it, pain, and most of all a wild, unrelenting anger. How dare the world allow this? How dare the world forget?

The next morning – or evening perhaps, depending on when this rain lets up – something will find this hole. A child, maybe, or a dog, or even an inquisitive drunk student: any of them will discover this strange pit, dug over a rock which was once a tombstone and has become a rock once more. They will frown, and stare, and perhaps wonder what happened there. Then they will touch it – gingerly at first, then with more confidence – until finally they are grinning, delighting in the pleasure of novelty. Not much changes in this little town – nothing other than the tides and the constant intake and release of students with interchangeable faces. But here is something old, something forgotten, that has become new and remembered again.

The dirt has ground Eleanor's fingernails to pieces before she finally uncovers a mark on the stone. Another hangnail flakes off when she runs her finger along the grooves. A common name: seven simple letters. Half an hour's work for the local stonemason. Yet Eleanor would know it in her sleep.

Her stomach roils. She staggers back: bile rises in her throat, and if she is going to be sick she has to do it right here, right now, where no one is around to stare or whisper.

The name on the stone, carved and weathered and forgotten, is Eleanor.

It's a prank; some elaborate joke. Eleanor glances wildly around the overgrown field, waiting for someone to jump out with a camera and delight at her humiliation. Raquelle, Gina, even Cheyenne – any of them could be wracked by jealousy. It is so much easier to assume it's a wicked trick, rather than the callous coincidence of the universe.

No one emerges. The rain patters on, unrelenting and uncaring. The dead lie in their graves, unmoving, forgotten.

Images of another graveyard flash in Eleanor's mind: another rainy field, another worn down stone. This time, the surname is visible: Sanders. There are no flowers lovingly placed at her feet, no devoted groundskeeper to trim away the encroaching vines. It is as dank and lonely as the grave before her.

It won't happen, Eleanor vows. She won't let it happen. She has Jack – and she can get Cheyenne and George and all the rest again, if she only tries. She can have it all.

She wanders home the long way, past the ditches and stinging nettles. The damp saturates her hair and runs down her limbs, making the mud on her hands drip behind her. She certainly looks like a witch now, with her earthen claws. Yet it's too wet to light the fire that would kill her.

In the dark and the rain, people light up their windows: a thousand picture boxes shining out onto the street. In one, a man sits shirtless, staring at a TV screen. In another, a group of friends chat as they cook a meal. A woman hunches over her computer, typing out the last few words of her dissertation. A child plays with their dog. A middle-aged couple share a bottle of champagne. A drunken hookup who have only just awoken sit awkwardly across from each other, both still naked. So many lives, so many loves and losses and desires and needs, all playing out next to each other. A different TV screen everywhere you look.

Not as good as Eleanor's scripts though. She has drama, tension, romance, all added in just the right amounts. She bakes a delightful cake, designed to wow the judges; these people are throwing together ingredients willy-nilly, desperately trying to survive.

The maid from this morning is still on the stairs when Eleanor returns: she really must be new, if she's only cleaned a few floors in all these hours. The girl starts when she sees Eleanor, she wiped the rain off her face without thinking earlier, so now her entire face is a patchwork of dirt. "Do you want something to clean yourself up?" she offers.

It's very forward of her, the staff usually keep quiet – but the back stairs aren't quite like the front rooms of the hotel. The boundaries are blurred, the distance between client and waitstaff trickier to define.

Eleanor shakes her head. "No. I have things in my room. Don't worry."

"I'll open the doors for you." The maid scurries ahead before Eleanor can protest. She likely took one look at the mud on her hands and decided she didn't want to spend half an hour polishing it off a doorknob.

Eleanor tries to dismiss the maid as soon as they reach the top floor, but she seems reluctant to leave. "Is something wrong?" Eleanor asks.

"My sister used to live with you," the girl says softly. "She said you were nice."

How hasn't she seen it? The hair, the eyes, the set of the jaw. The girl's a dead ringer for Liz. Then again, Eleanor hasn't seen Liz and been sober simultaneously for two years.

"She exaggerates. I was a nightmare." Eleanor's fingers rub nervously against her clothes, rendered skin-tight by the rain. "I went to see her this morning, but she was out."

The girl nods. "She always wondered why you didn't come back to live with her. But I suppose...'

"Yeah, well." Eleanor swallows uneasily. "I got lucky, I guess."

"And you met that man." This is an extremely unsuitable conversation for a maid to have with a typical hotel guest, but Eleanor isn't typical, and neither is this girl. "Is it true what you told the manager? That you're still dating?"

"You going to sell the story to the tabloids or something?"

The girl flushes an angry red. "No! I just... I wanted..."

Eleanor shrugs. "The allure of Hollywood gets to everyone." She frowns, runs her eyes over the girl once more. "What's your name?"

"Amy."

"And I'm Eleanor, but you know that already. If you repeat any of what I'm about to tell you, I will track you down and sue you for all you're worth. You understand?" Her eyes turn steely: she has done all this before.

Amy gulps. "Yes."

Eleanor recites the facts off in a monotone. "Me and Jack are together. I saw him at Christmas. The tabloids are saying we're on a break because the potential of him dating gets people interested. He won't be able to get another girlfriend, so I'm not worried. He needs me too much anyway." Somehow, it all sounded much more dramatic in her head.

Amy's voice is catlike-quiet. "Why can't he get another girlfriend?"

"That's something only friends can know. And I'm afraid I don't have any of those."

Amy shrugs. "You have people who would like to be your friend."

One sentence, the sort of thing a schoolchild might say to another on the playground, and yet it shocks Eleanor to the core. People who would want to be her friend? There are people who admire her, yes, people who wonder about her, respect her, work with her. But friends? She left that idea behind years ago.

"I think it's a bit late for that," is all Eleanor replies. When she moves to shut the door, Amy is still standing there, a sad look in her eyes.

April.

Three years and one month before the party.

Eleanor hadn't seen George for days. She didn't notice it so much on the weekends – their trio rarely had dinner together anymore, what with Henry on Cheyenne's side and swimming on Eleanor's – so it was only when he stopped turning up to lectures that she asked what was wrong.

Cheyenne raised an eyebrow in surprise. "He's sick," she said as if it were obvious. Behind her, Raquelle exchanged a knowing glance with Gina. Eleanor's chest burned in fury.

On their way home, Cheyenne swerved into the corner shop. "Food for George," she explained when faced with Eleanor's blank stare. "He can't come down for meals anymore." She paid on her own credit card and threw the receipt away without even glancing at it.

"I'll come with you," Eleanor said as they approached Cheyenne's hall. "I should go and see him."

She paused. "He might not want you there."

"I don't care. I'm his friend, I should be giving him support."

"This isn't about you, Eleanor."

She felt as if Cheyenne had slapped her. It wasn't her fault she didn't know what was wrong – and if she wanted to get closer to George, then seeing him was the way to do it.

But she couldn't argue. Not with Cheyenne.

Eleanor turned and strode away without a word, hands jammed into her pockets so Cheyenne couldn't see her fists clench. Tears pricked at her eyes as she walked, and thoughts swarmed her brain, turning more and more poisonous. Cheyenne couldn't mistrust her that much, could she? It must be George's fault. Not even his fault – a natural thing to do, her logical brain insisted, to confide in the one who lived closest to you. Cheyenne was the natural choice.

Yet, Raquelle had known. Gina too. She kept replaying their smirks in the lecture hall, the English – or as good as English – twins digging their claws into everything. They were the problem, really: they were the ones who were tearing Eleanor's friendships apart. They'd dragged Cheyenne in, entrapped her, and they were wrapping their tendrils around George as well.

Anger gave her strength of conviction. She turned again, paced back down the street to George and Cheyenne's halls. There was a small park opposite one of the building's walls – barely more than a patch of grass and a few scrubby trees, but it gave Eleanor a space to sit and conceal herself while she watched the windows. George's room was on the third floor, Cheyenne's on the second. Eleanor waited in the cold, her mind too furious to think about trying to get some work done, until Cheyenne's light finally switched on. George's room also remained illuminated. Perfect.

People were always coming in and out of the halls and she was let in without question. Once inside, she took the back stairs – the pit of her stomach was prickly with anticipation, and the potential of seeing someone was too much for her to handle.

She stood outside George's room for five whole minutes before working up the courage to knock on the door.

At first, she thought he wouldn't answer. There was no sign of movement, not even the creak of someone rolling over on the bed.

She knocked again: three hard raps.

This time, footsteps sounded. Eleanor braced herself as the door opened.

George looked awful. He was dressed in sweatpants and a hoodie – items of clothing Eleanor didn't even know he owned – and he had gone without shaving long enough to develop a thick dusting of stubble. His eyes were red and puffy as he took her in. "What are you doing here?" There was accusation in his voice.

"I came to see you," Eleanor replied simply. "To see how you're doing."

"I'm terrible. Is that good enough?" He tried to shut the door, but Eleanor stuck her foot in the frame.

"George, let me in."

"I don't want to."

Eleanor pushed with all her strength and flung the door open anyway. George stumbled to ground and groaned as he picked himself up. He really must be atrocious if he couldn't put up a better fight.

She could see why George hadn't wanted her in here. The room was filthy. It looked as though he hadn't left in days. The bed was in disarray, the floor covered in dirty plates and scattered clothes, and his desk, normally so neat, was covered in dried paint. As Eleanor got closer, she could make out empty paint tubes and stained brushes.

"Do you like it?" George said as she took the scene in. "It's my new masterpiece." He picked a fleck on paint off the side of the desk and blew it into the main collage. "It's like one of Goya's: a moving depiction of the loss of my mind."

"You know they'll make you pay for that," Eleanor pointed out.

George shrugged. "Who cares? I'll just buy the thing. It can get displayed in a museum one day – if I ever make it, which is looking less likely by the minute."

Eleanor made what she hoped was a sympathetic face, but she suspected was closer to a grimace. "Gallery submission didn't go well then?"

"Does it look like it went well?" George grabbed the nearest paintbrush and tossed it against the wall in anger. It left a faint yellow stain: one of many, Eleanor noticed, creating a strange mural of ghostly butterflies, a monument to George's anger. It must have been difficult to look at those each night.

She tried to keep her voice calm and rational. "You know you'll get a thousand rejections before an acceptance? It's the same with writing."

"But not this one!" Another paintbrush hit the wall. This one was purple. "You heard what Cheyenne said: the curator went to the same school as I did! If he doesn't take me, nobody will."

"Maybe that's why he didn't take you," suggested Eleanor. "He didn't want to be accused of nepotism."

"It was all the wrong theme anyway," George muttered. "Focused on identity – and I have an identity, goddammit, and I painted that! What it means to be young, uncertain, adrift. How it feels to have parents who don't quite understand why you're dooming yourself to poverty as an artist; what it's like being so subject to other's approval..."

"George, you're a white man who went to Eton. Your identity isn't very avant-garde."

"I can't help that!" he cried, and Eleanor got the feeling this was not what she was meant to be saying.

She tried a different tack. "Look, why don't you submit to one of the student art magazines? There were more than I could count at the club fair in September."

"I don't want the student magazines!" A blue butterfly hit the wall. "I'm worth more than their stuff! I work harder, I want it more! I deserve to be in something greater that the *Student Review of Arts*!"

"And if you get rejected from there, it'll be even worse." Oddly enough, everything George was saying made perfect sense. Eleanor knew the feeling, had sorted through it a thousand times when deciding whether or not to churn out some ditty for one of the endless student competitions. She knew she was better than her peers. To lose to them would destroy her entire sense of being.

For a second, she considered telling George this, sharing her connection. But the words that flowed so easily through her mind seemed to transform into clumsy, half-wrought sentences devoid of emotion. In the end, she settled for gentle reassurances. "It'll be alright. And look, you should come to lectures. It'll take your mind off it. Besides, if you fail your first year, you'll have an even harder time getting into galleries."

"Telling people to just do things doesn't do much for depression," George muttered.

"Then I'll come and collect you. Me and Cheyenne." Eleanor lapsed back into including Cheyenne despite the resentment bubbling up inside her. It was too unthinkable to leave her out. "And we'll find other galleries. Ones more suited to you."

George nodded slowly. He seemed on the verge of saying something – a word lingered on his lips that would sum up what he and Eleanor were. How they had started, where they had ended up, what they were going to do. But when he opened his mouth, he hit a wall. His eyes shone wearily as they met Eleanor's - but some of their despondency was gone. That was as close to a dismissal as Eleanor was going to get.

Her limbs were filled with adrenaline as she descended the stairs, and without thinking, she marched over to Cheyenne's door and knocked. It wasn't Cheyenne who opened the door.

Eleanor tried to keep a blank face as she took in Henry. "Can I talk to Cheyenne for a second?" she asked.

Cheyenne emerged, frowning, adjusting a jumper she'd evidently only just pulled over her. Eleanor could see flashes of skin from behind the zip. "What is it now?"

"I was just up with George." Eleanor paused to let the triumph exude from her, but Cheyenne was too busy glancing back towards Henry to pay any attention. "I told him we're going to be making sure he goes to lectures from now on. Walking him there and everything."

Cheyenne nodded. "Cool. We'll do that."

"So I'll be over here a lot," Eleanor went on. "To help George."

Her words had precisely no effect on Cheyenne, whose feet were already edging towards her boyfriend. Eleanor turned without bothering to hide her disgust, then shoved her way out the door, pushing past people as she rushed down the corridor. She couldn't stand another second in this godforsaken hall. As she walked away, even the heat of her victory with George faded to nothing more than a lukewarm ember, barely alive in the chill of her soul.

6th May.

Three years before the party.

Eleanor's birthday fell right after the end of exams. There was to be no repeat of the Nice trip – George hadn't been well enough to even think about travelling until last week, and by that time it was too late to book a trip. Nor did Eleanor feel like copying Cheyenne anyway. But she didn't have the time to think of something else to do in the midst of studying, so the sixth of May dawned with them still in their dorm rooms.

"We'll do something fun," Cheyenne declared when they met for coffee that morning. These hangouts were becoming less frequent: gone were the days of impromptu meetups. Now everything had to be arranged days before, and was always subject to someone rushing off for a class they claimed they'd completely forgotten about. "Find somewhere we've never been before."

Eleanor smiled wryly. "This town has about three streets."

She frowned. "You'll see."

The door creaked as it swung open. Eleanor glanced up from their table in the corner to see Gina, Raquelle, Henry and Sam walk in. She looked away immediately, but it was too late: Cheyenne stood and gestured them over.

Raquelle frowned at their little group. "I didn't know you drank coffee, Eleanor."

"It's tea," she replied bluntly. Raquelle's outfit could have doubled as a prep school uniform: pleated skirt, blazer, bow. Her socks were unusual: a sunset gradient, with chequers overlaid. Eleanor had never seen them on her before. "We're just here to meet up before my birthday."

"Where are you going?" Gina piped up. Despite the heat, she was wrapped in an oversized jumper emblazoned with the surf club logo: one of Sam's.

Silence. Eleanor fidgeted awkwardly, sure she was about to admit her lameness to this group.

Cheyenne jumped in at the last minute. "The castle," she declared confidently, as if it had been her plan all along. "We can even have some drinks." Eleanor's heart soared at her wry smile, only for it to sink when she added, "you can come along, if you like." She was looking at Henry as she said it, wrapping a coil of hair around her finger.

There was nothing to be done after Cheyenne had made the suggestion. Eleanor traipsed to the castle next to George, the beautiful weather only making her feel worse. It had been such a glorious day, why did that lot have to come and ruin it? Why did they have to take Cheyenne from her now?

The castle sat high on the sea cliffs, half a mile down from the beach where Eleanor took her swims. From the sand, it always seemed so imposing: a looming edifice sitting at stark contrast to the vast, open beauty of the ocean. Yet approaching from land, it seemed much less threatening: a squat, crumbling ruin; little more than a square of grass surrounded by half-collapsed walls.

When you crossed the green to the cliff edge and looked down, your whole view changed. Here was the drop, a precipitous overhang above jagged rocks battered by approaching waves. Their medieval predecessors had built a balcony here where you could sit and watch your domain, and contemplate casting your enemies into the abyss below.

"No one's ever fallen off this, have they?" George wondered.

"Probably," Eleanor said. "People get drunk, they get too close." *Drawn in*, she wanted to say, by the alluring beauty of the sea below and sky above. An endless void waiting for someone to fill it. "And I'm sure a few prisoners got thrown off." It was only after the words left her mouth she considered she might have been a little more tactful, considering George's morose state.

"They burnt people at the stake back then instead," Raquelle butted in. "You can see the dungeon over there." She led the way to a tiny room with a hole in the ground, leading to a pit that Eleanor couldn't see the bottom of. A nearby sign helpfully informed them that this was where prisoners would wait before their execution.

"I'd go insane." Cheyenne shivered. "All alone in the dark, cut off from everyone."

Gina shrugged. "People were cruel back then."

As they shuffled out, Eleanor found herself slotted behind Raquelle. She watched her feet to make sure she didn't miss a step, and she found herself drawn to Raquelle's socks. They really were distinctive.

"Raquelle," she said as they climbed, "where did you get your socks?"

Raquelle frowned and glanced down. "One of the shops in town maybe. I don't remember."

"It's just I have the same pair. Identical."

"And?"

"And I was just wondering – if maybe they got lost, or you picked them up from the lost and found, or…"

"Are you accusing me of stealing your socks?" Raquelle rolled her eyes. "Come off it, Eleanor. I'm not a thief."

"I'm not saying you are! I was just wondering…"

"What makes you think I'd want anything of yours that badly?" Raquelle turned on her heel and flounced off, leaving Eleanor floundering and alone. She waited a moment before rejoining the others, but Raquelle already had her arm around Cheyenne. The pair were laughing, and Eleanor felt her heart twist as she settled down a few feet from them.

She couldn't be bothered to talk. Instead she lay in the grass and watched the sky; made shapes out of the clouds as they drifted over the sun. Childhood games; simple things that could be done by yourself. Good for if you didn't really have any friends.

A bolt of anger shot through her and Eleanor pulled out her phone. In a few clicks, she'd got what she needed.

"Cheyenne, George?" she called. The two looked up. "I forgot to mention, but I made a reservation the other night for dinner. It's very early though: it was all they had available."

"Just the three of us?" Cheyenne said. She didn't sound overly enthused. Perhaps Raquelle had already whispered poison in her ear.

"I didn't know there would be more people when I made it."

"Hmmf." Cheyenne propped herself on her elbows to glance at her watch. The pose only made her look even more like a model, as if she were posing for an imaginary camera. "We have a few hours," she declared. "A few drinks at the beach with everyone, and then we go."

"Actually," Eleanor said, "I have to meet my flatmates for next year in an hour. They want to say happy birthday before they go home."

It wasn't quite a lie: Liz and Molly would be happy to see her. They'd messaged her a happy birthday that morning, said they would like to meet. But Eleanor had no intention of seeing them at this moment. Instead, when Cheyenne and George said a happy – if slightly confused – goodbye, and Raquelle and Gina only waved, Eleanor rushed back to her room, collapsed on her bed, buried her head in her pillow, and screamed until her voice went raw.

Three hours later, eyes empty of tears and throat lozenges sucked, Eleanor arrived at the restaurant with a smile on her face. She was a lovely girl, pretty enough and perfectly charming, and as they talked of banal topics and George smiled at Cheyenne's in-jokes, she could almost convince herself that things were alright.

6th May. 16:47.

Two hours until the party.

They say the mirror never lies. That may be true, but the thing reflected in the glass can be a conniving little fiend if it wants to be. Like all sorts of people Eleanor doesn't care to mention.

Thank God, Eleanor thinks, twirling a lock of hair around her finger, she isn't blonde. Not another California bombshell, row after row of them lined up like they just stepped off the manufacturer's line. No, in LA she is different. *Foreign*, Jack calls her, with silky hair and a silkier accent. Unique. Not like here, where she is nothing more than the girl who lives in the penthouse, not even pretty enough to warrant attention. Not that it matters, when she has a pretty mind.

Her dress is the colour of wine, just like Homer's angry sea. Comforting, in a way, to feel her beloved ocean surrounding her like a shield. Nothing can go wrong while she's shrouded in its waves. There are vague memories contained within the dress' fabric of another night: some LA party on Jack's arm, champagne fizzing up her nose, the smell of some mansion's bougainvillea rising above the reek of tarmac. What a life she has known.

The necklace is blue as well: a sparkling azure. Jack bought it for her six months ago and got it shipped from a London studio. He yearns to visit London. She could hear it in his voice when he spoke. Sometimes Eleanor wishes she'd gone there instead – swapped this tiny Scottish town for some cosmopolitan sinkhole. But then, she supposes, she wouldn't have met Jack at all. Would never have known Cheyenne. Besides, the last time she walked through London, out to dinner with her parents, she spent the entire trip green with envy. Incredulous that so many people could be so rich, so successful. She wouldn't return, she vowed to herself, until she could buy out the entirety of Bond Street.

Still, at least it wouldn't have been Scotland.

She must remember to talk Jack out of visiting the Highlands. Eleanor can't take another minute in this country.

She rummages through the detritus of the side table, searching for the hard glint of a mobile phone. Instead, her fingers rest on the corner of an envelope. An expensive one, made of thick, heavy paper. Her name and address are emblazoned on it in a fiery red, but they've been ripped in two by Eleanor in her haste to open it.

It came three weeks ago – an invitation from the university president, inviting Eleanor to a dinner for high-achieving students. *An invitation of highest honour,* the letter read. *A good networking event,* Eleanor translated it to. The letter was the sort of thing Eleanor had once dreamed of receiving, but now she tossed it to the side without a second thought. How meteoric people's rises could be. How equally quick the fall.

Her phone rests on a pile of makeup behind the envelope. The device is sparkling new, but when Eleanor flips it on, she can see a familiar home screen loaded onto it. The sim slot is blank for now, but tomorrow her American number will be loaded onto it, and her old phone discarded. University thrown completely in the bin.

Other things will be discarded as well. Eleanor dreamed of the castle last night – just as she has so many times over, beginning the night back in second year she prefers not to think about. In Eleanor's dream she flounders helplessly; she lets them drag her to her doom. Tonight, the castle looms large in her imagination. She will take them there. She will show them what Eleanor Sanders can do.

She steels herself one more time, runs her hands down her dress. She looks strong, like a goddess, and the mirror never lies.

September.

Two years and eight months before the party.

Eleanor didn't speak much to university friends over summer. Partly because she was too busy – there were swimming competitions to attend, shifts at the local pub to work, afternoons to sit lounging on the grass – but more pressing was that she had no one to talk to. Cheyenne was in Los Angeles (though she spent the end of July with school friends having their "hot girl summer" on the Continent), George declined her one request to visit saying he was "too busy with work", and all her swimming mates lived too far up north for her to bother with. So, she freckled and sweated and tanned and worked on her novel in the long summer evenings when the air still hung muggy and warm. Cheyenne, she thought, would approve of the romantic isolation of it all.

Cheyenne would also approve of her writing. She finished one novel, a fantasy lark with elves and dragons, then threw it away with disgust when she reread it. Her next project would be something more serious, something with weight – the sort that snatched up literary awards and had articles written about it in the New York Times. She set her sights on a sweeping critique of the military industrial complex through a soul-wrenching tale of war and woe, and she was quite pleased with her progress.

So, it was with excitement that Eleanor disembarked the train station in September, weighed down by her books and clothes. This was going to be a reset. They'd had their time away over the summer to decompress, to forget all the things they found aggravating about each other, and now they could kindle their friendship anew.

She'd found a flat with some friends from swimming, Liz and Molly. It was, by all regards, a perfectly lovely place. Tucked away down one of the alleyways in downtown, it got wonderful light in the morning to wake them up for training, and the pool was conveniently nearby. The pair she shared with were lovely girls, but she hadn't spent that much time with them last year. Whenever they were together, Eleanor's thoughts always strayed to wondering what Cheyenne was doing right now. But this year, things would be better: Eleanor had a lovely conversation with Liz as they unpacked, and she laughed with Molly as they made meal plans for the rest of the week.

But, as always, the real draw was to see Cheyenne.

She lived in a gorgeous townhouse one street off the main thoroughfare: Victorian, with sweeping bay windows and a spacious garden. Eleanor arranged to meet with her one sunny afternoon, and when Cheyenne opened the door, she grinned and waved her in like an excited real estate agent.

"Isn't it just wonderful?" she gushed. "And so *old*! There's nothing like this in Los Angeles! My house was built in 2015." Cheyenne's house was also – judging from the backgrounds of pictures Eleanor had ruthlessly scrutinised – extremely large and extremely expensive.

"And this is my room," she finished, pulling Eleanor into a sunny space that looked over the road – suitable, so mere mortals could look up and admire their goddess, and she could in turn smile benevolently as she surveyed her domain.

"Raquelle is right next to me," she went on, "and Gina across the hall. And of course, Henry's down the other end of the corridor – so I suppose where I sleep is really down to who decorates better." She winked.

"Still going strong then?"

"The best. He's so charming – really chivalrous. You know, you don't get that in America. Must be the culture here. And the *accent*!" She collapsed on her bed and pretended to swoon.

Eleanor forced her tone to teasing. "I've got the same accent as Henry, and you don't find me sexy."

Cheyenne tossed a pillow in her face. "Don't you start trying to seduce me now, Eleanor Sanders. Besides," she added with a twinkle in her eye, "you've got George to occupy you."

"*George?*"

"Don't look so shocked. He told me the other day he's in love with this girl, but he'll never have the guts to tell her. And when I prodded, he told me it was one of our friends. And you're both artists, and prone to being grumpy, and a little bit awkward – hey!" she cried when the pillow was tossed back at her.

"You're love sick," Eleanor declared. "Or love contagious. Not everyone has to be in love just because you are."

"Eleanor, staaaap!" she said in her American drawl as she writhed in fits of laughter. She looked so happy lying there, splayed out on the bed, crying tears of hilarity because of a joke Eleanor had made, that Eleanor allowed herself to imagine that it was she who'd caused Cheyenne's other happiness too. That Cheyenne was only distracting herself with Henry, that she couldn't live with Eleanor because she couldn't control herself around her, that she loved Eleanor best of all–

The door creaked open and Raquelle strode in. She'd cut her hair during the summer and it hung in a bob to her chin. It strengthened her resemblance to a 1940s schoolgirl. "Everything alright in here?"

Cheyenne waved a hand in Eleanor's direction. "Something Eleanor said – you wouldn't understand – had to be there."

Raquelle nodded and fixed her eyes on Eleanor. They weren't cold, not exactly, but there was certainly no affection in them. "Good summer, Eleanor?"

"Passable." She nodded politely. "You do anything interesting?"

"Just an internship in the city." Raquelle picked at her nails in boredom. "My uncle works in finance – dead boring, but what can you do? And I travelled around half the country to watch my brother play polo."

"Henry plays polo," Cheyenne butted in. She sat up on the bed, her eyes suddenly twinkling. "We went to his house together before we came up and he introduced me to his pony. Her name's Lucy and she's beautiful – he says he's considering shipping her up so he can play on her instead of renting a horse."

"He was amazing in the charity polo tournament last year," Raquelle said. Cheyenne nodded with pride while Eleanor stood back: she couldn't stand polo, and had rejected the polo tournament offhand without caring what noble cause it was for. Cheyenne, George and Cheyenne's flatmates had gone together without telling her.

She wasn't to think about things like that. This was a new year.

"Anyway," Raquelle went on, "Gina's debating where to move the sofa in the living room. Can you come and take a look? And then we have to decide on which set of cutlery we're using for the kitchen – you know it has to be coordinated…'

Eleanor slipped away as Raquelle led Cheyenne out, still babbling on about the slight differences between sets of silver spoons. As she marched back towards her flat, her heart throbbed. She had hoped to forget about Raquelle and Gina. And yet here they were, living with Cheyenne, locking her away, distorting her mind. What scum. She hoped Gina choked on one of the nuts she was always going on about being allergic to.

Her feet led her down to the sea, where she threw her shoes to the side and stood up to her knees in the chill. It hurt, but she welcomed the numbness: it let her forget about Cheyenne and her so-called friends. The water sang to her: she moved deeper, but edged back as it licked at her clothes.

Fuck it. She hadn't brought her swimsuit and the beach was too crowded to swim naked, but what did it matter? Eleanor slipped out of her clothes and dived in her underwear.

The impact took her breath away, no matter how many times she repeated it. Eleanor had been in the sea this term already of course, but she had been feeling more optimistic then. Now she was in the mood to conquer them, to show that she could at least manage something in her life. Her strokes were fast, ferocious and the ocean parted before her. She swam sprints until she was exhausted, then sprinted some more. When she finally collapsed back on the sand, the short Scottish afternoon was already fading to evening, leaving her a chilly walk back. At least she had her anger to fuel her.

"Good swim?" Lily asked when she walked in. Eleanor gave a grunt of approval as she went to drown herself in the shower. This water wasn't nearly as satisfying, but there was some relief in turning the temperature so hot it scalded her skin.

"You're very quiet," Molly remarked over dinner. Molly was never quiet: she was a playful, smiling young woman with a crooked smile and twisty red curls. She offset the more introverted Liz very nicely.

Eleanor shrugged. "Just friend stuff. You know it's not the same when you come back from summer…"

"Is it the American again?" Liz cut in. "The one you were going to live with before she dumped you?" Her eyes glittered with the malice you could only feel for someone when you didn't know them.

"Don't think about her," Molly said when Eleanor nodded. "Or any of her cronies. It doesn't do you any good. You've got us, and the swim team – you need to come to more socials this year; they're really good fun."

"I will," Eleanor said, but she didn't bother to try and sound convincing.

"Tell you what," Molly decided, "let's do something tonight. We could go out drinking: that's good for forgetting stuff."

"No." Going out meant there was the possibility of seeing Cheyenne and her friends, which meant that Eleanor would spend her whole night thinking of them. "Let's just stay in."

"I have some board games in my room," Liz suggested. "And we'll put a film on."

It was all refreshingly normal. But despite herself, Eleanor's thoughts kept slinking back to that townhouse, picturing Cheyenne wrapped around Henry in the same bed she'd sprawled over earlier that morning.

October.

Two years and seven months before the party.

It was a nightmare to get George alone. He was always either attached to Cheyenne or rushing off to his house to work. Any attempts from Eleanor to work on his mental state had disintegrated over the summer. "Cheyenne takes care of that," George said bluntly when she asked. She tried again, and again, the responses becoming more snappy – but she still wanted to help. He let Cheyenne in, let her be his friend, his confidant. They had a bond that Eleanor, despite all her attempts to claw her way in, could never manage slip inside and match.

He was talking to Gina, Raquelle, and Henry, she knew. She saw pictures of them together online sometimes, blurry photos of nights out. The faces were so indistinct that you couldn't tell who was who at a glance, but Eleanor had pored over so many she knew Gina's curls or Henry's shoulder at a glance.

When Eleanor finally cornered him, it was unexpected. She was drinking with the swimming club when she spotted him squeezed into the edge of a booth at one of the tables. The usual suspects were with him: Gina, wrapped around Sam, Cheyenne practically on Henry's lap, and Raquelle sitting bolt upright in the middle of them all, as though she was poised to discipline them if they stepped out of line.

She sidled up to George on his way to the toilet. "Fancy seeing you here!" she cried, and then grabbed his wrist so he couldn't get away – alcohol made her bold. He tried to struggle, but she shoved him against a wall. She was strong from swimming, and George spent all his time wilting away in his room.

"Eleanor, let me go!" George snapped. His breath stank of beer.

"Out again, I see," Eleanor sneered. "I didn't get an invite."

He shrugged. "Bring it up with the others. It's their house – they just invite me along."

And what have you done to deserve that? Eleanor wanted to scream. *Why you and not me?* She changed the subject to the first thing she could think of. "Cheyenne told me you liked me. Romantically."

He rolled his eyes. "As if."

"That's what I thought. So there's only one person left, isn't there, that you could possibly be head-over-heels in love with. Only you don't tell her because she's helplessly wrapped up in her posh little boyfriend."

George tried to wrench himself free; she nearly lost her grip. "I'm not in love with Cheyenne!"

"You follow her around like a lost little puppy."

"And you're just jealous because you can't do the same!"

"So what?" Eleanor shot back. "I'm in love with Cheyenne? It doesn't matter. It's not like I'm going to act on it."

George tilted his head back and unleashed a manic laugh. "You're not in love with her, Eleanor. You just want her because she's – what was it – 'rich and foreign.' You told me yourself."

"I said that's what everyone else likes about Cheyenne. Not that it matters now. She's dead set on being British. Though what she sees in this country I can't imagine."

"You only say that because you want her to take you to America."

"Sod off," Eleanor snapped. It wasn't quite true – she only thought about America occasionally, only scrolled through images of the mountains and the desert and the ocean – the Pacific Ocean! – every few nights. America was merely a plus that came with Cheyenne. What she really wanted was for Cheyenne to look at Eleanor and smile, to really see her and appreciate her like she had that very first day. Like she'd smiled when she'd seen Eleanor swimming in Nice, like she'd laughed that afternoon on the bed.

Deep in the recesses of Eleanor's heart, a creature gave a shudder. A miniature serpent, tongue flicking, beady eyes seeking prey. Eleanor had awoken it now, all she had to do was follow it, let it fill her with the courage she needed.

George's eyes were sparkling; he saw he'd hit a nerve. "You're such a fucking–"

"Who do you like then?" Eleanor shot out before he could get his final word in. "Because I'm sure Raquelle would love a little cuddle now and then."

"I don't have to tell you."

"Sam then? I always thought you were gay, to be honest. It's the sort of thing Cheyenne would like – a gay best friend, just like the movies."

"Cheyenne's a real person you know, not just your sick collection of thoughts."

"Gina's very pretty, too. No fucking personality though, but maybe that suits you. You don't have much depth when you're not playing the part of a starving artist."

"Eleanor, I am warning you."

"If you make a scene, I'll do the same," Eleanor's face was so close to George's she could taste his sweat. The snake within her hissed with pleasure. "*I'm* warning *you*, I can do a very good crying girl."

He froze. She could hear his heart over the frenzied chatter of the bar. "I'll kill you for this."

Eleanor leaned backwards, hard enough that George, who had been resting his weight on her, sagged forward, and she collapsed to the ground. The impact took the wind out of her and the floor stained her shirt sickeningly sticky, but she was too hot with hate and fury to care. "You fucking freak!" she shouted, as loud as she could, projecting for the bar. "You hit me! Fuck off to Hell!"

People surrounded her instantly. A hand from behind pulled her away and helped her towards the bar. "You alright, love?"

George's face was clenched in fury, but just as her view was blocked by a concerned passerby, she saw a gruff-looking man approach him with malice in his face.

Eleanor nodded shakily. "I'll be fine – he just tried to – I need air." She staggered towards the door and, as soon as she hit fresh air, sprinted for home.

What had she done? She was such an idiot. George would never speak to her again, and through him, Cheyenne never would as well.

Unless they didn't believe George.

But they would. He might have the personality of white bread, but he was faultlessly loyal to Cheyenne; would tell her the truth no matter the circumstances. She would believe him wholeheartedly.

Eleanor had fucked it. Totally and completely fucked it.

Normally in times like this, she'd go to the beach. But she was tired, the world was spinning and her mouth was dry. She stumbled up the stairs to her flat, pulled off her clothes, and lay in bed sobbing, too tired to bother with pyjamas. They'd only get covered in tears and snot anyway. Besides, she liked the feeling of nudity, it made her vulnerable. And God if she didn't deserve vulnerable, didn't deserve George to dig his teeth into her neck and Cheyenne to rip her heart out with her perfectly manicured California nails. What a lovely way to die, killed by her old friends. One final act to draw the line.

Her flatmates arrived after what felt like years, but must only have been a few minutes. "Are you alright?" Molly asked, opening the door a crack. She flung it open the whole way when she saw Eleanor's state. "Good God, Eleanor, what happened? Don't you have any clothes? Did he do something to you? Eleanor, love, answer me!"

Eleanor wrapped herself in a dressing gown and followed Molly to the living room, where Liz hastily set a cup of tea before her. They were still in their dresses and makeup, and Eleanor felt another pang of guilt: she'd ruined the entire swimming club's night. "Do you want to tell us?" Liz asked. "We don't want to push you, but..."

Eleanor shook her head. "We just argued," she said, her words monotone. "And then," the words seemed to stick to her tongue, "he hit me. Then threw me to the floor."

"I'm sorry – I thought you were close." Eleanor can't tell if Molly is talking about their relationship or just the press of their bodies in the pub.

"Yeah, well." Eleanor shrugged. "I guess our friendship isn't what I thought." That, at least, wasn't a lie.

November.

Two years and six months before the party.

Eleanor finished her book in record time. She had nothing else to do. Cheyenne and her friends were ignoring her, and she'd already finished all her assignments. When she wasn't swimming or playing cards with Liz and Molly, she was up in her room, typing furiously.

She was determined to finish. If Cheyenne didn't love her, if George wanted to toss her aside like a sack of old bricks, she could get back at them only by making herself unforgettable. And the only thing she had on hand to make herself unforgettable was her writing.

So, one afternoon in November, when the light had already faded ridiculously early, Eleanor found herself staring at a finished document. It was tense, and gritty and explored all the right topics in all the right ways. Unlike with her fantasy novel, she was satisfied.

There was only one problem. Its word count was forty thousand: surely too short for any publisher to front the printing cost for a debut author? But the book was tight already: to add more would be to bloat it, to compromise the quality of the art.

Perhaps she could work on the descriptions, be more poetic. Half the power was in the brutality and beauty of the landscape as it mirrored and contrasted the lonely soldiers and the pointless war they were waging. It was difficult to put such scale into words.

Such scale into words...

She tossed her head back laughing; it was that obvious. Hadn't the goal always been Hollywood anyway? Why not skip straight there? Write a script?

She was good, her history tutor had said so. So good she *must* take classes, Cheyenne had gushed in her fake English way – back when they were friends, when things *were* good, when Eleanor had watched her pull up her top to expose her bra and no one had cared. What better way to show Cheyenne what she had lost than to take her own accolades and toss them back at her?

Eleanor barely slept for the next week. It was just like that first night at the library, except she was punching her laptop keys so hard they jammed instead of blotting pages with ink. And really, nothing had changed since then – here was Eleanor, back at square one, forever on the outside looking in.

She threw away her first attempt – she hated the dialogue. The second draft was rebuilt from the ground up – she hated that still. A third attempt to rewrite the script – if this failed she would have to throw the whole thing away, but she could not, would not fail.

Fourth time around, she liked it a little better. Eleanor's mind was hazy – she had missed class, missed meals, missed entire days in a fervour of tears and writing and sleep. Her flatmates barely saw her – they knocked on the door, but Eleanor didn't answer, and so they flitted away and stopped asking after her.

Fifth time – she was getting somewhere. Lines were snappier, runtime was down. Eleanor's mind swirled with hallucinations and delusions – but the script was still solid. It held, at its core, a kernel of genius. No matter how much the walls swayed, this could not be doubted.

Genius or not, it wouldn't matter if she didn't have backing. Original scripts rarely sold in Hollywood; it was a tough business.

Eleanor's stomach twisted. This was the dangerous part.

She found the number online: the office had an inquiries line. She called late in the day, during California office hours, at roughly their two pm. They had just returned from lunch, but the meal wasn't so recent they would be feeling sleepy, only happily sated. Her hands trembled as she dialled the number.

"Leonsdale Associates?" a chirpy-sounding receptionist said into the phone.

"Hello. This is Eleanor Sanders, and I'm a friend of the Leonsdales' daughter, Cheyenne. I just wrote a script that she loves, and she told me to call you right away. I hope this is the right number – I thought about asking her to get her dad on the phone, but I thought it wouldn't be professional…"

"Normally we ask for queries to be made through an agent," the receptionist said. "We don't take unsolicited–"

"But it's not unsolicited!" Eleanor let out a light, tinkling laugh. "Cheyenne said you'd be trouble. But if you want, I can call Alan and Margaret – or Mr and Mrs Leonsdale, if you prefer – after work tonight. It's just that I didn't want to disturb them outside of business hours…'

Silence. For a second Eleanor thought she'd been too forward. Her heart flew to her mouth as she waited. A rush like a hummingbird pulsed through her head. Finally, the receptionist cleared her throat. "I've spoken to Mrs Leonsdale.

She's very busy this afternoon, as is her husband. But if you send either of them an email and mention what you just told me, they'll get around to you as soon as they can."

"Brilliant; thank you!" Eleanor said as she hung up. She hardly thought she'd be able to sit still, but somehow she managed to control her hands shaking for long enough to type out a formal query letter to Cheyenne's parents. At the top, she wrote the subject line: QUERY FROM CHEYENNE'S FRIEND. Then, after some deliberation, she added,

Hello Mr and Mrs Leonsdale. I've heard so much about you and your business from Cheyenne, it feels as if I know you already. I don't know if Cheyenne's mentioned me much, but we're very good friends; I've attached a picture of us in Nice together last year. Such fun!

Eleanor jumped up as if sparks were flying from her fingertips when she pressed send. This whole plan relied on Cheyenne not being close enough to her parents to tell them the ins and outs of her friendships. From the flippant way Cheyenne referred to anyone from LA, Eleanor got the feeling Cheyenne wasn't ringing her parents every night to update them on the shots she'd done at the club a few hours ago. Rich parents were all the same: hand the child money in place of attention.

The next week seemed endless: Eleanor's nerves were on edge, her hand always brushing her phone in anticipation of the fatal buzz. Whenever a message arrived, she held back in anticipation, only to finally open it to receive the disappointing blow that it was only some admin from the university office.

Maybe Cheyenne had told her parents all about Eleanor, and they'd discarded the message in disgust. Maybe they'd told Cheyenne about Eleanor's pathetic attempt to suck up to them, and the family had all had a good laugh about it. Most likely they'd just ignored it. Eleanor had resigned herself to her fate and was debating making half-hearted submissions to agents when her inbox pinged.

Dear Eleanor,
How wonderful to hear from you! I'm so glad Cheyenne has some friends interested in the industry, and that she thinks so highly of her parents to recommend us.

I'm sure you know it's ordinarily very difficult to sell scripts. However, one of the studios recently acquired the rights to a wildly successful First World War book that released last year, and are betting big on it being successful. A gritty, modern competitor could be perfect.

With that in mind, I would like to formally make you an offer of script purchase. The full documentation is attached. Please read the terms of sale carefully, and do let me know if you have any questions. You could even ask Cheyenne – I'm sure she knows more than she lets on!

Sincerely,
Alan Leonsdale
Leonsdale Associates

It was a dream. Some heady, wonderful dream that would be all the worse when she woke and returned to her living hell. It hadn't possibly worked; it couldn't have worked.

Eleanor opened the attached documents. The proposed sum was mindbogglingly huge.

"Oh Cheyenne," she whispered. "Thank you." Thank you for entering her life, for her status as a child of nepotism, for lighting the fire within her. Wouldn't Cheyenne seethe when she saw this? Or better yet, fall back in love with Eleanor for her ingeniousness.

Eleanor accepted the offer without any negotiation: there was room for that in the future. The next day, she walked down to the study abroad office and filled out her application to spend her third year at the Los Angeles branch of the University of California. It was so easy to do from a Scottish university: life had panned out perfectly. Maybe she had always been meant to forget this place, to leave George and Cheyenne behind her. Her degree was secondary now. She had a whole new career, a whole new life ahead of her.

December.

Two years and five months before the party.

Eleanor didn't talk to Cheyenne for the rest of term. Well, they did talk, but not properly. It was impossible for Cheyenne and her friends to avoid Eleanor in the lecture halls, and when they walked out Eleanor would stick to them like a barnacle. It gave Eleanor immense satisfaction to see them flash panicked glances and resentful glares and make excuses that they needed to pop into shops to get rid of her.

Cheyenne still didn't know about the sale of her script. Eleanor kept waiting for Cheyenne to bring it up, giving her an opportunity to gloat, but it seemed she was living in blissful ignorance. In a way, it was better for Eleanor: the script had already been sold, the money transferred, but the company could still halt production and lock it into development hell.

The emails kept coming from Cheyenne's parents. Cheerful notes updating her on movement in "the industry" and inviting her to Los Angeles during the summer. Eleanor finally and tentatively accepted when they said she could attend a gala with major figures from studios – people who'd worked on several major upcoming releases. *Good networking*, the note read, with the same relentlessly cheery attitude that made Eleanor suspect Cheyenne's parents were relived someone in their daughter's circle was showing an interest in their work.

Or maybe their never-ending positivity was just an American trait. Eleanor would find out soon. She was even more obsessed with America than before. She spent her spare time reading American newspapers, reading American travel guides, sighing over aesthetic videos of American influencers she found on social media.

"You realise there's a reason all the Americans here have left the country?" Molly said one afternoon, after fifteen minutes of listening to Eleanor wax lyrical about Californian beaches.

Eleanor shrugged. "Those people must not have surfed. Or hated warm weather. Or..."

"You could die," Liz cut in. Eleanor shivered. "There are so many guns there. And the healthcare. And the wild animals!"

"I won't live in those areas. Especially not after my film makes millions and everyone's queuing up for my stuff."

"They don't say queuing there," Molly teased. "You'll stick out like a sore thumb."

"America loves immigrants! There's a reason people are queuing – oh, sorry, *lining* up – on the borders to get in."

"America loves immigrants if they're the right sort," Liz remarked darkly.

"I *am* the right sort. White and, very shortly, rich." It was an attempt at a joke, but the words twisted and curdled in her stomach. To distract herself, Eleanor slumped back and turned to scrolling through pictures of California she'd saved to her Pinterest board. "How's the search for my replacement going anyway?"

"We're taking Avery. You know her?"

Avery was one a first year from the swimming club. Funny, outgoing and a phenomenal backstroke. She was apparently legendary at swim socials, but Eleanor was always too busy working to go.

"Of course I know her. That'll be... fun." She couldn't quite imagine Avery and quiet Liz fitting together, but perhaps Molly could bridge the gap.

"If it goes poorly, you can always move back in." The silence settled heavy after Molly's remark. Eleanor tried not to show her discomfort. She had another year in Scotland after she got back from California, and it was unlikely Avery would take very kindly to being kicked out of the flat. Eleanor seemed destined to spend her final year back in halls.

No, she wouldn't be in halls. She'd come back so filthy rich she could buy herself a mansion. She could buy the whole town. Lord over it in place of Cheyenne.

Cheyenne. Instinctively, Eleanor's eyes flicked to her phone, checking the date. The fourteenth. Cheyenne's birthday was tomorrow.

She had to tell her at some point. In the future, when the film was too far in production for Cheyenne to do anything about it. But that she was going to LA: *that* Cheyenne could know.

Somewhere, in the back of her mind, there was still an inkling of hope that Cheyenne would take her back. Perhaps she had seen through George, figured out Gina. She could have had some horrible realisation that her so-called 'friends' had been poisoning her against Eleanor in an attempt to hoard Cheyenne all for themselves. Really, it was Eleanor's own naivety that had doomed her – she was too kind, too sweet, too innocent to play the elaborate mind games Gina and Raquelle's ilk so loved. Cheyenne could see that. She was so clever – Cheyenne must see that.

Molly was still talking: something banal about an actor she'd read about in the tabloids. Eleanor daydreamed strolling down Ocean Boulevard with a tanned, blonde figure as she typed a messaged to Cheyenne. *Want to meet up? Got news.*

There was no response that day, or the next. Eleanor spent the evening pacing her room like a caged rat, gritting her teeth and clenching her fists. She'd have gone to the sea, but she didn't want to miss a message from Cheyenne.

Six o'clock came and went. Then seven. Then eight.

Eleanor punched a pillow, then kicked it, then bit into it so hard the pillowcase tore. She imagined the fabric was Cheyenne's perfect skin, so soft and taut over her throat. Even Cheyenne's blood, she was sure, would be perfect, delicate ruby drops that splattered artfully against her skin.

Enough. She grabbed her coat and a bottle of wine out the fridge. She drank half of it on her way to Cheyenne's street. As she suspected, the townhouse was lit up in every window. It was midweek, in the midst of exams, and Cheyenne wouldn't go out when her beloved Henry had a practical worth half his grade the next day. Eleanor could see them through the window, laughing in a circle, passing around drinks, and suddenly Eleanor was sixteen years old again, ignoring the gossip about parties she hadn't been invited to.

She was meant to have turned it around by now. Meant to have found people she loved. Meant to have been so, so lucky. And now it was falling apart before her eyes.

The door was unlocked. Eleanor strode in like she owned the place and followed the sound of voices to the living room. She threw herself onto a sofa and flung the bottle onto the table.

She smiled. "Lovely evening we're having."

"Eleanor." Cheyenne's voice was deathly cold. "You weren't invited." It was nothing like the understanding smile Eleanor had pictured; nothing like the bright and confident girl she'd fallen in love with. What had these people done to her?

Eleanor shrugged. "You needed your birthday wishes."

"You can't just…"

"I wanted to tell you something, and to do it in person. You weren't responding."

"You could at least knock on the door."

"I'm already late for the party!" Eleanor grabbed the bottle again and took a swig. It burnt the back of her throat, but she didn't stop until she'd chugged another solid third. Deep within her, the snake uncoiled in pleasure.

"You framed George at the pub," Raquelle warned from across the room. She was sitting bolt-upright in her armchair, looking rather like a queen. The little bitch. That was Cheyenne's role, and Raquelle knew it. Why on Earth was Cheyenne putting up with this?

"He assaulted me. A gentleman should never hit a woman."

"That's a lie and you know it!" It was George who spoke from his position, scrunched at the end of a sofa Gina and Sam were lounging on, as if they were guests at a Roman dinner party. Ideally one in Pompeii, right before the eruption.

Eleanor shrugged. "It doesn't matter what I know. It matters what people believe. And the whole town thinks George is guilty."

"I should call the police," Raquelle threatened. "You're breaking and entering."

"Doesn't Cheyenne want to know what I have to tell her?"

"Which is?" Raquelle barked.

"I'm off to LA next year."

Cheyenne rolled her eyes. "That's it?"

That was it. Somehow it had sounded more monumental in her head. Without the sting of the script, there was no glory in it. And the eye-roll: there was no love in that. Not even hate. Just the cruel, empty disinterest of a woman looking at something beneath her.

"I thought you'd be glad," Eleanor said spitefully. "No more me to run into during lectures."

"Look Eleanor, you have to understand…"

"Understand what? That I'm not good enough for you? That you love the others so much more because they're richer and posher and will help you become a Surrey housewife who goes hunting and plays polo on the weekend?"

"Says the girl who wants to be American, of all things." Cheyenne was spitting the words out, but she was still too calm for Eleanor's taste. All of them were. Where was the reaction: the awe, the fear, the realisation that the girl they'd abandoned had already achieved more than their meaningless little lives ever would? She couldn't be bothered with forgiveness anymore, she wasn't going to stop until they respected her.

"At least I love you for what you are! All your other 'friends' only care that you're exotic and glamourous"

Cheyenne rolled her eyes. "Don't act like that's not what you care about either. At least no one else is a fucking stalker!"

In the psychology lab, they would say what Eleanor did next was a function of the primitive amygdala overriding the advanced, logical, prefrontal cortex: a retreat to instinct, nothing more. On the street, they would call her insane, a psychopath, needing to be locked up.

In Eleanor's mind, she called it the weight of the glass in her hand, the rush of adrenaline as she charged at what used to be her friend, the sound of the shatter as she brought it onto Cheyenne's face. Cheap wine drenched her fingers, ran down Cheyenne's perfect collarbone to stain her top. The glass bit into her palm as she rubbed the shards into Cheyenne's smug little face. Let her eat her words with that.

Screams echoed under the living room's cavernous ceiling. Cheyenne made no move to push Eleanor away from her: she had become a statue, pale as marble against the wine trickling down her skin. Another liquid, thick and viscous, welled from her cuts. Eleanor stared as the blood inched down Cheyenne's face and dripped to the ground with a solemn thud.

Raquelle was crying; George shrieked insults. Eleanor couldn't hear either of them: her ears were filled with a rising static. Cheyenne's mouth parted in a horrified O, and her eyes blazed with something more than fear. It was fury – the same fire that had driven Eleanor to this house tonight – and Eleanor knew she was finished.

Rough hands grabbed Eleanor from behind. "Out," ordered Henry – he'd been there all along, the smarmy little shit. Eleanor twisted, lunged, found a patch of skin and bit down as hard as she could. He shrieked and let go in shock, and Eleanor sprinted for the exit. She crashed out the door, down the steps, onto the dreary street. She ran without a destination in mind, wanting nothing more than to get away from that awful house, those terrible people.

Finally, she stopped short in a park a little way from her old halls. She'd been there a dozen times before; on the way home from nights out they had often stopped there to catch their breath – they being a group consisting of Eleanor, George, Cheyenne and the rest of the fucking hangers-on. Not hangers-on anymore – people Cheyenne loved more than her. Perhaps had always loved more than her.

Fucking stalker.

At least she'd become what they all believed her to be. Stalkers were horrifying, weren't they, and she was as good as a maniac. It was only what they'd turned her into. Cheyenne had loved her, and she had loved Cheyenne, and spurned lovers couldn't be dropped without warning. And it been Cheyenne who had latched on to Eleanor first. Spoken to her in the lecture, followed her to the beach, let Eleanor lead her up the hill, watched Eleanor swim in Nice? Cheyenne had used Eleanor to fulfil her fetishist European fantasy, and dropped her as soon as she was no longer useful.

A thought nagged at the back of her mind. Could Eleanor have just played along? Perhaps it was her fault for not living up to Cheyenne's standards?

She'd live up to her standards now, all right.

Eleanor reached for the bottle to take a swig, only to remember she'd left it at Cheyenne's. Typical Cheyenne. Stealing everything from her.

Eleanor felt like stealing something back.

She couldn't get to Cheyenne directly: that was certain after tonight. But she could hit her lackeys.

Eleanor had been to George's flat back in September. It was a few blocks out of the main town, covered in a god-ugly 60s stucco. She made her way there down side streets and back alleys, in case someone decided to come after her – though in her heart, she knew no one was coming. A few lights were on: Eleanor could hear the tv blaring from the living room in the front of the house.

The back door was a flimsy, draughty thing George always complained about: the key was so stiff no one ever bothered to lock it. Eleanor slipped past the gate, through the door, and up the stairs. Adrenaline kept her steps swift and quiet and stopped her from thinking about anything more articulate than the roaring rush of rage. George's room, she remembered, was on the right.

It was almost identical to his bedroom in halls. The same paint-covered desk – he'd really bought the thing – and paintings still covered every open space. They were nice, Eleanor had to admit, in their own sort of way. They reminded her of the impressionists. His latest was still sitting on the easel. A group of friends, sitting on a hill. The colours were a beautiful blend of oranges and yellows: the sun, the trees, the dried grass. And the blonde hair of the central figure.

George never painted faces. But Eleanor could swear she could see a hint of blue: Cheyenne's eyes still glinting out, mocking her through layers of paint. Behind her were her friends: Eleanor would recognise Gina's hair anywhere, and Raquelle's stupid bow. And there was Henry, arms wrapped around his girlfriend: Eleanor's vision blurred with red. How dare they?

George's paint knife was lying to the side. Eleanor lifted it, felt its weight, then hesitated. There was to be no coming back from this.

She thought of her hands on George's body as he struggled in the pub; his threats to kill her – little did he know she was as good as dead already, shut out and forced to wander like a zombie.

She was determined take them all down with her.

Eleanor raised her hand and slashed down, right across Cheyenne's smug little face. The canvas flapped apart like a dead butterfly's crumpled wings.

She slashed again, and again, and again. Here: a picture of Cheyenne at a country club, there: Henry, Raquelle, and Sam strolling down a street. Another of his parents, three landscapes, two of a dog. And again Cheyenne: here Cheyenne, there Cheyenne, everywhere Cheyenne, all flapping their pathetic little wings, slaughtered at her hand.

The last ones to go were a stack of dusty canvases in the corner, hidden between piles of newer paintings. Eleanor had destroyed them all methodically, barely glancing at their contents. Yet, when she raised the knife to rip apart her final stack, she froze.

The top image was a beach scene. The day was sunny: the buildings perched on the edge of the cliff shone in the afternoon light. Seagulls wheeled above: Eleanor could see the light reflected off their wings as they spun and dove. And in the surf, elbows linked, were two girls.

They'd been so happy; Eleanor could tell, even though they were barely more than stick figures, that the girls were smiling.

The paint knife fell from her fingers: she tossed the canvas to the side, trying to find something underneath that would set her off again. But here was a tree in the university quad, with two girls lounging under it. So, George had taken up Cheyenne's suggestion after all. Finally there was a scene in Nice: Eleanor would recognise the street to the beach anywhere.

It should have made her angrier. Here was proof of what she'd lost, laid bare before her eyes. The fact that George hadn't got rid of them was only more of an insult: it showed how little her loss had truly bothered him. Eleanor should bring the knife down and forget about it.

But it was too late. The brief pause to look at the paintings had killed her adrenaline. Now there was only a gaping maw of horror within her. What had she done? How had the carefree girl in these paintings turned into this?

She backed away as vomit threatened to rise up her throat. At the last moment, her hand darted out: she grabbed a painting and tucked it under her coat. She had suddenly become paranoid that George would sense her crime and return, so she lifted the window sash, clambered onto a roof and scrambled down next to the bins. She let herself out the back gate and rushed away, heart pounding. It wasn't until she reached the park that she let herself cry again.

Molly found her in the living room, cradling the canvas in her arms like it was a child. "Oh Eleanor," she said wearily. "Was it them again?"

She nodded mutely.

"How many times do I have to tell you? Just forget those bitches."

If only it was that easy, Eleanor thought as she lay in her tear-stained bed. She replayed that moment in Cheyenne's living room: the rush of anger, the shatter of the glass, the blood coating her palms and covering Cheyenne's face. The screams she'd tuned out. George's shock and Cheyenne's hate. What enthralled her most was how easy it had been: in the work of a few moments, she had destroyed everything. Had made others long to destroy her.

Her thoughts dwelled on George: what would he do when he returned to his room? He would know it was her, of course. The portraits she had left would only enrage him further, instead of leading him to some twisted path of forgiveness. He'd surely call Cheyenne. Would they come to her flat? More likely they'd just stew. As long as Cheyenne didn't call her parents. Oh, God, what if Cheyenne called her parents? Eleanor would have to rely on the hope that Cheyenne's parents cared about profit more than they cared about their daughter.

Hour by hour, she worked through each and every thought: minimising the impacts, thinking about things logically. When she was finished, all was left was the image of George walking into a dark room and collapsing in horror when he turned on the lights. She saw the sobs wrack his body, felt the tears run down his cheek, let his grief mix with hers. Just a boy in a butterfly graveyard, returning home to find his friends massacred, to learn Eleanor had become a murderer.

She tried to console herself by staring at her painting: if she focused hard enough, her sleep-deprived brain could almost imagine it was still that day at the beach, and that everything since had been nothing more than a horrible dream. The illusion only lasted for a moment before reality broke though. Eventually, Eleanor gave up and shoved the painting deep under her bed. As she drifted off to sleep, the jagged lines of the painting – angry brushstrokes and even angrier swipes of a knife – played across her eyelids.

In her dreams, Eleanor strolled through a misty town. It had the vague outline of St Andrews, but everything was wrong: the streets too wide and empty, the storefronts too dark. Around the corner should have been Logies' Lane, but instead it was the wide shore front of Nice.

Her feet ploughed on desperately. She was looking for someone. Something gnawed away at the back of her skull, incessant and relentless. She knew instinctively it wouldn't stop until she found what she was looking for.

St Andrews castle emerged abruptly out of the gloom. It hung precipitously over a cliff, threatening to drag its inhabitants with it as it plummeted into the waves.

Across the drawbridge, through the portcullis were two figures, leaning against the crumbling wall, locked together in a conspiratorial whisper. An endless abyss of haze unfurled behind them.

Eleanor's footsteps made no sound, but the pair glanced up anyway. Cheyenne's face ran red: rivulets of blood seeped down her cheeks like tears. George's shape seemed to bend and fuel, like the jagged edges of the paintings Eleanor had–

They lunged. Eleanor grappled with Cheyenne's arms as they reached for her neck, George snuck around behind her and knocked her legs out from beneath her. Eleanor screamed, but this cold, desolate place was devoid of sound. Cheyenne Eleanor and George tumbled together until they reached the edge of the cliff, then suddenly they were falling down, down, down. Even as they hit the water, they still clawed at each other as they slowly, slowly sank.

Eleanor jerked awake, breathless and sweaty. In the dim light of the room, her bedsheets seemed to cling to her like the limp remains of George's paintings.

It was still dark outside. The moon barely made a dent in the damp November night. Nothing was outside her window, but something had awoken her.

A thump, echoing up from the floorboards. Voices down the corridor, one raised to a fever pitch, then softened again.

Ah, thought Eleanor with a rush of understanding. They had come. It was over. The police were on her. They would drag her away and lock her up. She could wave goodbye to California, to Hollywood, to any chance of escape. The lines slashed across Cheyenne's face became the confines of a prison, pinning Eleanor in. All fight had left her. She lay prone in her bed, waiting for the knock on the door.

When it came, it was barely audible: a faint tremor against the wood.

Eleanor swallowed. "Come in."

A thin beam of light cut into Eleanor's eyes as the door swung open. When her vision adjusted, it was not the hulking frame of an armed police officer that stood before her, but Molly, hair frizzy and still in her pyjamas.

She sat down on the bed. "We've had visitors."

"Send them up." The words were sawdust in Eleanor's throat.

Molly shrugged. "They went home."

Eleanor jerked up. "What? The police are gone?"

"There aren't any police," Molly went on, "but they were threatening to call them. Your... friends."

"Which ones?"

"George and that girl – Cheyenne." Molly swayed with uncertainty before continuing. "The face above her eye had been bandaged up."

"There was a fight." Eleanor could barely force the words out.

"They wanted–" Molly paused again, delaying the inevitable – "to make a decision. To see if we thought you should be reported for assault and trespassing."

When Eleanor was five years old, she started swim lessons. It didn't come naturally to her – it would be years before she could slip through the water, sleek as a shark. Instead, swimming was a cold, painful, torturous process: so horrible that before walking into the lesson, Eleanor would squeeze her eyes shut, as if not seeing the pool approaching would prevent the inevitable entrance.

Now, Eleanor squeezed her eyes shut again.

"I wasn't sure," Molly went on. "The girl in their story isn't the one Liz and I know. And one of them – George – didn't want to press charges either."

Eleanor jerked. "What? George said that?"

Molly shrugged. "Don't ask me why." She fixed Eleanor with a pointed glare. "Maybe he knows the real you as well."

The door slammed shut with a thud, and Molly was gone. Eleanor was left alone with her thoughts.

The sun began to leak through the windows, soft and rosy, but Eleanor's mood was anything but. Why hadn't George called the police? Why had Cheyenne given up so easily? Did they not want to rock the boat, to drop a stone into the perfectly still pond Cheyenne maintained around her image?

The other idea, the one that briefly jumped to the forefront of her mind, she tried to banish. What if Cheyenne, with her ponies and her parties and her perfect English friends, simply didn't care about Eleanor? What if Gina and Raquelle and Henry and all the rest had surpassed her completely in Cheyenne's mind?

Impossible, Eleanor told herself. No one could forget her.

But still, when she found herself biting her nails or chewing on the side of her mouth, it was always those same thoughts that plagued her, day in and day out.

6th May. 19:00.

The beginning of the party.

People start trickling in half an hour before the scheduled time. Most of them are nervous first years, trying desperately to sneak a peek at the Radcliffe lobby. Eleanor doesn't see the point. The lobby is public and looks the same as it always does, except for a few more tables stocked with food and drink. It is her twenty-second birthday, after all: people need to be refreshed.

No one important arrives until half-past seven at the earliest. Though importance is relative. One of the second years is the son of a duke; a first year is some Russian heiress. They're the sort that are used to having people fluttering around them. The old order. But all the cash in the world doesn't matter if no one knows your face.

If you measure success by notoriety, then no one here is more successful than Eleanor. Except perhaps Cheyenne.

But Cheyenne isn't here, so Eleanor is able to be the centre of attention without worrying. She smiles, she hugs, she giggles, she shakes people's hands. A great crowd has turned up, full of people who barely know her and who she knows even less. She can see a few classmates from when she used to attend lectures, some old faces from the swimming team, but beyond that – everything is a sea of unknowns. It's a strange limbo to move through, a thousand people coming up to her when she doesn't know a single one. And there is no one, not a soul, to talk to.

A group nearby are discussing their summer plans: trips to Spain and Italy and Greece. They ask her about LA, and Eleanor smiles as she licks a drop of champagne from her finger, so coquettish it's sarcastic. These are the nouveau-riche, from families that had become flush with cash in the post-war boom and had only grown fatter during the Thatcher years. Quite a position. Born a century earlier they'd have been down in the gutter, yet they hold themselves like medieval lords. An aristocracy that was blooming instead of withering.

They all seem so pathetic.

She wanders to another room, abandoning her champagne on the table as she goes. A few boys she vaguely recognises are sitting on the sofas having a hectic discussion about names she doesn't recognise: they could be polo players or politicians for all Eleanor cares.

She fidgets nervously. Where is Cheyenne?

The boys see her now: they're calling her over, handing her a shot glass. Eleanor stands and looks enthusiastic. She downs the first shot for courage, but lets the next one fall onto the floor when they aren't looking. They cheer anyway and press up to her, pulling her onto a seat.

She cannot do this. Not now. She needs to stay sharp.

Is it the alcohol that's made her impulsive, or is it her own mettle? Either way, she leans into the closest boy – she thinks his name is Tom – and kisses him. He tastes like alcohol and sweat. He is taken aback, but before he can try and reciprocate she pushes him headfirst into the bottles on the table. His friends erupt in laughter, and Eleanor takes the moment to escape.

It's getting so crowded: Eleanor presses herself into a corner and forces herself to breathe. An attendant hands her another glass of champagne, and she takes a sip before tossing the rest over her shoulder. She's happy to look like she's drinking, but she needs her wits about her.

"You could have given me that if you weren't going to drink it."

Eleanor blinks. She didn't recognise Amy out of uniform. Her dress is lovely: pale pink and girlish, fluffing up around her like she's a summer flower in bloom. "You came."

Amy shrugs. "You said every student was on the guest list."

"Is your sister here?"

She shakes her head. "Swimming."

"Like always." Eleanor cocks her head. "Do you swim too?"

"Hockey."

Eleanor grimaces. "Never for me. Too much teamwork. I could never figure out how I fitted in the lineup. You any good?"

"I'm alright."

"Don't be modest. Nothing good comes of being modest. Being too confident only means you'll turn away people who'd use you as a doormat." She's talking like she's drunk, but Eleanor can't be. She's only had a few sips at best. Maybe it's just the stress of the evening, the rush of its proximity, the high that comes from being near-victorious.

A hint of a smile cracks across Amy's face. "I'm not being modest. I'm being honest. I'm mediocre at best."

"Oh. So you won't be getting anything out of it?" She pauses to think. "You could always switch to swimming. Your sister's very good: you probably have a lot of potential."

"I like hockey," Amy replies simply.

Of course she likes hockey. Middle-class British girls always do – and middle-class is stretching it, if she's working at the Radcliffe. But to not switch – she must *really* like it.

How odd, to be so dedicated to something you weren't even that good at.

"You know Cheyenne Leonsdale?" Eleanor asks. Amy nods. "Have you seen her around?"

She shakes her head. "But I'll let you know if I do." She steps away, but something in Eleanor made her extend a hand.

"Wait. Stay." She gestures the waiter over – Amy must know him, she supposes. She grabs a flute and hands it over. "Have a drink with me, just for a bit."

Amy furrows her brow. "You don't have a drink."

"I'll have a sip of yours. Just stay with me for a while."

They don't talk much, and when they do it's banal stuff: what Amy studies, what classes Eleanor enjoyed. Nothing of substance, but it is nice merely to have someone next to her – almost like having a friend.

May.

Two years before the party.

Eleanor spent the rest of the school year in a daze. Her assignments were half-hearted, her swimming faltered. Nothing mattered other than California.

"Aren't you going to miss this?" Liz asked as they lounged on the grass in one of the old quads. It was the most beautiful part of campus (other than the sea). Eighteenth-century buildings clustered around a spacious lawn overlooked by a medieval clock tower. On sunny days like this one, the stone itself sparkled.

"What, the weather?" Eleanor replied. "That's better in California."

"I mean the history. Nothing like that in California."

Eleanor waved a hand dismissively. "I don't need dusty old buildings. Besides," she added, "the landscape more than makes up for it. This country looks so boring: flat and brown. Even its mountains are hills by American standards."

"I like this country," said Liz defensively. "It's got plenty of mountains –haven't you ever been to Glencoe?"

"No. And I didn't say *you* didn't like Scotland. After all, someone has to."

Eleanor left town on her birthday, laden down with all her belongings. Most would be left at her parents' house. She had the sense that America heralded a whole new her, stripped of all that she had been and, by extension, all she had owned.

Liz and Molly waved goodbye and handed her a cake through the car window. Eleanor even thought she saw Molly cry. It saddled Eleanor with an odd feeling of regret – she hadn't spent enough time with them.

She lingered at her parents' for a few days, soaking up the last of England she'd see for months. It was a sunny June, and the countryside days slipped by, slow and languid. However you left her village you could see cows in fields. Eleanor felt certain she would not be living in such close proximity to barnyard animals in Los Angeles. There, instead, she would have the sea.

She still had George's painting. Eleanor flinched every time she looked at it: first from anger, then from regret. She debated leaving it at her parents' house. Eventually, sheer practicality got the better of her. It was the sort of thing that might be useful to show to Cheyenne's parents, in case they needed proof of her friendship with their daughter. She was steadily becoming numb to the sight of it. If she didn't think too hard, she could convince herself it was a generic seaside image, with people and places conjured up out of the artist's imagination. The scene depicted was so far from Eleanor's current reality that might as well have been a true statement.

Eleanor's parents were seemingly unbothered by her departure. Her father remarked how ideal it was for a person to be internationally minded these days, and her mother told her they would top up her allowance for her travels.

Eleanor supposed her parents weren't any more involved in her life than Cheyenne's. Mostly they just seemed glad she wasn't as enamoured with Scotland as she had been when she started university.

On the tenth of May, Eleanor arrived at Heathrow and stepped on a plane to Los Angeles. She had just turned twenty, and life, at last, was beginning.

The first thing Eleanor noticed upon landing in LA was the heat. Warmer than England, certainly warmer than Scotland, but a different kind of heat. The dry kind, where your sweat evaporated rather than pooled.

The second thing she noticed were the cars. So many of them, on so many different highways, concrete bridges crisscrossing the skyline in angry grey streaks. The air was thick with exhaust fumes, and she coughed a few times at the shock of it after the recycled airport environment.

Her hotel was a no-nonsense franchise. She'd toyed with idea of spending her newfound fortune on something luxurious, but decided she needed to save money in case her career didn't play out. Instead, she quickly discovered she was to spend a small fortune on getting cabs everywhere, thanks to the almost non-existent metro system and a city that was too spread out to walk around.

But none of that mattered the minute Eleanor saw the ocean.

The ocean. It somehow looked vaster than it did in Scotland, but perhaps that was because it truly was. The Pacific stretched halfway across the globe, as far as Japan and China and the Philippines. It was bluer, too, but that was because the sky was bluer here, despite the smog. The waves seemed imposingly huge, clustered with surfers instead of swimmers.

It didn't matter. She was Eleanor Sanders. She could conquer waves.

She was right of course, and it wasn't the waves that did her in. It was the temperature of the water. The water was cold back in Scotland, of course, but she expected it there. In California, the chill of the water was a complete shock: she had to sprint up and down to keep herself warm.

She stayed at the beach until sunset, then returned the next morning before dawn. Jet lag meant she couldn't sleep, but the studio gala was that night, and she had nothing to do other than spend the day fretting. She swam, she waved at seals, she watched seagulls, she strolled along the sand, she swam some more. Before returning home, she wandered past the designer shops lined up on Rodeo Drive, her hair still dripping from the beachside shower. One day, she told herself, she'd shop here. It would be an essential part of her 'New Life'.

The gala was held in one of the studio executive's mansions. Eleanor tried to look confident as she rattled the Beverly Hills address off to her driver and smoothed her dress down every few seconds to keep her hands busy. She hoped she looked good enough. The cocktail dress was her mother's, some dusty relic unearthed from her mother's networking days, and Eleanor wasn't convinced it didn't scream 'poor' and 'old fashioned'.

The mansion was gated. Eleanor let the cabbie buzz for permission to enter and told him to give her name. There was a deathly pause, in which Eleanor was terrified the gatekeeper was going to say he was terribly sorry but it had all been a mistake... but the doors eventually swung open. The cab driver drove her down to the end of an extraordinarily long driveway and then he was gone, leaving Eleanor all alone.

Not quite alone. "Eleanor Sanders?" asked a shape emerging from the shadows. Some faceless aide stepped out from beside the doors and gestured for her to come in.

The place was cavernous: high ceilings, floors that echoed, everything sleek and white and modern. Eleanor's dress was green. She suddenly felt like she'd violated the dress code by not coming dressed as either a widow or a bride.

"Right this way," the person said, after handing Eleanor a flute of champagne. He led her to what must have been a living room, only it was so vast Eleanor couldn't fathom how anyone could possibly relax in it under normal circumstances. Huge glass panels had been slid aside to allow open-air access to the pool and veranda, and the hilltop dropped away behind the property to allow sweeping views of the city.

One day, Eleanor reminded herself. *One day you can have all this.*

"Are you Eleanor Sanders?" A tanned man with greying blond hair and a lazy smile on his face wandered over. His suit was impeccably tailored, but he'd left it unbuttoned, adding an air of confident nonchalance to his demeanour. "Your lost expression was kind of a giveaway. I'm Alan Leonsdale, by the way." He held out a hand and Eleanor shook it, shakily.

"I have to say," he went on, "what a fantastic script you delivered to us. I told you how well-poised it's going to be in the market. Rest assured, your royalties will be fantastic. Ah, here's my wife."

"Clarissa," she said, taking Eleanor's hand and shaking it with vigour. Her face was frighteningly identical to Cheyenne's and there were very few obvious signs of aging. Her hair, if possible, was even blonder, and, unlike Cheyenne's, cascaded in a flood of curls around her shoulders. "So amazing to meet you at last! Cheyenne's always so cagey about her friends."

"You know how it is," Eleanor said casually. "It's not very trendy to talk about your parents at uni." Behind her calm façade, her heart was singing victory songs.

"*Uni*!" Cheyenne's mother clucked. "Such a great little word. Oh, I just love the Brits!"

Evidently it ran in the family.

"You want a tour then?" Alan Leonsdale asked. "I can point out a few people you should know, even introduce you to ones you shouldn't." There was so much of Cheyenne in him, especially when he laughed at this own joke.

"Roger Fredericks," he pointed out when Eleanor agreed. "Heads a major studio. Kristina Randall. Produces a major superhero franchise. Jeffrey Henderson."

The names blurred into each other. Occasionally Mr Leonsdale would march Eleanor up to some executive or another, where they'd have a sparkling conversation in which Eleanor would be counted on to say something witty about the UK. They smiled and laughed, but the conversation inevitably moved on.

"Don't be discouraged," Alan Leonsdale said. "They're a little drunk tonight. Celebrating last week's release of *Sunset Boulevard*: already a rolling success. Bit of a gamble though – the script was unorthodox, and all of the younger actors are pretty much unknown." He winked. "I pushed for its production. Then they got Arnold Gissinger playing the male lead and it was set."

"Is he here tonight?" Eleanor asked. Everyone knew Arnold Gissinger. Molly liked to swoon over him whenever his face appeared on social media, even though he was over twice her age.

"He's around somewhere. But if you want an actor there's Jack Flannigan – he's the spirited young assistant. Good role for someone his age. He'll have a few casting agents calling him up soon, I reckon."

Eleanor followed the direction of his pointing finger. A youth was lingering by one of the drinks tables talking to some producer or other whose name she'd already forgotten. Her gaze would have passed over him in an instant if he hadn't been singled out. He resembled a score of other young white men that appeared in films. Strange, Eleanor thought, at how homogenous this room was compared to the city streets.

Still, at least he was her age.

"Flannigan!" Leonsdale called as he strode over. "Got someone I'd like you to meet." He pulled out Eleanor's hand for her so Flannigan could shake it. "This is Eleanor Sanders. She just sold a script that's perfect for you: starring sensitive young men in the midst of a brutal war zone. I thought it might be up your alley."

Flannigan frowned. "Are you offering me the role? Because I'd have to speak with my agent..."

"Not at all! Just letting you know of a future opportunity. And to meet this lovely young lady. She's friends with my daughter, you know. Goes to college with her in Scotland."

"Scotland?" Flannigan raised an eyebrow. "What's it like coming to LA then?"

Eleanor had been answering the same question all evening. "The water's freezing."

He laughed and Eleanor noticed how his eyes sparkled in the light of the Leonsdales' chandelier. "You didn't wear a wetsuit, did you?"

"I don't wear a wetsuit in Scotland either," Eleanor said impulsively.

"And I bet you were frantic trying to stay warm. In surfing, you've got to wait around: wetsuits are essential."

"You surf?" Eleanor had stared longingly at endless pictures of Californian surfers catching waves. Traced the curve of the water with her fingertips as she watched them race the breakers in a cobalt-blue tunnel on YouTube. They didn't have waves like that in Scotland.

He nodded. "Pretty often. I live kinda far from the beach though, so not as much as I used to. I went every day in high school."

"I'd love to learn," Eleanor said. "I just go swimming."

"It's amazing. No feeling like it. Though to be honest, I like snowboarding more."

"We can't do that in Scotland, either," Eleanor said in awe. "Well, we can, but it's rubbish. Everyone goes to the Alps."

He smiled. "Say that again."

"What? The Alps?"

"No, but I'd love to go there one day. What you said before."

"That snowboarding in Scotland's rubbish?"

"Yes! That word!" His grin widened. "I love hearing you say it."

"Rubbish? It means the same as trash."

"But I like the way it sounds in your accent. The way you just drop it in conversation. It's such a funny word." He handed her another champagne glass. "Want a pint?"

"You have no idea what a pint is, do you?" Eleanor laughed as she sipped the champagne. As she said it, a realisation clicked in her head. Everything Cheyenne had been to her – namely, talented, exotic, and, let's face it, rich – she was to these people. Well, maybe not the rich part, but she had the potential to be.

Therefore, all she had to do to succeed here was to become Cheyenne. And wasn't that the point of her coming here anyway? Taking the place in the film industry that could have been Cheyenne's? Returning to Scotland worshipped in Cheyenne's place?

Be Cheyenne. She could do this.

Eleanor placed her head into a coquettish tilt, giggled, and stared adoringly at Flannigan as she lowered her eyelids in what she hoped was a flirtatious manner. "So Jack – can I call you Jack – what's your favourite thing about LA?"

"Depends who's asking. Are you staying long?"

"I start a year abroad at UCLA in August. But I don't have a place to stay until then, so I'm travelling around the country."

His eyes brightened. "You've got to get up to the mountains: I love Mammoth Lakes. And Yosemite! And Lake Tahoe!"

"I sort of wanted to see the coast."

"Then go down the mountains on the way back. Skip Death Valley, though. it'll be way too hot now…"

"Okay, okay!" Eleanor's laugh was tinkling and bright. "Do you know if they work you hard at UCLA? I want to continue writing while I'm here."

"I wouldn't know; I just did two years of acting school. But they have screenwriting classes. You can take one of those."

"You're finished with school then?"

He shrugged. "I've got jobs now. I'm not going back to where I don't get paid. You know," his voice dipped to a conspiratorial whisper, "they paid me enough from *Sunset* that I've bought a house. It's not as nice as this, but it's up in the hills, so it's got a great view."

Be like Cheyenne, Eleanor reminded her pounding heart. "You'll have to show me sometime."

"I can point it out. Come outside; I'll show you." Jack took her hand and led her to the garden, past the pool, and into a secluded corner. "On that hill over there, see?"

She could see, but what was more concerning was how close his body was. How tight his hand was around her waist; how long his fingers were when he brought them up to stroke her face.

"You're very beautiful," he said in an awestruck voice.

Be like Cheyenne.

"I think you're beautiful too," she responded.

In the dark, late at night after Cheyenne had left her, Eleanor had imagined what it would have been like to kiss her. How she would smile, would press eagerly against Eleanor, how her body would give under Eleanor's touch. Then, as it grew even later, the thoughts would turn torturous: would Cheyenne push away, scream, snarl like a wildcat and bare her fangs? In her worst thoughts, Cheyenne sank those perfect teeth right into Eleanor's face. Blood poured out of her, just as it had flowed from Cheyenne after Eleanor picked up that glass.

Kissing Jack was nothing like those fantasies. He was gentler than either Cheyenne – the real one, or the one that lurked in Eleanor's imagination – would ever be. When he pulled her towards him, there was no underlying surge of passion. He just touched Eleanor, who wasn't furious or envious or in love at that moment. Instead, all she felt was an icy, pulsing anxiety, slowly replaced with something warmer bubbling up within in. This was, for all intents and purposes, nice.

And he was an *actor*. Cheyenne would find that so romantic.

And rich. Cheyenne would like that too.

Yes, he was perfect. A Californian Henry. Funny, how things worked out.

Jack took her back to his house. Why not? Eleanor had nowhere else to go, no one who would care to check. The feeling was equal parts liberating and lonely.

He kept apologising for the state of the place. "Haven't had the time to buy furniture yet..." But Eleanor didn't care. They had a bed, wide enough for two, and that was enough.

It was Eleanor's first time. She thought that might mean she would feel something, but there was nothing other than a furious desire to get it done, to conquer him. When they were finished, she wasn't relieved or apathetic, but nor was she triumphant. There was a slight kindle within her of something close to affection, but that soon disappeared – replaced with thoughts of Cheyenne.

Cheyenne definitely felt something when she fucked Henry.

She woke to find Jack lying propped up on his side, peering over at her. There was an expression in his eyes

Eleanor couldn't quite place. A mix of reverence, desire and utilitarianism.

"How long are you in LA for?" he asked.

"The whole year, remember?"

"I mean, how long until you go on your road trip?" He reached out and brushed a lock of hair out of her eyes. It felt strangely intimate, which was odd since they'd had sex the night before.

Eleanor shrugged. "Depends how much there is to do in Los Angeles."

"Loads." He sat up and grinned. "You said you wanted to go surfing?"

"Anything to do with the ocean," Eleanor replied. "But swimming's my main love."

"And writing, I presume?"

She smiled. "You'll be seeing my name in lights, soon."

"Mine will be larger," Jack teased "Actors come first; screenwriters barely get a mention."

"There's still a category for them at the Oscars."

"There are lots of categories at the Oscars." His eyes twinkled – they really were very blue. Almost the colour of Cheyenne's – a thought which instantly struck Eleanor with pangs of guilt. "What you need is to become an author. Write the next 'Great American Novel'."

"I tried that. Couldn't manage it. They were too long, or too short, or I thought they were rubbish."

"Rubbish." He tried the word over and over again, until it sounded like nothing more than a strange collection of sounds devoid of meaning. "Rubbish. Rubbish. You'll never write the next Great *American* Novel, that's for certain."

"I can write the next Great British one."

"*Or*," he said with a grin, "you stay here and write screenplays. Movies are better than books any day. You can even do a play if you want – everyone loves Arthur Miller; he was serious enough."

"I've already written a serious screenplay. Weren't you listening when Mr Leonsdale explained?"

"Tell me again." He took her hand and kissed it. "I want to hear your version."

Eleanor intended to brush over the general outline before he lost interest, but Jack seemed truly engaged, leaning closer with every plot point she explained. By the end, she was going over the minute details; painting the full picture to ensure the perfect emotional response.

"And so finally, as the perspectives blur, we hear a gunshot. Cut to landscape and a shot of a flock of fleeing birds. The camera lingers for a moment, letting the audience take in the juxtaposition of beauty, ferocity, and astonishing indifference within both the landscape and human beings. The shot pans out to the silhouette of a surviving pair on their horse, and they turn and ride away. At least," Eleanor said with a blush, "that's how I'd film it. If I were the director. Which I'm not."

"It's gorgeous." Jack lay back and breathed a sigh of appreciation. "Which role do you think is more affecting? The hero or his ill-fated lover?"

"They're all emotionally affecting. That's the point."

He cocked his head. "Then I suppose my question is, which of the two do you think I'd play better?"

"How am I supposed to know? I haven't seen you in anything."

Jack shot up in excitement. "That's it! We'll go and see *Sunset Boulevard* tonight. Right after surfing and dinner. My agent can get us tickets at one of the old movie theatres downtown. She'll be delighted: I'm supposed to be showing my face."

He grabbed her hand and pulled her to her feet. They were still both naked – Eleanor thought she should be embarrassed, but instead there was only a heady sense of joy caught from Jack's enthusiasm. They rushed through empty rooms to the kitchen, where Jack dragged her out the door and into the garden. Even at this hour it was already warmer than it ever got in Scotland, but the crisp freshness of the dawn still lingered.

"You have a pool," Eleanor remarked in awe.

"Never mind that. Look at the view!"

Jack's house didn't face the city, nor overlook the ocean. Instead, its garden was angled towards the mountains: towering peaks that loomed above the smog. There was nothing so tall in all of Britain, nor anything so golden.

"They're very beautiful," Eleanor said.

"I love mountains," Jack sighed. "If I had my way I'd live up in the Sierra Nevada, but I have to stay in the city for work. So, I look at these instead. And run up them when I have time."

"You like to run?"

"Love it." He smiled. "It's a lot like swimming or surfing – you feel free."

"Surely not on the slog up?"

"Ah, but then there's the way down." His eyes twinkled.

He made her breakfast – toasted bagels with cream cheese, since he didn't have anything else in the house. It was a far cry from the avocados and organic protein shakes Eleanor had been expecting, but she found she didn't mind – she hated avocados anyway.

Eleanor had left her suitcase at the hotel, so she wore one of Jack's t-shirts – designer – and a pair of jeans at least three sizes too big for her. He put his arm around her as they drove to the beach. Eleanor lent out the window and luxuriated in the smell of palms, then ducked back in when hit by exhaust fumes. Jack kissed her again when they arrived at the beach – he parked in a shifty-looking corner, but shrugged when Eleanor raised an eyebrow. "The car's a wreck. Who'd want to break in?"

"You don't have another one? For driving to work and auditions?" Eleanor had presumed show business entailed making a good first impression.

He shrugged. "I can get a taxi. Besides, I spent all my money on the house. I'll get a car with my next pay check – maybe when the royalties start rolling in."

Jack had his own wetsuit – along with gloves and a hood, he told her, but it was too warm in LA for them. He picked a rental out for Eleanor with practised ease and zipped her up when she'd struggled into it. His fingers brushed her nape as he pushed her hair out of the way; her heart fluttered. No one had ever touched her like this before – no matter how much she'd wanted them to.

Eleanor's nerves disappeared the second she stepped into the sea. This was home, even if she was wearing a strange neoprene contraption where the water took several seconds to seep through and cocoon her skin with its coolness. She laughed, and Jack grinned back at her as he lugged a surfboard into the waves.

Surfing was more difficult than Eleanor imagined. Padding out over the incoming breaks took effort, learning how to read when a suitable break was coming took time and trying to stand always ended in a wipeout. But they were in the ocean, Eleanor's domain, and the sea wrapped comfortingly around her every time the board tipped and she was thrown into the waves again. And of course, Jack was there, holding her waist and instructing her when to "Stand! Stand now! Move your right foot; you're unbalanced! Arm out! Yes! Yes, yes, yes! Yes – oh shit!" Jack panicked when Eleanor inevitably fell off, in the moments before she popped up laughing again like a particularly jovial seal.

When she'd had enough, Eleanor swam while she watched Jack surf. He hadn't lied when he said he knew what he was doing. He was as elegant as the cormorants that glided overhead. He popped up effortlessly and careened across the waves, balancing like a ballet dancer. In that moment, Jack became as beautiful as he had when she was tipsy – prettier than Henry ever was.

They drove to Eleanor's hotel: she thought of telling Jack to wait outside, but her heart craved company. He followed her to her room, watched her pack her bags, and laughed when she fell into bed with him. It was odd to do it in the light of day, while the sun still baked the sea, but Eleanor forgot her qualms when she tasted remnants of salt on Jack's skin. Did Cheyenne taste like this, Eleanor wondered, when she lived in California? What did Cheyenne look like in a wetsuit, water sluicing off her curves as she stepped out of the ocean?

"You're amazing," Jack whispered. "You're... you're bloody brilliant!" His attempt at an English accent was so poor that Eleanor burst out laughing.

"I thought you were an actor!"

"I play Americans."

"Not very versatile."

"I'm still young."

"I'll write something British for you," Eleanor declared. "Then you'll be forced to learn."

"Can I be a Scottish rebel?" Jack's eyes sparkled with excitement.

"That's overdone."

"What about a prince?"

"Overrated."

"Or a cockney – it can be just like Mary Poppins!"

Eleanor buried her face in a pillow. "You'll be from Stroud."

"What's in Stroud?

"Nothing."

Jack was still scrolling through his phone, examining the profiles of various UK towns and cities to decide which was best for his heroically tortured protagonist, when Eleanor checked out. He chatted non-stop about Eleanor's country as they drove to the restaurant – "Do they really wear kilts in Scotland? Do you hear bagpipes? How often?" – and listened intently as Eleanor described her village. It was only as he grabbed the bill and paid without looking, that he begin to grow quiet.

"Jack, is something wrong?"

"No." He blushed an angry red. "It's just – there might be some people at the cinema. Taking pictures and things. My agent says I'm supposed to be seen. It reminds people I exist. Big publicity push you know, since it just came out…"

"It's fine." Eleanor squeezed his hand. "I don't mind at all." In fact, she luxuriated in it. As she stepped out the car and they walked past a row of flashing cameras to the cinema door, all she could feel was a feverish heat burning within her. She pictured Cheyenne seeing the photos – would she pore over them, searching for every detail to try and discover what Eleanor had that Cheyenne did not? Would she seethe in jealousy? Anything would do, as long as Cheyenne saw, and cared, and she remembered the name of Eleanor Sanders. As long as she remembered how she'd hurt Eleanor.

Sunset Boulevard was excellent. The whole thing was a vast reflection of Los Angeles and its multifaceted cultures; a sea of identities blurring into one. Jack was a confused young man, set adrift in a tumultuous world as he desperately tried to discover himself. The camera work was shaky and disorienting to mirror Jack's inner state: the only stable shots were wides of the landscape. The final act of violence culminated with Jack's character, bruised, bleeding, and bloody-knuckled, walking along Sunset Boulevard towards the sunset. Eleanor wasn't sure she'd ever loved a film more.

"You like it?" Jack asked with a blush as they stepped out into the lobby. He was oddly bashful, but perhaps that came with trying to view your own work through the eyes of others.

Eleanor smiled and brushed his cheek, just as he'd done to her that morning. "It was amazing. You'll be at the Oscars in no time."

"I wouldn't be that sure."

"It's Oscar-bait!"

"It's also been released under a different studio name: it's a branch of one of the mains that specialises in experimental, art house films. It doesn't have the name recognition."

"But the executives said it was sure to be a success!"

"Executives say a lot of things. We don't know what the Academy will decide."

Eleanor leaned against Jack and angled her shoulder so his arm fell naturally over her: she'd seen Cheyenne do it a dozen times with Henry. "But you'll get work from this. There were already photographers outside: people love you."

"They've gone now." Jack was right: when they stepped out into the cool night air, the paparazzi had disintegrated, drawn like moths to other celebrity sightings around the city. "The promise of me doesn't hold them for that long."

"They just won't make much selling pictures of us walking by the same place, wearing the same clothes."

Jack gave her a pensive look. "You sound like my manager."

Eleanor shrugged. "My flatmate loved celebrity gossip. I picked things up from her."

He ruffled her hair playfully. "Are you old enough to drink in this country?"

She wasn't, so they ended up back at Jack's house, sipping American beer brands Eleanor had never tried as they lounged by the pool. Eleanor's eyes kept being drawn to the mountains. They were a hypnotic black abyss against the sky, in stark contrast to the lights from the valley. Haughty, remote, threatening in their wilderness, yet peaceful all the same.

"Jack," she asked over the crickets, "when's your next job?"

"There's a credit card ad on Thursday." Jack made a face. "But the exciting stuff starts in two weeks – I've got an indie film. Nowhere near as hard-hitting as Sunset, but my agent says she'd make some calls so I can start sending some tapes in."

"Forget the credit card company." Eleanor was feeling strangely bold: it must be the alcohol. Or perhaps it was the sensation of being wanted. "Come with me on holiday. Just the first part. Then I'll keep travelling and you can go back to work."

"I've got a better idea." His hand trailed up her side. "We go on vacation for a week or two. Then we both come back to LA. You stay with me and write scripts. You could finish another one by September."

"What about Yosemite?"

"We'll see Yosemite. We'll see the whole state." He kissed her cheek. "And then you get to spend the summer with me."

It was a horrible idea. Eleanor didn't know much about relationships, but she knew that you didn't move in with your fling after twenty-four hours together. But Jack was sweet, and funny, and attractive, and he would make Cheyenne jealous.

"Okay." She kissed him back. "I'll stay."

June.

One year and eleven months before the party.

Eleanor loved California. She loved the cliffs towering over the ocean, the redwoods and sequoias stretching to the sky, the vastness of the mountains, the majesty of the granite. They skipped San Francisco – Eleanor had wanted to see the bridge, but Jack said he thought it better to avoid his parents – but they made up for it by spending longer near the alpine Lake Tahoe. This seemed to exhilarate Jack: he loved nothing more than charging up mountains, then bounding back down like an overexcited puppy to see where Eleanor had got to. Every night, they curled up in a cabin Jack had found for them – usually remote, though sometimes near a small town. Eleanor exalted in walking the streets: smelling the pines, seeing the pickups, letting the shopkeepers marvel at her accent. Once they even saw a bear.

"It's a pity we don't have time to stay in Mammoth Lakes," Jack said as they sped down a highway where the imposing mountains met the endless expanse of sagebrush that was the desert. "That's my favourite place in the world."

"Next time," Eleanor assured him, delighted with the promise of future trips. She stared out the window and grinned at the strange plants whizzing past, so different to anything back in Britain. Things were *dry* here: gone was the constant damp ache that permeated everything in her old country. Dry and spacious and beautiful.

"At some point we should see the Grand Canyon," she announced. "And Arches. And Yellowstone. And the Tetons."

"Next summer," Jack promised. "Or in one of your breaks – as long as I'm not working."

That was easier said than done. Jack was working a lot: he seemed to have one indie film after another. Nothing from the big studios yet, but Jack assured her it was only a matter of time. Meanwhile, Eleanor spent her time making edits to her script as the Leonsdales discussed production with her. They kept suggesting she found an agent for her next script, but Eleanor had to write the thing first. She was stuck on the topic: maybe she should adapt her fantasy novel? Or do another gritty, realist piece? Or a totally different direction? Nothing seemed satisfying.

When her mind wandered, she thought of Jack. She studied his IMDB religiously, poring over indie flicks he'd grabbed bit roles in out of film school. They were arty and depressing, about teenagers shooting heroin and having sex in high schools and looking moodily out windows. None of them were particularly inspiring.

Once she tired of Jack's work, she turned her attention to his personal life: she relentlessly stalked his social media. Then, when her curiosity wasn't sated, she turned to glitzy Hollywood tabloids. Most of the press coverage focused on *Sunset Boulevard* – but there, at the bottom of a paragraph summarizing the film, lurked a niggling sentence. *With Jack Flannigan, former boyfriend of Janette Reed.* Clicking on the blue hyperlink revealed several pages of articles dedicated to a glossy-haired model with pouty lips.

She wasn't successful, not really. No Vogue covers or perfume ads. But she had walked a few runways, worked with some high-profile designers. Every one of her pictures, from the moody side profiles to the glamourous full body shots, bore a striking resemblance to Eleanor.

Not totally, of course. Eleanor was no supermodel – that was always the purview of Cheyenne – but they both had dark hair and a square face, and large eyes –they couldn't quite be sisters, but they could be distant relatives.

Three months ago, Janette had landed a magazine gig. Since then, nothing – except for one string of comments, posted on a fashion message board. *She smashed up a bar near Yosemite,* one comment read. *Punched a bouncer. My cousin's friend saw it.*

Can't be. It was just someone who looked like her.

No, I saw it. She was screaming at him, flashing her ID. And then she started wailing about meth.

That's why she went out to Arizona – the agency forced her out there at gunpoint.

Is she clean?

No one knows.

Eleanor slammed her laptop shut and pondered. An ex-girlfriend gone to seed on drugs. Another girl, bright and naïve, who bore a striking resemblance to the old one, falling right into Jack's lap. Him taking her home; everything moving so quickly.

It wasn't strange, Eleanor told herself. Jack wanted companionship; he wanted to fix the void Janette had left within him. So what if he wanted what she could provide him? She wanted what he could provide her. And if she could get a girl who looked like Cheyenne – who could one-up Cheyenne, but succeeding in her own right and supporting Eleanor where Cheyenne had failed – wouldn't she take it?

Cheyenne didn't seem to have realised Eleanor's presence in her hometown, yet. Or if she did, she was being awfully quiet about it. Her social media told Eleanor she was working an internship in London – something in finance that she'd got from Henry's parents. The pictures were all of her looking beautiful and imposing in a suit, sipping cocktails on some company's rooftop bar.

George, Gina, and Raquelle were in an infuriating amount of them. They were all pretty enough, but Cheyenne, as she always had, outshone them all. It was something to do with her Americanness. Try as she might, she still hadn't shed it, that veneer of confidence everyone from this country carried with them. It was in her hair, her teeth, her posture, the glint of her eyes. She was forever destined to be 'Other' in Britain, but that only made her a greater object of desire.

"Who's that?" Jack asked one night when he leaned over to look at Eleanor's screen. In this picture Cheyenne was on a yacht zipping down the Thames.

"A friend from uni. She's American," Eleanor added, and just as she'd predicted, Jack's eyes glazed over in boredom. "You've seen her in the painting in the study – the one of the sea." She'd moved everything she owned into Jack's house by now – so much so the property was beginning to become not his but theirs. She'd dreamed of this, back in St Andrews: that someone would want her enough to take her into their home. Yet when Jack grew bored or irritated, her status as an interloper only opened a gulf between them. She tried to keep him happy, to make him forget those troubles.

"I thought that was you."

"There are two of us." She tried to keep her face neutral. "We used to be better friends – it's why I haven't put it somewhere nicer." She passed it often enough that the painting no longer shocked her every time she walked in the room, but Eleanor had no desire for George's art to be the centrepiece of their home.

Jack nodded. "She looks like one of the girls down on Rodeo Drive."

"She's from LA."

He snorted. "Nothing like you." Then he swung an arm around her, and Eleanor muttered something suitably British into his ear.

Still, the thought of Rodeo Drive girls struck with her. The blonde ones that lounged around in Beverly Hills mansions. Eleanor poked her head out of the window as they drove around; kept her eyes on a swivel when Jack took her downtown (always in a taxi – said his car was too bad to show to the public). There were girls of Cheyenne's type, of course, but none with the Cheyenne glow. And plenty of foreign girls from every country under the sun: Americans of course, and British, but French and Italian as well.

"Didn't she have the most beautiful accent?" Eleanor sighed after hearing a French woman on the phone pass by.

Jack shrugged. "Nothing as good as the English."

"You're just saying that."

"I'm not." He pulled her into a kiss. "I love your country best."

She laughed. "Is that code for: 'I want a visa'?"

"Can I make movies – or *films* – there?"

"Not as many as here," Eleanor said quickly. She didn't need him getting ideas of relocation But there *is* a nice cinema in Leicester Square."

"Much better name than movie theatre."

"Now you really are flattering me."

"I mean it!" His eyes misted over, almost dreamlike. "It's so much more romantic."

The words hit like a gut punch. Eleanor was back in Scotland, sitting under a tree near a quad; she was in Nice, watching the sun sparkle on the sea and illuminate the shore. And everywhere, everywhere, there was Cheyenne.

"I'll tell you what's romantic," Eleanor declared. "The sunset over the sea. You can't see that in Scotland in the town I'm from. Can't in London either."

"But you must have a west coast! What about the Highlands?"

"Hardly anyone lives in the Highlands. They're very rugged." Immediately, Eleanor realised she'd said the wrong thing. Jack's entire face lit up in excitement; even his body seemed to tense at the prospect of steep climbs and sweeping views.

"Mountains?"

"A few. In Scotland and England and Wales." Eleanor leaned into him and managed to nudge his body so it faced the San Gabriel mountains: dramatic spires that towered into the clouds to the east of the city. "But none so tall as here."

Jack brushed her cheek and smiled. "I really need to take you to Mammoth."

August.

One year and nine months before the party.

It was much easier to socialise when there was an end goal: she aimed for a touch, then a kiss, then a hand snaking dangerously low, then finally onto the bed to shriek and tumble and grin. She liked him then: seeing him slumped next to her as the evening light leaked through their bedroom window. The air smelt of bougainvillea and the sea glimmered, and if she forgot who she was she might almost think this was paradise.

But then they stepped outside, and the cameras flashed, and she remembered why she was there.

She pretended she didn't relish them. Jack was a gentleman: he tried to shield her from the lenses, usher her out back doors or take her out in the early morning when the swarms were less likely to be awake. But still, he had to play the game. His flinch was different when he was guilty: a sure sign his publicist had called the paps. Eleanor just applied another coat of lipstick and looked demure.

One morning, she woke early and tiptoed out of bed, careful not to wake Jack. She knew his house better than her own home now and she deftly manoeuvred down the corridors to the kitchen in the dim morning light. The sun was barely cresting the peaks of the mountains, and they were so majestic Eleanor almost understood why Jack lived up here, in the hills, instead of down by the sea. She fetched a glass of water, so cold it made her teeth ache, and sipped it while staring at her phone.

All those articles. So many pictures, so many clicks. All of them saying more or less the same thing: Eleanor Sanders, whose script they claimed was still stuck in development hell (it had only been a few months – but that wasn't fast enough for them, nor for Eleanor). Eleanor Sanders, screenwriter. Her heart throbbed with a strange sense of joy. She wanted this, but she wanted to do it herself. Not through her link to a man.

Or maybe this was why she'd picked Jack in the first place.

"Eleanor?" She started. Jack was standing by the doorway, wrapped in a terrycloth robe. "I woke up, and you weren't there."

She shrugged. "I felt like rising early."

"You scared me." He frowned. "You look cold. Do you want my robe?" He wrapped it around her before she could protest.

"Now you'll be cold."

"It doesn't matter." He bent down and kissed her on the forehead. "As long as you're alright."

She laughed. "You worry too much. I'm from a much colder place than here."

"That doesn't mean I can't make you warm." That garnered a smile from Eleanor – a real one, though she instantly panged with guilt.

Jack smiled too, though perhaps that was because he caught sight of the mountains. They were glowing pink now, the sun making them soft instead of harsh and fiery with heat. "They're so beautiful," he said in awe. "Just like you."

Another flinch. "They are lovely in this light."

"They're lovely in every light." He smiled wistfully. "But wait until the spring, when the fields are green and the flowers are blooming. In August the plants are dead, the grass is yellow. Everything smells like decay."

"I thought you loved this place all year round."

"I do. But it's best when there's enough water. Then you can swim as well." There was no malice in his voice as he said this, nothing but unadulterated joy as he imagined his perfect world. A world with Eleanor in.

She took another sip of water to numb her mind.

"You know," she said at last. "I don't mind yellow. At home winter is just grey and brown. At least here death is golden."

"You're so poetic," he remarked with a smile. "Such a brilliant writer." And he was kissing her again, tender and gentle and with nothing but love and delight in it. Eleanor should have been happy, should have been smiling and laughing and jumping for joy because she had everything she'd ever wanted, and yet inside her there was only a dark hole, gaping and empty. She shouldn't be here. It was deeply wrong.

When Jack pulled away, he told her they should go hiking, right that minute while the sun was still casting rosy shadows on the hills - Eleanor didn't protest.

6th May. 19:52

Amy doesn't stay, of course. She lingers for a while, out of politeness, but then she spots a real friend and disappears into the crowd. There is no reason she shouldn't: she isn't on the clock and has no reason to attend to Eleanor like a needy customer. Yet her departure still leaves Eleanor with a sour taste in her mouth. Another disappointment, another betrayal.

She takes another flute of champagne, swirls it around as she does the rounds again: smile at him, exchange artificially cheery hellos with her. It's oddly like LA, at another party where she knows almost no one. But there she had Jack to steady her. Here, she is alone. A glamorous hostess with an air of foreign intrigue about her.

Eleanor smooths down her dress. *Look like a warrior*.

She spots them out of the corner of her eye: Raquelle's willowy figure, Gina's gorgeous curls. And there, in the corner, coat still wrapped around her shoulders like she might decide to turn and leave, is Cheyenne. Back again for one last round.

Eleanor can't contain herself. She slips through the crowd towards them, snatching a drink from the counter as she goes. "Cheyenne!" she calls as she pretends to take a sip. "Cheyenne, you made it!"

Her California blue eyes – the Pacific shines like that, in the right light – flash back warily. "Happy birthday, Eleanor," she says at last. And so it is settled. They will be cordial here – there will be no scene. Just the way Eleanor wants it.

"And George!" Eleanor waves to him over Cheyenne's shoulder, the picture of the excited hostess. "So good to see you!" Then, a careful jab – against her better judgement, but she had to know: "How are your paintings?"

He looks down to hide his red cheeks. "Doing fine," he replies. "How's Hollywood?"

"Wonderful," Eleanor purrs. Her eyes flick to Cheyenne, whose expression is carefully blank. "It's a lovely town. Or city really – if you call LA a town, then what does that make this place?"

"Cosy," Cheyenne retorts. Eleanor nods, seemingly demurely, the picture of innocence. "How's the boyfriend?" Cheyenne asks.

"Lovely too." Eleanor moves towards Cheyenne, so close their breath mingles: Eleanor's hot with adrenaline and alcohol, Cheyenne's still frosty from the walk over. "You know he bought the penthouse flat? You can come and see it, if you like." Cheyenne, she remembers, never bothered to visit her when she lived with Liz and Molly.

"I think we can enjoy ourselves down here," Cheyenne says. As Eleanor moves ever closer, Raquelle steps in to cut her off. The two glare at each other, and Eleanor entertains the thought of yanking that bow straight out of her hair.

"Drinks," Eleanor says at last, tossing her hair. "There's plenty on the table over there. Or you can ask the barman: he'll mix you something. On me, unless you don't want American money."

"I think we'll manage," says Gina coolly. Her hair is so beautiful: the kind of salon curls girls dream about bestowed upon her by chance. Or luck. Or genetic nepotism. It's very neat tonight: she must have spent time getting ready. What does Gina envision this night looking like? Or is she simply excited to get home and wrap herself around Sam?

Speaking of, Sam is standing a little way off with Henry, both of them fidgeting as they watch the girls and George. Eleanor waves them over and flashes them a smile. "You two want to see upstairs, don't you?"

"Not particularly," Henry says, but Sam is too polite. He gives an encouraging nod.

Eleanor grins. "I'll take you up after drinks," she promises with a wink, and rushes over to the bartender to request that the drinks for the girls over there be extra strong. "Friends of mine," she promises. "They deserve it. And I'll have another vodka lemon soda, while you're at it." She takes one sip, then rushes off with it to the toilets. When she returns, the glass is full of nothing but water, which she drinks with abandon.

She circles a little more before returning to Cheyenne and Co. Everywhere she is loud, everywhere she is rambunctious, everywhere she pretends to go wild. She shoots shot after shot that end up over her shoulder or in a nearby plant pot. She dances with anyone who offers her their arm, stands on every table and bounds across every sofa. She makes sure everyone sees Eleanor Sanders, young and carefree and having a wonderful time at her twenty-second birthday party. Yet the whole time, she keeps a careful watch on the figures in the corner, still being plied with free refills from the bartender.

Eleanor slips back over when they are at least three glasses down. "Let me show you the place," she says with a grin. "Least I can do." As planned, they are too drunk to properly resist. For a moment, she thinks of Jack: wonders what happens to him at parties like this, when he's incapacitated and she is thousands of miles away. Is he scared? Helpless? Or does he enjoy it; fall into bed with some other girl?

Eleanor told Amy he could never leave her. Seeing Cheyenne in front of her, letting desire rise inside her, she is not so sure.

Not that it matters, after what she has done to him.

September.

One year and eight months before the party.

Eleanor approached UCLA with a determined detachment. She knew what university was like, understood the way students moved through the halls, the invisible hierarchy, the way they whispered and tittered as they discussed hookups and parties and how heinous it was that their comp sci professor assigned them *that* much homework. She was tired of it all by now, tired of spending her entire life in school, but she'd sunk enough time and money into her degree that she wanted to see it through. Especially as she had yet to sell another script.

It would come, Jack promised her. Especially now she was enrolled in her screenwriting course, where she'd be forced to write and ideas would start to flow. Something about California, he suggested, would be good.

"That's just another *Sunset Boulevard*." Eleanor wrinkled her nose. "I want to be original."

"All the best ideas are already taken. Your job is just to rework them into something that feels new. Besides, people love nostalgia."

"A film that came out three months ago isn't nostalgia."

"But I was good in *Sunset*. They'd give me a part in it without thinking."

Though they never discussed it, *Sunset* hadn't been the boon to Jack's career that he'd been hoping. He was still puttering along with his indie films, receiving minimal pay and recognition at best. The one he shot all September might go to Cannes, he told Eleanor, but his optimism was strained.

Finally, at the end of the month, Jack received a call from his agent. He'd been offered a supporting role in a historical drama from a major studio. It was fifty-fifty whether the thing would make any money, but Jack jumped on it anyway. They had no other options. Unfortunately, filming wasn't scheduled to start until February, and until then, Jack was forced to retire back to commercials.

"Are you sure you can't get the Leonsdales to pull some strings?" Jack asked one afternoon as they lounged in the living room. There was still no real furniture – there wasn't the money – so they lay on cushions Jack's old roommate had been throwing out. It was not, Eleanor thought as she watched a beetle make a daring crawl up the kitchen step and into the living room, the sort of glamour Cheyenne would envy. Hers was a love of paraquet floors and gilded curtains: this minimalist block Eleanor found herself in would not excite her.

But she would make it work, Eleanor assured herself. She and Jack would turn the house into a home. They would have the money to buy decor: a splash of colour, to make the place less sterile. Cheyenne would never touch her again.

"They can't do everything for me. Nepotism only goes so far when you're not actually their kid." Eleanor didn't mention that she didn't want to risk the Leonsdales mentioning her to their daughter. Jack only sighed and flopped dramatically over the cushions.

Without anything to do he paced around the house like a caged animal. It was easier for Eleanor: she had her classes to escape to, a swim club she intermittently attended (she found it difficult to make friends since she didn't live on campus, but she told herself she wasn't interested in that sort of thing anyway. Friends, as she had learnt from experience, only caused problems. She had Jack, and the ocean, and that was enough).

Jack had nothing. Some days he was rambunctious, jumping around the house and suggesting wild adventures that Eleanor couldn't go on because she had school. Other days he lay in bed all day, barely bothering to get up. When he got like that, it could be bad enough that Eleanor sometimes considered moving into her college dorm. Guilt immediately prickled in her stomach, and she tried to banish it, instead, her mind moved onto all the little things about Jack that annoyed her. His insistence upon running at odd times, his slight snore in his sleep, his melodramatics, the way he refused to buy them any goddamned furniture.

It would be better, she told herself, when Oscar nominations were released. They had to wait until January, and in the meantime, Eleanor flew back to London to spend Christmas with her family. Things were just as tense there as they were in LA: her parents, focused on nothing more than village politics and a distant cousin's wedding, irritated her. Fed up with their myopic view, Eleanor would often storm into the winter's endless rain, shivering, sulking, and soaked. California couldn't come soon enough.

Jack was even more tanned when she got back to LA, if it were possible. "High altitudes increase sun exposure," he said with a wink. "I was snowboarding all Christmas. With my parents," he added before Eleanor could ask how he'd paid for all that. He was in good spirits: he was convinced he was in the running for a best actor nomination at the Oscars. "Well, maybe best supporting. But my role's better, so they should focus on me. Arnold Gissinger has enough awards."

They sat together on the couch to watch the nominations. Eleanor kept trying to reach out to Jack – an arm around the shoulder, a squeeze of the palm – but he couldn't hold still for more than a few seconds before jerking away. Over the winter his fingernails had been bitten to the quick: their jagged corners scratched at Eleanor's skin when Jack pulled himself from her grasp.

Things started off well. *Sunset* nabbed a nomination for best cinematography: the announcer hadn't even finished reading the title before Jack leaped up, punching the air. Eleanor screamed in delight alongside him. He spun her around the room, the nearly sent her careening into a stack of magazines when his attention returned to the television.

Best Supporting Actor came and went without a mention of Jack. He pretended not to care, but the way he was furiously picking at a cut on his palm said otherwise.

'Where'd you get that?' Eleanor asked.

He grunted. 'Surfing.'

'Do you wanna go down to the ocean now?' Eleanor offered. It was still early – if they hurried they could catch the sunset. She shifted herself so she was between Jack and the television.

'No,' he demanded. 'Wait.'

And so they stayed on what passed for a sofa, watching the slick graphics whizz past their eyes and listening to the chipper voice of the announcer. The pit in Eleanor's stomach only grew as the show went on.

Finally it was time for Best Actor. Jack squeezed his fingers into his palms so tightly they turned white. Eleanor was frozen – but in the interminable pause before the names were read out, a sudden flare of hope burst within her. Maybe Jack was right. Maybe, just maybe, he'd made the cut. His dream would come true, and he could be happy.

There were five nominations per category. Jack wasn't the first – it went to a grey-haired man in a period piece. Nor was he the second – that was a young hotshot, not yet twenty-five. He wasn't the third, or the fourth.

Eleanor closed her eyes before the fifth name was read, as if by not seeing it the nomination would cease to exist. In the darkness, a rasping sound echoed on repeat. Eleanor thought the speakers were broken until she realised the sound was distinctly human: Jack whispering "please" on an endless loop.

Eleanor wanted to reach out and embrace him; to whisper in his ear that she had been the one begging so many times before. But she already knew that sympathy wasn't what he was looking for. He was determined to weather this alone.

"And finally..." another excruciating pause, "the fifth nomination for Best Actor goes to Arnold Gissinger."

Eleanor didn't get to see Arnold Gissinger's smiling face fill the screen, because Jack had already thrown a pillow at the television. It bounced listlessly off the screen as a short scene from *Sunset Boulevard* played. To add insult to injury, all of Jack's lines had been cut.

"Next time," Eleanor murmured endlessly. "It'll all work out – we just need to wait."

"You were considered," Jack's agent assured him over the phone an hour later. "Sometimes it's just the way it goes."

Jack sulked around the house for days after that. The only thing that improved his mood was going for runs or checking up on Eleanor's writing.

"Anything good?" he would say when he walked into her office for the third time that day.

"It's the same idea I told you about this morning."

"Can I read it?"

"Tonight. I'm in the flow."

"As long as there's a part for me," he muttered as he returned to pacing the kitchen.

That night, Eleanor woke to the sound of smashes. Her heart stopped: a burglary? Jack's side of the bed was warm, but empty. Had he tried to stop them? Was he hurt?

Another crash. Heart in her mouth, she tiptoed down the hall towards the kitchen. Her tongue was dry with fear, her stomach prickled with nerves. Should she get a weapon? Should she call the police? Where was Jack?

Glass shards splintered at her feet as she rounded the corner. She jerked back and tensed with fear. Jack was surrounded by open kitchen cupboards and was smashing their contents on the floor. Broken china surrounded his feet like he was a detonated bomb.

"Jack!" Eleanor called. She couldn't approach him, not barefoot. "Jack, calm down! You'll hurt yourself!"

His face was red with fury, though it darkened to a shade of embarrassment when he looked up and saw her. There was no need: Eleanor understood the urge for violence, the need to let the destruction you felt bubbling up behind your teeth out into the world. She remembered another smashed glass, this one cutting human skin. It was terribly familiar.

Jack said nothing, only stood deathly still while Eleanor found a broom and cleared a safe passage. It wasn't until he staggered out of range of the splinters that Eleanor saw the tear tracks staining his cheeks. She embraced him.

"The twenty-second of February," she murmured into his ear. "You just need to hold out until the twenty-second of February. Then you're working again." He made a small sound at the back of his throat, something helpless, like a child. It was remarkably alien: Eleanor had never held anyone so close with the intent to comfort them.

She would have liked to have held Cheyenne like this. Even George, as a friend.

"I'm sorry," Jack choked. "I woke you up. You have class in the morning."

"It doesn't matter." And suddenly she wasn't thinking of Cheyenne anymore, only the boy clutching onto her for dear life. "Let's go back to bed."

"I have to clean up."

"We can do it in the morning." She led him down the hall like a toddler and let the tears rain onto her shoulder as he cried himself to sleep.

February.

One year and three months before the party.

Jack's film shot in New York: he kissed Eleanor goodbye as he tossed her the house keys. "Now you can finally get some writing done," he teased as he stepped into the car. "And call the Leonsdales about your script's production!"

It was strange, being in LA by herself. Eleanor felt as if she'd just arrived anew: the streets seemed warped without Jack's arm around her, the mountains vaster without him to lead the way. The only thing that was the same was the ocean, and her near-endless swims. She spent more time on the beach now that Jack was gone – something about the empty house perturbed her. Once again, she considered moving into the student housing at UCLA, but she had no real friends there to make her any less lonely.

In another life, this would have been the time to stake her name as a strong, independent Hollywood player, who could create brilliant films without a man's name attached to hers. But her scripts, even as she finally managed to churn some out, weren't selling. She sat in her empty room, drinking from a water bottle now they didn't have any glasses, sending out query after query to agents, all of them ending in rejection.

Maybe Jack was right. Maybe she should swallow her fear and pride and write to the Leonsdales. But if they hadn't managed to get her first script into production – and therefore hadn't managed to net Eleanor any extra profits – what was the hope they'd buy a second from her?

Besides, the Leonsdales only made her think of Cheyenne.

Without Jack as a distraction, there was nothing to stop her from spending all day stalking Cheyenne online. She saw her strolling down the same familiar streets, arm in arm with those same hateful faces, even standing in the sun at some beach – fuck, was that Nice?

Eleanor tossed the phone across the room in disbelief. Unfortunately, that only made her focus on the painting on the wall, taunting her with its deceptively happy faces. She'd chosen the study unconsciously, as a way to casually link her with Cheyenne – as if she could still feel their connection across thousands of miles, two years, and five layers of paint. Now she felt as if the painted figure had reached out and slapped her across the face. Nice was *their* place, the one Cheyenne had dragged her around smiling after she watched Eleanor frolic in the sea. Their memories there were irreplaceable – or so she'd thought.

Gritting her teeth, Eleanor scrolled through her camera roll until she found some suitable photos: palm trees, sunsets, Jack. She posted them with some suitably cheery caption and then slammed her phone down on the table.

It was the first time she had publicly acknowledged Jack as her boyfriend – he was in some photos from back in June, but they were far back on a slideshow; easy to miss. Now he was front and centre, with her arms wrapped around him as he kissed her cheek. Officially, Jack would have said, she should have run it by his agent.

Not like it mattered. He wasn't famous anyway.

Three days later, Molly sent her a story. Eleanor had to do a double take: Molly had barely talked to her since she left Scotland. It was a link to the Mail Online: a short yet bombastic article claiming actors in New York had been filmed doing coke. The text was short and sweet: *is that ur boyfriend?*

Eleanor's boyfriend. Famous enough for papers to write about him allegedly doing cocaine in the back room of some New York City club. A strange sense of satisfaction pulsed through Eleanor. If she couldn't make it herself, at least she could do so through her boyfriend.

And Cheyenne would have to see.

Still, a nagging feeling raced through her mind – the old girlfriend, who liked meth and was still in rehab. She thought of Jack's outburst, the glass on the floor. He was no addict with anger problems. He liked her, and she liked him, and most importantly, the whole world knew it.

She busied herself with writing and swimming until Jack got back. When he returned, she'd managed to churn out another script – some fantasy/horror combo that sounded a little strange but had all the right buzzwords – and been to a depressing swim meet where she'd raced well but had sat on the stands by herself, shivering, while the rest of her teammates chatted about boys and grades and the other teams. Jack was delighted by the writing and was suitably disparaging about her teammates – and couldn't shut up about New York.

"It was so professional! Proper high calibre stuff, like I haven't had since *Sunset*! And the director – she's just as amazing as they say; I've never been given so many inspiring notes. It was like I suddenly understood. And the actors were all so brilliant – I was practically the only one without an Oscar. And the food–"

"Did you really do cocaine in a club?" Eleanor teased.

He blushed. "One of the other actors brought it in. He does it all the time – God, it felt amazing!"

Jack brushed off any further questions about drugs. Instead, he leaned back and talked about how he was sure to be on loads of panels this summer, how calls were going to be rolling in once people saw he was good enough to work with such cinema legends. It was a similar rhetoric to what he'd been saying after *Sunset Boulevard*, but Eleanor didn't question it. As long as he was happy: as long as he was staying with her. She was a good girlfriend: she didn't nag, or prod, or threaten to usurp his spotlight. She simply stood next to him and glowed in her own, lesser way: a moon to his sun.

He made her happy, too. One night, he took her out to eat with some of his co-stars. They were huge names, ones that made Eleanor shake with nerves in the car as they approached. Yet, when they arrived, she smiled politely, laughed in all the right places, told her funniest anecdotes. Her accent was out in full effect.

The paparazzi came that night. Eleanor brushed off any attempts from Jack to shield her: instead, she walked as close to the cameras she could, a grin plastered across her face. She looked as though the world was her oyster, and it had just been served to her on a silver platter.

The other actors were famous enough for the pictures to be published everywhere. The next morning, Eleanor received a call from an agent. Three days later, she had sold her next script.

"Isn't it *marvellous*?" she told Jack. "I've got a career again!" *And all it took was one pap walk*, she thought, silently.

He blushed. "I'm just sorry it didn't come sooner. If *Sunset Boulevard* had got me more roles..." He would be out more, and Eleanor would be with him. People would see her online and learn her name. The jobs would come rolling in, and so would the money. Cheyenne would look up from her corporate job in London, and George from his second-rate art fairs, and both would seethe.

But she wasn't to think of Cheyenne and George now.

"But you've got some roles now." Just yesterday a call had come in from Jack's agent.

He shrugged. "Thanks for not leaving me. You had every right. I had no money, and I was acting like – what would you say – a prick?"

And you had no cultural capital. But Eleanor couldn't say that: she was his loyal girlfriend. "I'm just glad it's all working out now."

He kissed her, and Eleanor couldn't stop herself: she imagined Cheyenne, tears running down her face as she thought of how she'd treated Eleanor, and a desperate desire to win her back. Eleanor would oblige, but only for a minute. Then she'd kick Cheyenne to the curb and spit on her, right on the spot she'd cut her with the champagne glass.

The thrill of revenge burnt through Eleanor. Deep within her, something stirred: a serpent, slithering through the ashes of her heart, fanning the flames of her victory. When she was this close to Jack, it was easy to pretend it was passion.

Eleanor leaned in and kissed her boyfriend harder, with enough force to send him rocking back. He gave a sigh of pleasure, but she wasn't listening; instead, her tongue traced the spot on his lip where she had cut Cheyenne. In one quick moment, she bit down: not enough to break the skin, but enough to make Jack stiffen.

"Sorry," she whispered. "Sorry, sorry. I was thinking of something else."

"Don't worry," he replied with a smile. "We've got work: everything will work out."

Eleanor wasn't worried. But even as he held her, high on their victory, the force that kept her kissing back was that image of Cheyenne, watching them with green-eyed jealousy.

April.

One year and one month before the party.

The pleasant fizz of champagne shot up Eleanor's nostrils, and she gulped her drink down. Applause erupted around her as she wiped her mouth triumphantly and raised her arms. Unfortunately, the world started to spin; she staggered and had to clumsily stagger down from the coffee table that was her makeshift podium.

"3.2 seconds," read the scorekeeper, one of an endless rotation of actor friends Jack had amassed. This one was more successful than most of the others, though he owed that to the cut of his jaw rather than any actual talent. Eleanor thought his name was Steven, but her head was too fuzzy to remember. "Not bad, but pretty far off Samantha Flores' record of 2.6."

Heads swivelled towards the romantic comedy actress standing on one edge of the crowd, who giggled and waved. Samantha was just as funny in person as she was onscreen, but far more raunchy. Cheyenne, Eleanor was sure, would not have approved.

As a reality TV star and a comedian rivalled to be next to chug champagne, Eleanor slipped away from the living room, towards the bar in the kitchen. A real bartender had been hired for the night, who handed her a glass of water on a napkin emblazoned with the words, *Brian Schlieman's 27th Birthday*. Eleanor wasn't a particular fan of Brian – his bland DJing got on her nerves, and his eyes always seemed to glaze over whenever a woman started speaking – but he'd invited so many stars to his party and pitched it as the event of the year that she and Jack had decided they had to go.

And now look at Eleanor. Downing champagne with Samantha Flores. Thank God Brian had hired enough security to patrol the grounds and keep the paparazzi from sneaking through the fence – though she wouldn't trust him enough not to pay someone to come and capture the carnage if it would boost his profile.

Eleanor sighed and stumbled towards the bathroom. She was so drunk she didn't hear the noises inside until she'd already flung open the door.

"Oh," Eleanor should have slammed the door, but her legs were giving out, and she ended up leaning on the door frame for support. "Oh fuck, I'm sorry, I should have knocked..."

"I was the one who forgot to lock it," said Penelope Hale. "Are you going to vomit too?"

Eleanor had known in the back of her mind that the singer was going to be at this party; anyone who was anyone would be. But she hadn't actually thought about the real, concrete possibility of running into her until now. Penelope, after all, was Cheyenne's girl, and Cheyenne was an entity that Eleanor always tried to force from her mind.

Cheyenne was right, Eleanor thought, glancing down at Penelope's fingers. Her nails were a mess. She'd worn fake ones earlier in the night – Eleanor could see them, torn off and sitting next to the sink. Her real nails were short and chipped, with several breaks that looked fresh.

"I might," Eleanor admitted. She stumbled inside and shut the door behind her; Penelope didn't seem to mind. "I chugged too much champagne."

"Dangerous, that." Penelope hit the paper towel roll with such ferocity it started unrolling quickly enough to cover the entire area around the toilet with damp paper squares. She dabbed around her lips and made a face in the mirror. "Fuck, my makeup's ruined. Is there anything on my dress?"

"No. Still beautiful." Eleanor wasn't lying. Penelope's outfit was a dashing blue ensemble that seemed to snake around her body as it hugged her curves. Artful slits in the skirt and bodice created the illusion of near-nudity, even though the vast majority of her skin was under wraps. Even after being yanked back over the toilet, her hair still fell in soft waves around her face, and the dark makeup that ringed her eyes was untouched.

"Thank God." Penelope sank to the ground and groaned in relief. "Do you mind if I stay here while you're sick?"

"I think I'll be alright," Eleanor replied. "I just need some proximity to the toilet bowl."

"Then we'll sit and soak in our misery together." Penelope leaned her head back and sighed. "Fuck, my head hurts. Maybe I need more tequila."

"I'm not sure that's the solution," Eleanor cautioned.

"Coke then? My boyfriend told me Brian's got a whole stash upstairs."

Now it was Eleanor's turn to groan. "My boyfriend got papped doing that in a club in New York. Just my luck I'll have some right as a photographer breaks in."

Penelope's laugh turned into a hacking cough. Eleanor rushed to help her, but she brushed it off. "Just the last of the sick caught in my throat. Really, it's too disgusting for anyone else to deal with." She fixed Eleanor with a quizzical look. "Which one's your boyfriend, then?"

"Jack Flannigan."

She nodded. "I think I met him once – maybe at a *Sunset Boulevard* launch party? He was in that, wasn't he? Nice boy. I don't know you though."

You will soon. That was Eleanor's typical mantra whenever a greying producer appraised her with a bored expression. Normally the phrase stirred rage within her – but with Penelope, that malicious serpent was silent. Instead, there was something fresh and unfamiliar: a curiosity she hadn't felt since meeting Jack. "I'm Eleanor. Eleanor Sanders. I write scripts."

It sounded lame, but Penelope cocked her head. "Anything I'd know?"

"Nothing that's out yet. Leonsdale Associates is producing one of mine though." There was a twitch from Penelope at the name Leonsdale: almost imperceptible if you weren't looking out for it. Eleanor knew she had to tread carefully, but the allure was too great to resist. "I go to university with their daughter."

"Ah." Penelope's eyes were dark and sad. "Cheyenne?"

"The very same. She said she went to high school with you."

"Yeah." Her voice sounded far away, as if she were talking on the other side of a deep valley of memories. "I remember."

"She called you a bitch." That was the champagne talking; Eleanor cursed herself the moment the words left her mouth.

A slight smile, the hint of a laugh. "She's right about that. Poor thing."

'Poor thing' wasn't a descriptor Eleanor would ever have used for Cheyenne. Thankfully, she was saved from opening that can of worms by another desperate pounding at the door.

"Shit," muttered Penelope. "We should go." She tossed her crumpled collection of fake nails into the bathroom bin then strolled out. Eleanor scampered behind, trying to ignore the shocked face on the girl waiting.

"They'll be spreading rumours about us in no time," Eleanor cautioned as Penelope struggled to mount the steps.

Penelope shrugged, but the movement set her off balance and made her grasp the banister for support as her feet collapsed under her. "My boyfriend won't care. Or if he does, I'm breaking up with him anyway: might as well go out with a bang."

"My boyfriend will care," Eleanor protested.

Penelope gave her another one of those inquisitive, appraising looks. "And I don't suppose you can break up with him either? Not when he's so much more famous. Oh well, I'll set him right. Maybe give him some coke to say sorry?"

"You can't be having cocaine in this state," snapped Eleanor. "You need water."

"I'm not going back to Brian Schlieman's kitchen. The man's a raging misogynist, and I wouldn't put it past him to try and peek up my skirt."

Eleanor sighed. "Then you probably should go home. Do you want me to get your boyfriend?"

"No! I told you, I'm breaking up with him!" She crossed her arms and delivered a pout that was so juvenile Eleanor couldn't help laughing. "Are my relationship troubles funny to you?"

"You're a riot," Eleanor declared. "Come on, I'll help you to a car."

"I'd rather walk. It's only a few miles. The night air will clear my head."

"Don't be ridiculous. The paps will get you."

"What about your boyfriend? The one with the ridiculous last name?"

"I'll text him." Eleanor wrapped her arm around the singer's shoulders: they seemed immensely skinny to hold the weight of all that fame, let alone a drunk young woman trying to leave a party. "Let's get you out of here."

For all his faults, Brian Schlieman had arranged for a row of blacked-out limos to escort guests home. Eleanor helped Penelope into the nearest one, then crawled in after her: she wasn't sure she trusted the girl not to throw herself out at the nearest opportunity.

"See?" Eleanor tapped the window as they pulled out the drive and into the flash of cameras. "You'd never have got them off your tail. And imagine the stories they'd print in the papers. Your career would be over."

"My career would enter a new wave of excitement as I pivot towards a rebellious, avant-garde image." Penelope raised an eyebrow as Eleanor fought and failed to contain the urge to break out into a smile. "Maybe that's why your boyfriend needs you. You double as his publicist and his mother."

"You'll thank me tomorrow." Eleanor leaned against the window and watched Beverly Hills flash by. There was always light in LA, a haze or a halo depending on your outlook. The glow illuminated the canyons, cast the mountaintops with a strange orange filter. They seemed mysterious, magical, the sort of place where anything could happen. Where you could sell your script, go out with a film star and end up in a limo escorting a drunk pop star home.

Cheyenne had never seen such magic. How could she, and still have chosen to leave?

Penelope couldn't get out of the limo without assistance, so Eleanor had to grab her waist, helping the singer down as she gripped her hipbone. She had planned to only take Penelope to her door, but she was in no state to be left alone.

"Could you stay?" Eleanor murmured to the driver. "I just have to make sure she gets in."

Penelope and Eleanor stumbled towards the gate. "Do you have a key?" Eleanor asked.

Penelope shook her head. "Under that panel." She pressed a shaky hand on a slab of marble in the wall next to the door, which slid back to reveal a sleek keypad. It took her four tries to enter the code.

The house was dark and cavernous. The ceiling in the hall stretched so high, Eleanor couldn't make out the top. Penelope seemed unperturbed by the gloom. She skipped forward, suddenly full of energy from being in her own home, humming a tune under her breath. She switched on lights as she went, creating a will-o-the-wisp trail for Eleanor to follow.

Eleanor finally found Penelope face-down on a sofa in the living room. She rushed towards her, but the singer only looked up with a grin from a very furry pillow. "Ssh," Penelope commanded. "You'll wake her up." Two orange slits on the pillow's edge slid open, and Eleanor realised she was looking at an outrageously fluffy cat.

"I know darling," Penelope cooed to her pet. "You're tired and we woke you up. Do you want a midnight snack?"

The cat yawned, stretched and trotted off in the direction of what Eleanor presumed was the kitchen, which seemed to answer that question.

"Her name's Calypso," Penelope explained as she climbed off the sofa. "She's my baby."

Calypso. Like the character from the *Odyssey*. "You like that poem then?" Eleanor asked.

Penelope shrugged. "I was named after it. And it's not a poem, it's a song. The bards used to perform the whole thing live. It would take them several nights. Can you imagine? The longest song I've written is five minutes and thirty-two seconds. Six if you include the bonus instrumental. Then again, Homer wasn't writing radio-friendly singles." Her face seemed to sour slightly. "You could write an adaptation you know. A good *Odyssey* for the screen. I could play Penelope."

Eleanor raised an eyebrow. "You can act?"

"Only if I'm drunk enough." She made what was probably meant to be a dramatic face. "Like now."

"I'm not sure you'll get many jobs that way." Penelope's hand was shaking as she poured the cat food. Eleanor reached to steady it so the food wouldn't spill over the floor. Calypso happily began to gobble up the pile. "Besides, I prefer to write my own stuff."

"So do I. But maybe an *Odyssey*-themed song? Or a reference in a line?" She chewed on her lip. "Can you text me that idea? I need to remember it, and I don't know where my phone is."

"I don't have your number."

"Then I'll do it." She snatched Eleanor's phone without asking, demanded the password, and spent a furious minute typing away. "Keep that chat open in case I get another idea."

"Are you likely to?"

"It's one in the morning. The creative hour. Of course I'll get another idea." Penelope flung her arms out and began walking on an imaginary balance beam, one foot in front of another, teetering over the hardwood floor. Then she tossed her head back, laughed and hopped about manically. She only stopped when Calypso jumped and scampered to the other side of the room. "Sorry darling."

Eleanor was beginning to get the inkling that Penelope Hale, international pop star and Cheyenne's sworn enemy, may not be entirely sane. But then again, Eleanor had smashed a glass in Cheyenne's face and destroyed George's life's work: she was throwing stones from a palace of glass.

As if to prove her point, Penelope let out a sudden gasp that sent Calypso bolting. "I almost forgot! Do you want a drink? There's good gin. A tiny bit of weed, but not much because I hate using it. I'm all out of snow. And there's not much real food, I'm sorry. Calypso eats better than I do."

"Just water for us both. And then you're going to bed." Eleanor stumbled around, found two glasses and filled them up from the complicated tap. The fine crystal clinked against her teeth uncomfortably. "You'll feel better in the morning if you eat something."

Another tiny flinch. "No need. I threw up everything toxic anyway."

Eleanor only gave her a sad look as she started turning off the lights.

It seemed to take them an eon to find Penelope's bedroom. Her house – or mansion, rather – was a maze, filled with carbon copies of the same room, all tastefully decorated but lacking in any real warmth or soul. "Does anyone live here with you?" Eleanor asked.

Penelope shook her head. "Sometimes my parents come to visit. Or a boyfriend sleeps over."

In the end, it was Calypso who saved them. The cat trotted up from behind, snaked through their legs and deposited herself by a door at the end of the hallway, where she started meowing loudly. Penelope rushed inside and collapsed face-down on a plush king-sized bed.

Eleanor found herself unsure of what to do. She didn't exactly want to undress Penelope and tuck her in, but neither did she want to leave without a cursory goodbye. She was rocking awkwardly back and forth in the doorway when Calypso mewed and Penelope looked up at her.

"You're a good friend," Penelope murmured. "I'm glad Cheyenne found someone." Eleanor was no Jack, but her acting can't have been too bad: she'd fooled Cheyenne's parents, after all. Either the drink was getting to her head, or Penelope was remarkably attuned, for she narrowed her eyes and frowned. "Is something wrong?"

Eleanor was drunk enough to loosen her tongue. "We're not quite friends," Eleanor admitted. "Not anymore."

"You had an argument?"

"You could say that." In this half-light, hazy, dream-like setting, the girl richer and more famous than Eleanor looked up at her with ocean-deep eyes and clung onto her every word. Eleanor was filled with a sudden desire to tell her secret. To share what she'd been holding in, even if it ruined her.

No. Perhaps it wouldn't ruin her. Perhaps it was the lateness of the hour, or the alcohol in her blood, or the love with which Penelope cradled the cat, but Eleanor felt certain she could trust her with her life.

"I smashed a glass into Cheyenne's face," Eleanor admitted. "Then I rubbed it in."

"Oh God." She seemed remarkably concerned for someone Cheyenne had called a bitch, and Eleanor began to regret telling her about the attack. "Why?"

"We were good friends. Great friends, even. Then she ditched me for people she liked better."

However Eleanor was expecting Penelope to react, it wasn't what came next. The singer threw her head into the air and let out a chocked sound: some strange combination between a laugh and a sob. "Oh Cheyenne," she choked as she gasped for air. "Good for her, in a way."

Eleanor sat down on the bed, her hand brushed Penelope's. She didn't seem to notice. "What was Cheyenne like?"

A dreamy smile snaked across Penelope's face. "Wonderful. Spectacular. We were best friends, you know. Inseparable. She fawned over me."

Eleanor couldn't quite imagine Cheyenne fawning over anyone who wasn't suitably English. "Did she leave you?"

This time, the sound that came out of Penelope's mouth was a proper laugh. "Oh, doll. I left her. Not for other people," she added when she saw Eleanor's shocked face. "I left her for myself."

"You mean to sing?"

"Oh no. I was very sick. Strange thing, anorexia. It hits you like a wasting disease but it's all in your head." Another laugh, a manic one. "It's a selfish thing. Makes you used to getting your own way through sheer force of will. Nothing matters except having no food left inside. She tried very hard, Cheyenne, to reach out, but I shut her off over and over and over again.

"I think everyone thought things would be better after a stint in rehab. But when I came back there was only that horrible school, with those terrible memories, full of people who had forgotten their bonds, without me. I was bored. I started writing songs, turning up for classes less and less. I barely even staggered along to graduation: I liked being the opening act at celebrities' stadium tours more than flunking out of some stupid high school. All this time, Cheyenne kept asking, over and over again, to see me. Every time I said no, or just ignored her, and eventually those invitations started dwindling.

"She texted me one final time, before she left for Scotland. One of my songs had just gone viral, and the invitations to parties and dinners and charity galas kept rolling in. But Cheyenne didn't want any of that: just something casual, a coffee downtown. But I didn't want to see her. What the fuck would I say? Sorry? How does that capture it?"

"You could write her a song," suggested Eleanor.

Penelope shook her head. "Not yet. Hurts too much to think about. Maybe one day." Her fingers traced the curve of her body, counting her own ribs, lingering on the protrusion of the hipbone. Her hand trembled, so frail it was blown by an undetectable wind. "It would be a terrible apology anyway. The selfishness isn't just the eating disorder, it's in me too. There's no great revelation and reforging. I haven't fundamentally changed."

"But you regret it."

"That doesn't mean I wouldn't do it all over again." Penelope heaved a sigh. "I'm just fundamentally terrible with people. Is it any wonder I've got no friends?"

"You have a lot of fans."

"They're not the same, and you know it." She flopped down and screwed her eyes shut, then took a deep breath and propped herself back up. "Sorry, I'm just unloading on you. I know it's annoying. I'm just really drunk."

Eleanor shook her head and squeezed Penelope's hand. "Don't apologise. I don't mind."

"You need to get back to your party. I'm sorry, I took you away–"

"Someone told me Brian Schlieman's a raging misogynist anyway." This got Penelope to crack a smile. "You'll be alright tonight? You're not going to be sick again?"

She waved a hand. "That's all gone now. I'll be fine." Gone was the emotion of a minute ago: it was as if it had been purged and had flowed down a drain, disappeared from her mind.

"Okay." Eleanor turned to go but lingered at the door. She turned back for one last look, and said, hesitantly: "Just so you know – if you want – or you're ever feeling lonely – you can call me. Or text, or whatever. I would be happy to be your friend."

Penelope's smile was the softest Eleanor had seen the entire night. "You sound like a schoolgirl."

"Sometimes that's what people need."

She nodded. "Thanks Eleanor."

Eleanor flicked the light switch off like she was a mother bidding goodnight to her child. "Goodnight, Penelope." Her only answer was a contented sigh and a quiet purr.

The limo was still waiting, but Eleanor was in no state to be taken back to the party. Instead, she texted Jack and ordered the driver to take her home.

The night was quiet and calm, but Eleanor was in no mood to go to bed. Instead, she sat on the patio, sipping water and staring at the silhouette of the mountains amidst the stars until Jack came home.

"Are you alright?" he demanded. "I couldn't find you."

Eleanor shrugged. "I had to take Penelope Hale home. She was wasted."

"*The* Penelope Hale?"

"Is there another?"

His shoulders sagged. "Just checking. It's just – Penelope Hale. There's big and there's Big."

"She was very nice." Eleanor didn't add just how lonely Penelope had seemed.

"Of course she would be, when she's with you. Who could you possibly offend?" Jack took her in his arms and kissed her, leaving Eleanor to smile and laugh while her mind raced with thoughts of Cheyenne with glass in her face, Cheyenne alone in high school, Cheyenne kissing Henry, Cheyenne sitting in a coffee shop waiting for a girl who was never going to show up. Cheyenne, Cheyenne, Cheyenne. If only Jack knew a fraction of it.

6th May. 21:25.

Two hours into the party.

She stuffs them in the lift, because while Eleanor finds the gold filigree gaudy, Cheyenne will see it as a hallmark of British refinement. It is for the same reason she redecorated the flat with Waterhouse prints: they're exactly the sort of thing Cheyenne loves (not to mention it gives Eleanor a strange sense of catharsis to examine *Ophelia*).

"It's nice, isn't it?" Eleanor gestures around as they file through the door of the penthouse. "A lucrative place, America. Look around, if you want – but stay away from the kitchen, Gina. I think I left the nuts out from earlier."

They are cautious in the extreme. Raquelle, especially, creeps around as if every surface is radioactive, every cabinet hiding a bomb. George stays rooted to one spot, swaying uneasily. Cheyenne strolls around with an air of confidence masking her uneasy stagger.

"Come see the view," Eleanor says when Cheyenne is suitably isolated in the sitting room. She reaches out to grip the other girl's wrist. Cheyenne draws away, but it is enough for Eleanor to feel the pace of her pulse. Quick, but not butterfly-fast: alcohol has steadied her.

She follows Eleanor quietly to the balcony. All the pride from the coffee shop means nothing now.

"You can see the ocean." Eleanor points to the beach. "If it wasn't for the noise downstairs, you can hear the waves lapping on the shore. Or crashing, if there's a storm."

"Do you still swim every day?" Cheyenne's voice is husky, whether from drink or fear.

"Every day." Eleanor's hand inches along the guard rail, closer and closer to the other girl's skin. "Just like in Nice."

"Nice," Cheyenne echoes. She cocks her head, as if trying to recall. "We had fun there."

"We did." She presses her wrists against the cool metal in frustration. "What changed?"

"You were fucking annoying, that's what changed." Cheyenne laughs, but somehow it isn't a cruel sound, just factual. "And so bloody possessive. Good for us to grow apart."

No, a serpentine thing within Eleanor hisses. *No, that isn't true*.

But another quieter part of Eleanor, one worn down by time and endless attrition, points to memories Eleanor prefers to forget. All those times she tried to snatch Cheyenne away when she chafed at others coming close.

She wishes, unbidden, that Penelope Hale was here. She understood what it was like to have a troubled past with the girl standing before her.

"I rubbed a glass into your face," Eleanor admits.

"Because you're mental, Eleanor Sanders. I told you before and I'll tell you again."

It stings, but not like it did before. Somehow the alcohol has taken all the aggression from Cheyenne's body.

"You can see the castle from up here," Eleanor goes on. "Remember my birthday?"

Cheyenne laughs "It was fucking terrible."

"Because Raquelle and Gina were there, and I hate them."

"You only hate them because you're clingy. It's one of your many problems."

"Guilty as charged." She looks over and grins. "We should head over there?"

"What the bloody hell for?" Her accent has shifted enough that the words sound natural.

"One last hurrah." Eleanor leans over the terrace and sniffs the night air. "A toast to the end of our relationship, dead and buried forever."

"Not so dead and buried if we're toasting it."

"Are you coming or not?"

Cheyenne blinks those baby-blue eyes. She really is beautiful tonight. Her hair straightened, her cheeks glowing red, her dress the amber of the sunset. Desire wells up inside Eleanor, banging on her chest like a restless tiger in a cage.

But it is a unique idea, held in a quintessentially British castle, and Cheyenne will never be able to resist something special and British.

"Fine," she says, and satisfaction uncurls within Eleanor.

June.

Eleven months before the party.

Jack was practically jumping around the house. He couldn't contain his excitement, especially now Eleanor had finished the year, and all their things were boxed up in the car.

"You'll love Mammoth," he kept repeating. "You'll just love it. The views, the hiking, the fresh air – it's nothing like LA."

"Jack, we went skiing there a few months ago."

"But this is Mammoth in the *summer*." He babbled on about everything they would see, how she would get to see Yosemite again, that he's desperate to get close to a bear – so that all there was left for her to do was sit back and listen with a smile. He was like a child when he was excited, so full of innocence and awe.

"And the lakes!" he finished. "Eleanor, there are so many lakes – and they're all so beautiful. Clear and blue and cold. You'll be right at home."

He should be the poet, Eleanor thought to herself in the car. The way he waxed lyrical about the Sierra Nevada, he could be the new John Muir. But as the sagebrush turned to rocks that scrape the sky, as the petrol fumes faded to pines, as she grew restless and stuck her head out the window and screamed in delight at the peaks before her, more golden than anything in the city of angels, she thought she understood.

"One day," Jack said as they pulled up to the cabin they had rented, "we'll have a house up here. A little cabin just like this, for you and me."

"Ah," Eleanor teased, "but there's no ocean for me."

His eyes twinkled as he kissed her. "But there are lakes."

And what lakes they were. That first day they scrambled up a mountainside, leaving the tourists behind, racing each other through the trees as they lugged their bags to the top. There was nothing like this in Britain – it was too sunny, the air too warm – nor in Los Angeles – the air was fresher, the sky clearer, the wind cooler. And then, when Eleanor doubted she could get any happier, they saw the lake.

Crystal blue and fed by a snowmelt stream. The rocks they'd been climbing over faded away to sand, while bushes a perfect shade of green hugged one edge. Above them, a picturesque peak just brushed the clouds.

"You were right," she said as she turned to him, a little breathless from the hike and the view. "I do love it."

She'd worn her swimsuit under her clothes. Within seconds, she was in the water, surrounded by the perfect cold. It made her gasp in shock, then bubble up with joy as energy filled her. She was flipping, twisting, flicking in and out of the water, her muscles flexing in perfect harmony. She was the most powerful thing in this whole lake, on this whole mountainside, in this whole world. Let everyone on it see her and quiver.

She was halfway across the lake, somewhere so deep she couldn't see the bottom, even in water this clear. Jack was reduced to a dot on the shore. She wondered if anyone had ever been in this spot before, anyone else ever dared to swim the distance. If anyone had ever swum further.

Without thinking, she turned away from Jack, shooting off to a distant shore.

"Eleanor!" She heard his voice before she touched the other side. For a moment, she panicked: he hadn't followed her out into the lake, had he? But no, there he was, cocooned among the trunks of the pines; he had walked around while she swum. He was waving with one arm, in the other hand he held her shoes.

"Eleanor!" he called again as she crawled onto the shore. An expanse of blue stretched out behind her. The shore Eleanor had departed from seemed sickeningly small. "What did you think you were doing? You scared me half to death!"

She gave a half smile. "I wanted to prove I could do it."

"But what if you couldn't?"

"But I knew I could." She smiled again. "And it was wonderful out there, just like you said. And now I feel ecstatic." She flung out her arms and grins. For a moment, he shook his head, but then a smile broke out on his face, too. "It's just like climbing mountains," she murmured to him. "Only my way."

He kissed her. "As long as you *walk* back with me."

He wrapped his arm around her as they strolled along the shore. It was comforting, and warm, and steady, but Eleanor's mind kept flicking back to the lake. Just her, the water, that chilling emptiness, and the knowledge that she'd been the one to conquer it. The victory that tasted so sweet upon her tongue, that filled her limbs with heavenly fire.

That evening, they lounged on rocks at a lake near the car park. The sunset was glorious, but Eleanor's mind couldn't focus. All she could imagine was what Cheyenne would think if she saw Eleanor swim that lake. Would she fret like Jack, or would she have jumped in with her? Something in Eleanor is certain it would be the latter, that she and Cheyenne would conquer the water together.

No. This was Jack's place, not Cheyenne's. Eleanor and Cheyenne hadn't so much as laid eyes on each other for over a year, content on clawing their way into each other's countries. Cheyenne had probably never even been to Mammoth Lakes.

But oh, wouldn't it be wonderful to see her reaction?

She became aware that Jack's eyes were weighing heavily on her. "Is something wrong?" she asked.

"I could ask you the same. You look thoughtful."

Eleanor bit her lip. "Just thinking of Scotland."

"Are you excited to go back?"

Her silence told him everything he needed to know.

"Here's an idea," Jack went on. He chewed his lip and whispered something inaudibly, like a line he'd been rehearsing, of a silent prayer to God. "Don't go."

Eleanor frowned. "What?"

"It's not as crazy as it seems. You've got a job here, one that's becoming very successful. You have an excellent college you can transfer to if you really want to finish your degree. And you've got me." When she stared out over the water, not daring to meet his eyes, he added: "You're always going on about how much better California is than the UK. So why not stay?"

"I need a visa," she blurted out, the quickest thing she could think of to get him off her back.

Jack only shrugged. "So? We could always get married."

And there it was. On one side, life in California: fame, money, a house on a mountain, the sea. A boy who loved her, who she loved back. Someone who could match her in every emotion.

And on the other side: Cheyenne.

She doesn't love you. She told you herself.

But to see Cheyenne's reaction to 'Eleanor Flannigan', to force her to notice, to force her to care. Let Eleanor live her fantasy just once.

"I have to go back," she choked out. "There are people I have to see – have to say goodbye to. But after... After I finished, I would very much like to live here with you."

He raised an eyebrow. "And what about the visa?"

Eleanor was twenty-one years old. She'd had her birthday last month. A massive blowout, with all of Jack's actor friends invited. They travelled to, what felt like, every bar in LA to celebrate Eleanor reaching legal drinking age. Their photos were in every Hollywood magazine; their publicists on the phone doing damage control the morning after (Eleanor shared Jack's, she'd handed her social media over to them ever since posting that he was her boyfriend).

Twenty-one years old, and a man she still thought of as a boy was asking to marry her.

Not even Cheyenne, she bet, was engaged to Henry.

She leaned in and kissed Jack's cheek. "I'll have to think about it," she whispered. "But that marriage idea isn't a bad one."

He beamed, and just for the moment that was enough.

August.

Nine months before the party.

Jack was determined to make up for the time he would miss with Eleanor. As her departure date grew closer, he seemed to spend every minute in her arms or in her bed. It would be charming, Eleanor thought, if he didn't pepper every kiss with a whimper of 'stay'. He was filming most days, and in some ways it was a relief to have him out the house. Though now he kept insisting on taking her to film sets. His current project was a Western being filmed in the canyons near LA, so Eleanor spent several scorching afternoons watching actors repeat the same takes over and over again before ducking into one of the trailers to get some writing in. Jack seemed to take personal offence every moment she didn't watch. "Do you not think my job's interesting?" he pouted.

Eleanor shrugged. "You wouldn't want to spend all day watching me write, and I don't want to spend all day watching you repeat the same three words."

"But the emotions–"

She silenced him with a kiss. "Look even better on screen, when I can see the close ups instead of standing fifty bloody feet away." The British slang seemed to calm him down.

The only time Jack wasn't with her was when he was disappearing off to cast parties. Often, he wouldn't return until the next evening, with bags under his eyes and red veins visible in his eye. In films, this was the sort of time the leading lady worried about her husband straying to another woman. But somehow, Eleanor didn't care much. Jack was too obsessed with her to stray.

If anything, his absences gave her time to build connections of her own. She saw Penelope Hale again, at the singer's invitation. She drove up to Eleanor's house while Jack was away and the pair sat morosely across from each other, Eleanor sipping a drink while Penelope worked away at a salad she'd brought with her. Every bite seemed a hassle, but Penelope was insistent Eleanor watched. "It's good for me," she said with a wince. Eleanor just swallowed and tried not to think of Penelope even frailer than she already was, lying in a hospital bed with a plastic tube down her throat, hooked up to a machine.

Afterwards, Penelope blinked those lovely eyes and demanded they turned on the radio.

"We don't have one," Eleanor replied. Who had a radio these days? Let alone at her and Jack's house and the lack of furniture she'd been trying (and mostly failing) to conceal.

"Your phone then," said Penelope, eyes fixed somewhere in the distance as she thought. So like Cheyenne in some ways, with a list of demands. So unlike her in others, in her utter disregard of the objects and people around her, preferring to be lost in her own fantasy world.

They started with the radio hits. Penelope managed to find the only sheet of paper they had in the barely-furnished house – some old receipt from one of their countless takeouts – and wrangle up a pen. She sat intently as every song played, jotting notes down at breakneck speed. Eleanor could barely hear the music over the scratch of her pen. Finally, the song would end, and Penelope would demand a pause. She would then proceed to walk through every one of her notes with Eleanor.

"You heard the end of the second line of the chorus? I would have added another drum there. It sounds empty."

"Intro is too long. It's boring."

"I don't know why they introduce 'high' into the rhyme scheme so early. They would be better off choosing the obvious and satisfying alliteration by sticking to something starting with ch: chase maybe? Or chasm, if you get a metaphor going about a deep hope opening beneath your feet. But you'd have to pronounce it strangely, with the h sound – it could work, but it would be messy..." She would have launched into a lecture about poetic devices had Eleanor not stopped her.

"You sound like my English lecturer."

Penelope wrinkled her nose, perhaps unsure if this was a compliment. "As I should. Aren't I the best at lyrics?"

Eleanor tsked. "You're so arrogant," she teased.

"I have to believe I'm good at something. Otherwise I'd just waste away in despair." The look she gave Eleanor was strangely vulnerable for someone who just moments ago had been so aloof. "And we are, aren't we? We're the ones who got here, who rose above the rest. It isn't just chance. It can't be, because then, what's the point?" She scratched down something, crossed it out with harsh, violent strokes, then shook her head and wrote it back down again.

"Go on," Penelope prompted when Eleanor continued to stare at her. "It's creative hour. Work on your script."

And just as it had been with Cheyenne, Eleanor, ever-obedient, obeyed. They sat in Jack's garden for hours, working until Penelope decided all of her salad had been digested and it was safe to leave. "Besides, your boyfriend will be back soon," she remarked, sliding off her chair and making for the exit. "The young man carbuncular." Her tone held a hint of derision.

Eleanor said nothing, tried not to imagine what he could be up to. Instead, she focused on Penelope's words, oddly familiar. Not from the Odyssey, nor one of the songs she'd heard.

"It's T. S. Eliot. *The Wasteland*. You must have read it." Penelope blinked incredulously.

Eleanor had, once, in a dusty university library, so long ago it felt like another lifetime. Cheyenne had sat next to her, George on her other side. The air had been heavy, but not oppressively so – it was more like a comforting blanket, wrapping Eleanor in security. The fog-clad city of the poem, inhabited only by throngs of the dead, had seemed a lifetime away.

"Unreal City," Penelope quoted again. "You know, the Los Angeles smog isn't too different from the London smog."

"They don't live that same awful half-life here," declared Eleanor. She tried not to think of Jack, slipping in and out of consciousness at some party. "They can't."

Penelope clicked her tongue. "So you think you brought that with you from your gloomy country?"

"Yes. No. I don't know." Eleanor struggled to find some kind of thought. "I'm different. I hate it there."

"That's what they all say," Penelope said gloomily. "You know T. S. Eliot was American? I'll give him some praise though. I won't correct a word of that poem. Nor *Cats*, for that matter. You know he wrote the poems the musical is based on?"

The notion that Penelope liked *Cats* was too much for Eleanor's sleep-deprived mind to wrap itself around. "He was British in the end though. He must have liked the country. Loved it even."

"A veritable Cheyenne." Eleanor couldn't tell in the darkness of the driveway, but Penelope's eyes seemed damp.

After she left, Eleanor was alone in the dark, ready to embrace the sagging, sweaty Jack that would eventually stumble home. Eleanor kissed him on the temple when he did, poured him a glass of water and dragged him into bed, where he lay still on top of her and whispered how much he loved her, wanted her, needed her. No, Eleanor told herself, it was not so bad.

And it wasn't – not until another night came, identical to so many others that spooled out ahead of and behind her. They were lying, clammy, in bed. Jack had just come home. They were in the midst of sex, about halfway through, when Jack suddenly tensed. His fingers began to dig into Eleanor's shoulder blades.

"Jack?" He didn't seem to hear her. "Jack, get off!" She tried to shove him, but that only made his grip stronger; instead, she kicked with all her might. He stumbled and she scrambled off the bed. "What the fuck's got into you?"

"Don't go," he said. His eyes couldn't focus on her. "Stay here with me."

Eleanor's skin tingled with unease; she shrugged on a dressing gown to try and take the edge off. The fabric only felt sickeningly artificial. "I'm leaving. You can't stop me." He was standing, she noted, between her and the bedroom door.

Jack made an awful groan from some dark recess of his throat. "Don't," he repeated. "Please."

"Let me leave the room." She could sleep on their cushions that still passed for a sofa.

He shook his head. "You can't..." And then, as if in a trance, he was charging at her, his hands around her neck, his breath hot in her face. She kicked, she punched, and then finally, when he still refused to let go, she bit down hard, right on the back of his arm.

The skin tasted different than when she was kissing him. It reminded her of Cheyenne's skin beneath her fingers, glass splintering into it: the same love, the same hate. Was this how Cheyenne had felt, when Eleanor lunged at her? Of course not. Cheyenne had dug that particular grave herself, shutting Eleanor out shovelful by shovelful. Eleanor, she reminded herself, had done nothing.

Jack bellowed and set her free. Eleanor ducked around his frame and dashed down the hall, past the office, the bathroom – she could have ducked in there and locked the door, but it was too late now – the kitchen. She reached the garden and stumbled into the bushes at the very end, where she lay in the dirt, concealed. It smelt of rot in there: suitable for the occasion.

She lay prone, ears pricked for any sign of Jack's pursuit. When none came, she finally allowed herself to relax. It was cold, but she must have slept a little, for when she woke up, the sun was cresting the peaks of the mountains. The entire interior of her bush was cast a shallow pink: beautiful, in its small, self-contained way.

Eleanor scrambled out of the bush and sat down at the kitchen island. Her feet were brown and covered with dust, there were twigs in her hair, and her palms were covered in scratches. Yet she sipped a glass of water and waited, like an ecological Madonna, for Jack to arrive.

His face was red and patchy. "Eleanor," he choked out, his voice hoarse. "Eleanor, I'm–"

"Where do you keep your drugs?" she demanded.

His shoulders sagged. "At the back of my closet."

"You need to get rid of them. If they make you act like that."

"They must have been laced with something. Eleanor, I'm so sorry, I…"

"Then get a better dealer." Eleanor set her glass down and glared. "Though if Hollywood actors can't use a trustworthy one, then I'm not sure there's much hope."

"Eleanor, sweetheart…" He reached out to try and brush her face, but she flinched away. "It won't happen again."

"It won't happen again because I'll be in Scotland."

He nodded morosely and started to make himself a cup of coffee. It was only when he sat down that he announced: "I've been given a part in your film."

She blinked. "My film?"

"It's not official yet. But I had a few talks, and it's basically confirmed. I'm playing one of the male leads."

"The one who lives or the one who dies?"

"The one who dies."

She nodded blankly. "I didn't even know it was in production."

"Like I said, it's unofficial."

Eleanor's mind swirled. Maybe Cheyenne had told her parents everything. Maybe all contact was being broken off. Or maybe she'd just been too stressed to answer her phone.

"I read the script," Jack said at last. "It's – it's very good. You could be such a hit. Even better if you didn't take a year off."

"We've talked about this. I have to go."

"Eleanor…'

"And you're not doing cocaine at parties anymore."

His face hardened. "You can't tell me what to do if you're across the ocean."

"You'd be moronic to keep taking it." She gave him a patronising glare. "It would ruin your career."

That did it. Jack sank into his seat, more rejected than ever.

That afternoon, Eleanor packed up her clothes without looking at Jack. She didn't want to take anything – everything in the house was tainted with the memory of the night before. The next day, she was on the plane to Scotland. She made it all the way to the airport before she started to cry.

September.

Eight months before the party.

Eleanor now hated Scotland. She hated the dampness of the air, the weak, petering sunlight that never seemed to warm you, the resulting mould on every building, the sickeningly ugly council houses that dotted every town, the ever-encroaching darkness. Most of all, she hated the brown on every branch and bush that marked the coming of death. Much better for winter to be marked with gold and green.

She arrived with no accommodation arranged, instead walking into the fanciest hotel the town offered and taking the penthouse suite when she discovered it was available. It was gorgeous, with a full kitchen, sitting room, dining area and two massive bedrooms. Eleanor chose the one with the sea view and tried not to think about how empty the bed felt.

After two weeks, she finally picked up Jack's calls. She told him where she was staying, said the view of the sea was lovely, told him she missed LA. She said nothing about what it was like being back at university, for what could she say? That she spoke to no one, made no eye contact except to glare, and marched down the street in black like an out-of-work assassin? That she hadn't so much as texted

Molly and Liz to let them know she was back in town? That the one glimpse she'd had of Cheyenne and her entourage laughing while they got coffee had filled her with so much rage that she hadn't been able to sleep. Instead, she spent the night salivating over various ways she would torture them. Rip out their throats, yank out their hair, bite their breasts until rivulets of blood flowed alluringly over that tanned, American skin.

Better not to say anything.

She took a break from scripts to focus on her dissertation: some convoluted exploration of the overlap between literature and cinematic cultures in the twentieth century. She found it tedious and a waste of time, but Eleanor had told Jack again and again that she would finish her degree, and she wasn't backing out now. In a way, it was nice to write something that didn't consist solely of dialogue tags.

"It's good to branch out," Jack said when she mentioned her dissertation. "You'll come back refreshed. Or maybe you'll discover something else you're great at: have you ever written a song?"

"Not since I was about six."

"You should try it. I'm thinking of becoming a singer. All the front members of bands are on drugs anyway."

"Can you sing?"

"Not really. But neither can Penelope Hale."

"She's got that air of authenticity about her though." Eleanor frowned, picturing the drunk girl she'd led to bed, trying to imagine what kind of life she led day-to-day. "And a kind of raw vulnerability I'm not sure you could capture."

"I'm a good actor."

"But people don't want acting from pop stars. They want something real."

Jack cursed over the phone. Eleanor waited a while before she started to prod. "How are the... you know... the drugs?"

"Better." He must have realised his answer was too quick because he rushed to elaborate. "Really Eleanor, so much better. I've cut back, I've talked to friends to find out which are the better dealers, I only take them with others..."

"Are you sure you don't need to see a doctor?"

"You said it yourself: rehab will ruin my career."

"I said addiction would ruin your career." But he was right. To be publicly revealed that he was in intensive treatment for drug addiction could be devastating to his brand. "But it doesn't have to be scorched earth. You could just have therapy sessions, find some talk groups?"

"I don't want to."

"Do you not have any friends that have tried to quit? You could talk a bit with them–"

"I already do!" For a second there was stony silence, and Eleanor feared Jack would hang up. Then there was a sigh. "It's easy for you to say all this when you're not here."

It hit like a punch to the gut. Eleanor often imagined Jack, all alone in that empty house with nothing to distract him, but to hear him say it crystalised the thoughts she'd been trying to ignore. It was all too easy to succumb with no one around you.

"I'll be back in December," she vowed. "Right at the beginning – all my classes are completely coursework based this semester, so as soon as it wraps up, I'll fly back." She'd been meaning to visit her parents, but she could see them another time. "I promise."

"Maybe I should come over," Jack suggested. "I don't have any work next week–"

'No!" It came out more forceful than she intended. But Eleanor couldn't have Jack here, not in this foreign world. He was her rock in LA, her image of safety (if he wasn't high), peace (sometimes), prosperity (occasionally). To have him in Scotland ran the risk of him becoming Cheyenne. "Look, I couldn't give you the attention you deserve here – I'm too busy with uni. And it's important to be in LA. You never know, you might meet someone or have some great publicity opportunity."

Jack's voice was weary. "But you'll come for Christmas?"

"More than Christmas. All of December." She tried to force comfort into her voice. "I love you."

He suddenly sounded very, very young. Like a child as you turned off the light at bedtime. "Love you too."

Eleanor cried again that night. This time she was on the balcony, staring out at the sea. Beneath her the town swarmed, lit up like a stage, but she was invisible to them. She tried to imagine herself as some kind of silent ruler or omniscient god, but it fell flat every time her eyes fixed on a figure on the street. Was that Cheyenne down there, her golden hair gleaming? Gina behind her, curls perfectly coiled? Henry, with his arm wrapped around Cheyenne's side? Or was it one of a hundred other groups of laughing young people, all seemingly without a care in the world while Eleanor languished alone in her ivory tower?

The mist over the town had turned to drizzle. Eleanor couldn't stay up there, damp and shivering. She was struck with a sudden desire to get out, to escape the tiny confines of this austere hotel room. The rain would hide her tears.

She had walked the path to the club a thousand times, with swimming friends or girls from class or with Cheyenne. Rather, Cheyenne and the rest of her group, Eleanor more often than not relegated to the outskirts. The memory was as bitter as the alcohol she used to swallow to forget.

There was a queue: the same old press of faceless humanity, crammed against each other so the sweat and scent of strangers become one's own.

A zebra can tell different members of its herd at a glance; a mother bear knows at once which of her cubs is the strongest and which the runt. Yet to most humans, they are all interchangeable. All stripey, all furry, all foreign. An animal would not have been able to tell this mass apart. Eleanor wasn't sure she could either. Did that make her an animal? Sometimes she thought she had the instincts of one.

A bored security guard checked her ID, without even a flash of recognition on her face. What did she expect? Eleanor thought bitterly to herself as she strode inside and out of the rain. That Eleanor was even well-known enough to garner a reaction?

She pushed her way to the bar and ordered a gin and tonic. Jack had introduced her to them, and she'd grown accustomed to their tang. Yet it was odd, drinking one there, in this club that hadn't changed a bit. Every previous visit, almost two years ago now, she had ordered a vodka lemonade. Cheyenne's favourite.

"Eleanor!"

She turned abruptly. There, hanging off the side of the bar as she chugged a glass of water, was Liz's beaming face. "Eleanor, is that you?"

"The one and only," she said drily. She slipped through the crowd towards Liz. "How are you?"

"I'm here with Molly and Avery – the girl who lives with us now – and some other friends. You should come meet them!"

"I'm not sure–" But Liz was already pulling her into the crowd, over sticky floors and against sweaty backs. Eleanor's protests were drowned out by the droning bass, which only grew louder as they penetrated further and further into the club's depths. Someone's drink sloshed against her, and she winced as the damp seeped into her shirt and onto her skin.

Somehow Liz located her friends and squeezed Eleanor in. Molly gave Eleanor a hug and concerned look, Avery squealed and tried to kiss her cheek, and the other girls cooed over her outfit. One of the boys frowned as he ran his eyes up and down her.

"You're that writer with the actor boyfriend?" he asked.

"Yeah," Eleanor admitted as she took a sip of her drink. "I just got back from LA."

"You like it there?"

"Love it."

"The boyfriend rich?"

Eleanor's skin prickled. "My script sold for plenty of money as well," she snapped. She turned away so he didn't see her cheeks redden.

He grabbed her hand, not letting up. "What's the gossip in Hollywood?" His breath was hot on her cheek as he pressed himself closer. "Movie stars all hooked on drugs or hooking up?"

"Fuck off," Eleanor snapped. When he didn't relent, she thrust her glass forward and emptied the contents all over his face. It had been a terrible gin and tonic anyway.

In her dreams, the crowd parted before her like the Red Sea, recognising she was someone important: a genius, a star, a god on earth. In reality, she was barely anything, and so she had to shove to get people to move out of the way. A few people cried out as Eleanor ran into them, but Eleanor paid them no notice: they were weak, wallowing in mediocrity.

Outside, the rain had turned into a downpour; Eleanor was soon wet enough that it was irrelevant how many drinks had sloshed onto her. It was just like her first night here, where she had stood dripping in the library and dreamed of grandeur. But there was no library, no collected works of others' brilliance. There was only Eleanor, and her cold, empty room, and the dream of a brilliant career. Jack, who could have helped her, was thousands of miles away and hooked on cocaine – or was it meth by now? Liz and Molly seemed to live impossibly distant lives. Cheyenne wanted nothing to do with her.

Her feet took her the same old route, down the beach path to the ocean. Eleanor dropped her clothes in a pile on the sand – they were soaked anyway – and strode into the surf in her underwear as if being reeled in by the sea's line.

The waves were rough thanks to the storm, but as soon as Eleanor ducked under the surface the world turned quiet. Calm. Manageable. Even as the infinite blackness stretched beyond her. She could control herself here. A mistake in the ocean was hers alone, a triumph equally hers. Glory and death held in her hands.

Yet something stopped her from swimming out into the inky depths. For the first time, Eleanor hugged the trail of the cliffs, staring up at the bright lights above. Somewhere up there was Cheyenne: visions of dancing and drinking and kissing as the music blared danced in Eleanor's mind. Down below was Eleanor, watching.

She thought of the little mermaid, staring up from the water at the parties above. How she had longed for that place so much, and yet how it cost her so much pain to get there. How she loved a man who never loved her back.

It was too much to stare for too long. Instead, Eleanor swam on to the dark shape at the end of town – the castle ruins, looming over the ocean. The waves were rougher there. Eleanor paddled further out to avoid being crushed against a rock, only for her foot to scrape something jagged. She cursed inwardly, then frowned when her foot brushed it again. The grooves in the rock were strangely even.

Ah. She realised. The old castle decoration. Doorways and window arches decorated with grooves and crosses and meticulously carved likenesses of saints. Here was a piece, fallen from its post, still in the water all these centuries later. Waiting patiently for someone to take it home.

Tears, from something more than just the salt water, prickled in the corners of Eleanor's eyes. So much work had gone into that, so much care. Such an attempt to be remembered, to display your skill, your faith, your life, just to be dropped in an ocean and forgotten. So much excellence, lost. How cruel, to do that to someone and something they loved.

Eleanor dove down, scrabbling at the rock with her fingers. She got a purchase, but it was heavy, and half of it proved to be buried under the sand. A wave hit Eleanor unexpectedly and she lost her grip, sending the stone tumbling back to the floor. A burst of sand floated up and twisted around Eleanor's toes before the incoming currents washed it away.

Hopelessness surged through her, followed by harsh anger. If she couldn't do it, who would? Did the stone not want to be rescued? Did it want to rot in the sea forever? Did it want to be ground to dust?

It does not think, she reminded herself. *It's only rock*. But it was rock imbued with spirit and legacy.

She would tell someone tomorrow, she vowed. The university history department, perhaps? Or the archaeologists. They'd love a chance to do some fieldwork.

She turned to swim back, when another wave hit her: much larger than any of the ones before. Eleanor scrambled in panic as she was dragged towards the rocky coastline: she drew a breath in, and her mouth was flooded with salt. A few hideous moments later and she surfaced, spitting frantically, and paddled like hell out of the surf. She didn't stop until she was bobbing in the middle of the ocean, the lights of the town distant as she approached the far end of the beach. The waves might have been larger out there, but Eleanor could let her body float with them. Much easier to lurk in the abyss, surrounded by water, then in that liminal space where water met rock.

Eleanor crawled back onto the sand, what felt like hours later, on some deserted part of the beach. The town was over a mile away now, the lights dim enough that Eleanor could look up and see the stars in all their glory. It was like another sea up there, except with the company of the other constellations.

She didn't shiver the entire walk home, not even when she scooped up her clothes and felt their cloying dampness press against her skin. She wore her nudity like armour as she slipped along the empty path up the cliff and through the back door of the hotel no one ever used. It was meant to be locked, but Eleanor had taped the latch open as soon as she moved in. Never be without an escape or an entrance – she'd learnt that with Jack

This was the time Jack would have had a line. The moment of inspiration, he said, was now: the small hours, when emotion had come and overcome, snatched your soul away and left your body a shell. Seize the moment when your mind was elsewhere, and work.

But Jack might have had too many lines and smashed what little decoration his house had. Eleanor couldn't bear to think of it.

Instead, she lay in bed and thought of smashing a glass into Cheyenne's face. Then kissing her, then assaulting George, then fucking Jack, on and on and around and around forever.

29th September.

Eight months before the party.

For all Eleanor obsessed about Cheyenne, it wasn't her she encountered first. Instead the call came when she was walking down the street after a lecture, head down, dreaming of California.

"Bitch."

She stopped dead in her tracks to meet his glare. "Hi George."

He said nothing, only scowled stonily in her direction. Maybe he hadn't intended her to hear him. But Eleanor wasn't in the mood to brush the barb off either, so the two stood there, stone still, as hordes of students flowed around them: two stubborn rocks amidst the river of humanity.

He broke first. "You think you're so clever. Swanning around in your Californian clothes, preening up in that flat. I should tell them what you did: how fast would your script be out the window?"

Eleanor shrugged, refusing to let him see she was bothered. It was one thing to vaguely understand George would know who had destroyed his art, and quite another to hear him spit venom to her face. "They only care about making money in America. If the Leonsdales drop it, someone else will pick it up. Especially once Jack gets some more hits out."

"That boyfriend will drop you stat if he knows how evil you can be – if he knows how you ripped up–"

"Ripped up what?" Eleanor stared stonily across at him, trying not to let her panic flash in her eyes. She wasn't prepared for this: after all this time bracing herself for their vitriol, in its face she wanted to crumple like one of George's ruined canvases.

"You fucking bitch."

"I could sue you for libel, you know. A jealous uni friend out for revenge after I exposed him for being a woman-beater."

He narrowed his eyes and seethed. "Raquelle was right about you," he muttered.

So Raquelle *had* been muttering poisonous things into his and Cheyenne's ears all the time after all. Not that there had ever been any doubt, but it gave Eleanor sick satisfaction to have proof.

Deep in her stomach, something uncurled to whisper poison in her ear. If Raquelle could play at this game, so could she. "Your paintings were terrible anyway," she retorted.

"Not terrible enough that you didn't leave a few untouched."

Eleanor flinched: she tried to avoid remembering that particular weakness. While she'd shipped George's beach painting back with her, it was still wrapped up safely in a box, she hadn't yet had the heart to drag it out. "Maybe I was feeling sentimental. Emotions have been known to colour opinions."

His eyes flashed. "I've thrown them in the bin. I don't want anything around that you thought was worth keeping."

"You wouldn't have been able to get them shown anyway. You only managed your one exhibition because Cheyenne fluttered her eyelashes."

"Like your writing's any better? You've just extorted Cheyenne's parents!"

Eleanor shrugged airily. "At least my stuff exists."

"Your script will be terrible. Overloaded and melodramatic, just like you."

No time for tears, no space for flinching. Cold and callous, Eleanor repeated to herself: that was what she had to be. It got easier as she went on: a sick adrenaline engulfed her every time she spat back at George. "But it's interesting. Not the same few stripes on a canvas over and over again."

"They were all that kept me fucking going!" He was getting louder. People nearby were turning to stare. Good. Let them see Eleanor Sanders keeping her cool while a highly-strung boy exploded next to her. "When I wanted to kill myself, they were the only thing I had!"

"No," Eleanor replied bitterly. "You had Cheyenne." More fully than Eleanor had ever had her, with the exception of those scant few moments alone, up a hill or on the beach. How wonderful those had been: just the sun, the sea, and the girl she loved.

She'd thought Cheyenne had loved her too. In hindsight, perhaps it was only the sun and the sea. Or the blind adoration, or England and Scotland and France.

George snorted. "You could at least pretend to be sorry."

She had cared for George once. She'd helped him through his depression, tried to worm her way in even as Cheyenne pushed him away – why else would she have buried herself in her room while Eleanor had to sneak in to see George? She'd wanted to be in with him, in the know. Or maybe she'd just wanted to take Cheyenne's place in his heart.

"There are certainly things I regret," Eleanor said at last. Before George could say anything more, she turned and slipped away into the mass of people. Anonymity was nice sometimes.

She didn't bother returning to her flat. The hotel was bland and cold, with nothing of hers beyond a few books and clothes she disliked enough to taint with a trip back to Scotland. Nor was she in the mood to work. So Eleanor wandered. Up and down the same three streets she'd strolled a thousand times. How small it all seemed. How suffocating.

There were art galleries on the south side of town, tasteful places with minimal decoration and large, polished windows displaying their beige interiors. They catered for rich tourists, those who came for the golf and would return laden with new outfits, whisky bottles and home decoration.

George would have done fine here. He didn't need to be displayed in Edinburgh. Get a few wealthy Londoners – or better yet, Americans – to buy his art, and he'd be in. But Edinburgh was elite, and he got to go with Cheyenne.

Eleanor hadn't contented herself with this town. She'd gone straight to Hollywood, using Cheyenne along the way. The difference between them was Eleanor had succeeded. George simply floundered.

Then again, no one had destroyed all of Eleanor's work.

This was unhelpful thinking. Eleanor stumbled in the opposite direction, past the ruined monastery and the rotting chapel. How much time the builders must have spent on those buildings; what care they must have put into every carving, every vault, every stained-glass window. All for it to crumble to nothing because a man in Germany nailed commandments to a door, and a king in England wanted to divorce his wife, and an English queen had no children.

Sometimes destruction was out of an individual's control. George would do well to heed that lesson.

Was he telling Cheyenne about her now? Telling Raquelle? Sam? Henry? Gina?

What did it matter? Eleanor had already burnt her bridges. But Cheyenne...

Forget her, she told herself. *Forget her*. But the blonde's face flashed relentlessly through Eleanor's mind, pounding against her skull until she wanted to lean against the cliff railings and scream her pain to the world.

Oh, Cheyenne. Cheyenne, Cheyenne, Cheyenne.

Think of Jack. But even the brightest California sun couldn't cut through the haze in front of his face, while the shadow of Cheyenne loomed above him.

4th October. 10:31.

Seven months before the party.

Eleanor sat perched in the coffee shop window, eyes unfocused. Now she was here, her heart was beating so quickly it threatened to burst out of her chest. What had she been thinking? Stupid of her to do this. They probably wouldn't even come anyway, and if they did, they would turn away as soon as they saw Eleanor in the window.

But she was here now.

She glanced down. Her nails were chewed to the quick: a terrible habit, one she'd never had in LA. It was the stress of being here, surrounded by *them*, always watching, always worrying about being watched.

She was supposed to be reading a book. Should focus on that, not the time.

10:35. Almost time.

Try and type something, Eleanor.

10:37. She was late.

No, she couldn't be late if she didn't owe Eleanor any responsibility to be here. Probably she'd already glimpsed her and scarpered.

10:38. The bell rang.

It was getting cold in October, enough for scarfs and coats

to come out of storage. The girl in front of Eleanor wore browns and greys and tied her scarf the way they did in Paris, but her shirt was too casual; showed too much skin. An American holdover after all this time, as distinctive as the rush of blonde hair that cascaded down when she took off her hat.

Cheyenne had a lecture of an hour and a half on Tuesday mornings, beginning at nine. A terrible time, but to her credit Cheyenne attended every one, no matter what she'd been up to the night before (she worked hard on her economics. Eleanor often spied her in the library, poring over her calculations. Her furrowed brow was identical to the one she wore when sizing people up). Afterwards, without fail, she traipsed over to a tiny corner coffee shop, where she took her drink sickeningly sweet: another American taint she couldn't wash off.

She saw Eleanor instantly. She had positioned herself next to the counter. For a few seconds, Eleanor pretended not to notice her, waiting to see what she'd do. Cheyenne seemed unfazed, she strolled up to the counter without giving Eleanor a second glance.

How infuriating.

But there was no avoiding Eleanor after Cheyenne had given her order. She loitered awkwardly, a fly caught in a spider's web. Eleanor looked up and grinned. "Cheyenne!"

Her eyes flicked back and forth warily, like a blue-eyed deer. "Hello, Eleanor."

"How have you been? It's feels like ages since I've seen you."

Cheyenne frowned. "I think we both know why that is."

"Do we?" Eleanor said cooly. "I can't recall."

"Let's see." Cheyenne's lip curled unpleasantly. "You assaulted George in a pub and tried to blame him for it. You invaded my home. You destroyed George's art and half his career."

Eleanor furrowed her brow. "What art?"

"You know exactly what art! His paintings. The ones going to the gallery!"

"They were destroyed? How awful. What happened? Was it flooding? I seem to remember that was an awfully wet winter." She twisted her face into a picture of innocence. Jack's acting skills had rubbed off.

"You cut up his paintings just like you cut up my face!" Cheyenne pushed her hair aside to reveal a half-moon scar intersecting her right eyebrow like a fingernail. "You're insane, Eleanor!"

She shrugged. "Hollywood doesn't seem to mind."

"That's because you fit right in. California's full of wackos. You're probably the tamest of the lot."

"Penelope Hale told me about you. She said she was sorry." For the first time that day, the dam Eleanor had built within her began to crack. She'd been so determined to stay suave – cool, calm, and collected; an unflappable ice queen. But the mention of Penelope thrust an all too human image into her mind: a girl curled up on an oversized bed, longing for her lost friend. Penelope and Eleanor coalesced, and the memory of all those days spent longing and lonely flooded Eleanor from within. *Come back,* she wanted to cry. *I'm sorry.*

"Of course she'd tell that to you: you're like two fucking demented peas in a pod. Three, if you count the boyfriend that's a drug addict, or so I hear."

Eleanor's fingers curled into her palms. There it was, she told herself. Cheyenne was a vicious shrew who had drawn her in with honeyed words and false promises: really, she hadn't been at fault at all. She shoved any nagging doubts away and forced herself to spit venom. "Your parents don't seem to mind. They've hired him for one of their films."

This was dangerous territory. But it was worth it to see Cheyenne's reaction. Her narrowed eyes, her bit lip, her hair flip. "Doesn't matter what my parents think. They're just as bad as anyone out there."

Eleanor felt heady: she was racing along a tightrope, dodging projectiles while she avoided toppling into a pit of regret. She couldn't stop, couldn't falter, couldn't even think. For once, she wasn't plagued with regret: a weight had been lifted off her shoulders, and she was free to fly like a missile. "Bet they'd rather have me as a daughter than you."

"And thank fuck for that. Then I could be from a sane country instead!"

Cheyenne's shout was the final straw in a conversation that had already been drawing eyes from all over the cafe. The room fell silent, placing a glaring Cheyenne in centre stage. It was normally the sort of thing she loved, but this time she buried her face in her scarf, marched to the counter for her drink, and stormed out. As the door slammed shut and the bell tinkled all faces turned to Eleanor.

Eleanor took her time packing up. She let everyone see her as the calm, collected, rational participant as opposed to Cheyenne's wild fury. Really, Cheyenne should know better. That frenzied emotional output was so American of her.

Yet as Eleanor walked away from the coffee shop, the bitter, stinging victory began to feel hollow. It was biting at her too, not just Cheyenne. Eleanor really had ruined it, smashing that glass in her face and cutting up George's art. All that was left in Cheyenne's eyes was hate for her – the laughing girl on the bed was long gone.

As she climbed the stairs to her apartment the phone rang. It was Jack: it was only ever Jack.

His voice was urgent. "You live at the penthouse of the Radcliffe, don't you?"

"Of course. The one with the view of the sea."

"And you're paying per week?"

"I'm using my advances from my script." In truth they were running dangerously low. Eleanor had an allowance from her parents that she didn't use for accommodation, but circumstances were forcing her to consider dipping into it. She had confided these things to Jack only once, when both were alone in their rooms, she incredibly drunk and he incredibly high.

"I got my advance too," he told her. "For signing onto your script."

"Probably much more than mine."

"Loads." There was a nervous silence, then a gulp on his end of the line. "Eleanor, I'm buying the penthouse."

She nearly dropped the phone. "What?"

"I'm buying the penthouse. We can rent it out when you're not there, don't worry. But I want to know that you have a place to live, and that there's somewhere I can visit."

Eleanor's hand shook. "You know I never want to see this town again after I graduate." She was jetting off to America, never to be seen again on anything other than a TV screen.

But it was what Jack wanted. He had been so unhappy this past year. And he was trying – clumsily – to form a connection to her.

"But I might visit," Jack went on. He didn't need to: Eleanor had already let herself be convinced. "And think of the profits we can bring in."

Eleanor sighed. "Have you even bought yourself furniture yet?"

An awkward pause. "Some. But it's better to keep the place empty. Sometimes – in the night – I don't know what I'm doing. I stumble around... I've smashed things again."

"How many people know about this?" Eleanor demanded. Cheyenne's smirking face rushed through her thoughts. "That Leonsdale girl knew today."

"A few. Some. A lot. Look, I'm doing what you said and talking to my friends about it. They gossip. What else do you want me to do?"

Jack was right. Completely right. And Eleanor had been all for it, hadn't minded the word getting out – because she hadn't ever expected it to reach Cheyenne's ears. But what did it matter, she told herself. Jack would get better, and then she would be known as the woman who'd valiantly stood by a suffering man's side and helped coax him back to health. Cheyenne's perfect Henry could never compare.

"I'm sorry," she said. "Of course she might know, being from LA and all. It just blindsided me because she's here."

"Well speaking of gossip," Jack added, "my agent and publicist were talking about you the other day."

Eleanor frowned. "Saying what?"

"Well, they don't want you to disappear, especially now that you're not writing any scripts. And it's bad for my image as well – they don't want people to forget we're an item."

"Jack, I'm not sure you're in a fit state to be seen..."

"Exactly. So they were thinking you should write something."

"I told you, I can't even look at another script right now."

"That's not it. They want something nonfiction, something commercial. A little book about a wide-eyed English girl breaking into the film industry, and all the amazing things she found in America. And of course, something about me."

"And the drugs?"

"The part where I'm getting better, yes."

Eleanor's mind churned. "When do they want this done by?"

"This time next year, ideally. Good for Christmas sales, and you'll just be re-entering the public eye by that time. It should give you plenty of time…"

"I'll do it," Eleanor said breathlessly. A book! A real book! About her! She was deemed interesting enough of a subject to have a book about her!

Cheyenne had no book. *Ha.*

Jack was babbling on. "They said they'll send over some info and strategies other writers have used. It can be especially tricky writing about adolescence – and you might want to think about how you'll treat your college friends. Maybe change some names or…"

"I know what I'm doing," Eleanor replied. That would be the best part.

After Jack hung up – he seemed placated enough that Eleanor didn't think he would go feral for at least a few hours – she went down to the beach. There she kicked off her shoes and swam, length after length after length, ducking and diving and dreaming of the Pacific. A book. She really was famous in her own right then. A *book*!

She would have to work in the swimming somehow. Maybe it would be a good theme: a point of constant return. She could emphasise the differences between the North

Sea and the Pacific, yet also describe how their similarities enabled Eleanor to conquer them both. Yes, there really was something there.

A group of surfers approached as she clambered out onto the sand. "You swim without a wetsuit?" asked one, a dark-skinned girl with hair arranged in delicate braids.

"I don't do as much sitting around as you surfers." Eleanor repeated the mantra Jack had said to her. She frowned at the other girl's accent. "Are you American?"

"From Texas." She smiled, and her teeth were just like Cheyenne's: straight and white, fixed with braces and chemical toothpastes.

"Then you must really need a wetsuit!"

Her laugh was bright and clear. "'Like you said, you get used to it. But the bonfires we have over here are a big plus. You ever go to them?"

"I'm not in surf club." She wasn't in any clubs. But the thought of surfing was especially painful, with it came memories of Jack gripping her waist as he steadied her while they floated under the Californian sun. She missed him so much: missed when she could be the person he thought she was.

"Come anyway." The girl tossed her head, making her hair fall beautifully over her neck. "There's plenty of alcohol to warm you up as well."

"I think I will." Eleanor started down the beach with her, still dripping. "I'm Eleanor, by the way."

"Kirstie."

Eleanor was cold: Kirstie was warm. Even the bonfire didn't seem to help. Only nudging closer and closer to the other girl did. They drank and sang, and gripped ice-cold fingers on each other's arms, and the thought of Los

Angeles swirled through Eleanor's head. She was going to be famous – a gifted writer, an actor's wife.

"You know," Eleanor slurred into Kirstie's ear. "I rent the penthouse of the Radcliffe."

Her eyes widened. "You're that girl?"

Kirstie's surprise filled Eleanor with glee. She knew of her. Of course she knew of her. Everyone knew Eleanor Sanders. "Fresh from LA," she replied.

Kirstie's smile was awestruck. "The one with the actor..."

"We're on a break." Who cared about Jack now? Eleanor was the star of the show, not him. Not now. Not here on this beach, with an American girl who actually wanted her.

Eleanor leaned in closer. "You want to see the place?" *Want me want me want me want me want me.*

Kirstie grinned. "Show me the way."

Eleanor relished in Kirstie's excitement at sneaking in through the back stairs, her awe as she saw the size of the place, her delighted giggle as Eleanor kissed her in the shower. She was eager in bed, eager to fuck someone famous, someone who she could brag about to her friends and whisper of to future boyfriends. Eleanor had never slept with a woman before either, but it was so easy to forget yourself: to caress the right body parts and murmur the correct things. As long as she didn't think at all: as long as she let the present dissolve before her as her mind soared into oblivion. It wasn't that difficult, was it Cheyenne? Wasn't difficult to do obscene things in bed with your lover while going on to marry a bland English man and pop out little posh children.

"Eleanor!" Yes, that was what Cheyenne would say: how she would call her name when Eleanor was on top of her.

"Eleanor!" How she'd writhe when Eleanor ripped out her insides.

"Eleanor, you're hurting me!" Kirstie choked out.

Eleanor jolted back in shock. She'd been gripping the other girl's shoulders, digging her nails in to leave angry red indentations. One of them was leaking blood.

Jack had never made her bleed. And Jack had been on tainted drugs.

Jack...

"Get out!" Eleanor yelled as if she'd been shocked. She stumbled away to the other side of the room. "Out, now!"

Kirstie's brow furrowed in confusion, but she was so taken aback she did as Eleanor said. She climbed out of bed, moved to put on her clothes...

"Don't stop!" Eleanor yelled again. She tossed a pillow at the poor girl. "You can't stay here! Just... just leave!"

"I – I don't – I'm sorry!"

"OUT!"

The door slammed behind an only half-dressed Kirstie, and Eleanor slumped to the floor. What the fuck had she done now? Kirstie would tell. Of course she would tell: who wouldn't? And then it would get to Cheyenne, and then to Jack, and then...

She could call a lawyer. Sue the girl for slander. Was that how it worked in the UK? Or was it the US that had freedom of speech laws? But either would mean that Jack had to know, and that...

It didn't matter. He'd probably slept with a dozen other girls in her absence. All those parties had to have turned into orgies at some point. Right?

Her head was pounding. Eleanor lapped water from the tap like a dog and then paced the room in a daze. She understood what Jack had said; how it was dangerous being alone. But she couldn't exactly have company either, as she'd just proved.

In the morning, she woke collapsed on the living room floor with a throbbing headache. The night was a blur, but she was naked, and that told her everything she needed to know. She showered three times, scrubbed all over with every brush she owned, emptied an entire bottle of shampoo over her head, and still it clung to her like a stain. Not even the ocean would help: she swam until her arms were about to give out and yet the taint remained, mixed in with the salt. Finally Eleanor vomited, as if the guilt was inside her stomach, but she puked up nothing but bile and still felt it clawing within her. She was the girl George had accused her of being – cruel and callous and prone to violence. She had left the man who loved her to mutilate another girl. And she knew – could feel the darkness clawing within her, scrabbling for release – that when the moment came, she would do it again.

6th May. 22:03.

Two and a half hours into the party.

"Are you insane?" Raquelle's voice carries across the room. "We're not going out to the castle with *her*."

"Oh fuck off Raquelle," Eleanor shoots from her perch by the window. "Cheyenne wants to go, and that's that."

"Henry too," Cheyenne says decisively. She hooks an arm around her boyfriend's body, like nothing can go wrong while she's tethered to him. "It's a good sendoff."

Gina's eyes flick back and forth like she's watching an especially anxiety-inducing tennis match. "I'm not going," she finally declares in a quiet, sullen way.

"Fine," Eleanor mutters as she cracks a nut into her mouth. She smiles silkily as Gina leans away and Sam puts a protective arm around her. "George?"

His gaze darts towards Raquelle, arms crossed like an Amazon, but ultimately nods his head and says, "Fine'.

And there it is. Eleanor, George, and Cheyenne against the outsiders. If it weren't for Henry, it would be just like the old days. How easily things fall into place.

Raquelle seems to know she has lost, for she turns on her heel and marches into the lift. Her henchmen scuttle behind her like overly obedient ants. Eleanor gets one last glimpse of that hateful bow as the doors ping shut, and an idea floats into her mind.

"You go get your coats," she orders those remaining in the flat. "I'll meet you outside once I get my things."

Henry starts to leave, but George remains in place, fixated on the painting hanging over the far mantlepiece. From afar, it blends in beautifully with the Waterhouse – it uses the same colour scheme as *Ulysses and the Sirens* – but the style is closer to impressionism, like a Monet or a Sorolla. George could never resist staring at artwork – nor has he forgotten his own brushstrokes.

"I knew it," he mutters. "I knew there was one missing."

Eleanor glances over lazily. Pretends to be surprised. "Isn't it nice? You must have given it to me."

"You took it."

"It's a happy memory," Eleanor remarks. She stares not at George but Cheyenne, cocking her head. She forces her eyes to a soft and gentle expression, like a newborn fawn. Living with an actor has taught her well. "And such a beautiful composition. It almost feels like we are still there."

Cheyenne looks away. Even after all these years, it still sends a stab of pain through Eleanor's chest: a dark part of her mind still holds out that someday, somehow this will work, and Cheyenne will remember. The delusion is half of what keeps her going.

"And we are going back, aren't we?" Eleanor goes on. "You can see the beach from the castle in the light – it's only a stone's throw away."

"Eleanor–" Cheyenne murmurs.

"And George–" his eyes are as hard as granite – "it'll be so good for you, to have it hanging in Jack's house. We've already had people asking about the artist, and where to get one like it." If George only cooperated – if he had only seen the light all those years ago – he could have been so famous. He could still be now, if he makes the right choices tonight.

George and Henry turn away, but Cheyenne fixes Eleanor with a strange look. "We're still not friends, you know," she says.

Eleanor shrugs. "We're whatever you want us to be."

"Then we're acquaintances. Out for a final sendoff."

"Of course."

"And I'm getting out of this drug-infested room."

"Confused me with the boyfriend!" Eleanor calls after her. Cheyenne, of course, does not look back.

Now she is alone, she must act quickly. Eleanor nabs a bottle of wine from the fridge, stuffs it in some oversized trench coat she picked up during her first winter here – a Cheyenne approved style – and grabs two phones from her desk. She checks them carefully, assuring she knows which is which. Then, right before she goes downstairs, she nabs a spare tray of cupcakes from the fridge. Gluten free, saved especially for the celiacs. She balances it on one hand: the perfect hostess.

She slips down the back stairs, enters the lobby from the side. It doesn't take long to find Gina, Raquelle, and Sam – they're loitering in a corner by the door, downing drinks. Gina looks worried, while Raquelle's face is an angry red.

Eleanor swoops towards them. "Nearly ready!" she proclaims brightly. "I just need to find a place to set these down. Do you want one?" Already Raquelle's head is shaking no, but Eleanor forces one into her resisting hand. "No – they're really good. And Sam – you too, Gina!"

Eleanor leaves them to sashay around the room, handing out cakes to other guests with various levels of persuasion. She has made it to the back of the hotel when the screams begin.

She shoves her way through an ever-growing crowd to find Gina sprawled on the floor, gasping for breath. Against the marble, her porcelain skin appears wan and shallow; her perfect curls spiral out beneath her like blood. Raquelle kneels over her. When she sees Eleanor, her gaze turns from panic to fury.

"You!" Raquelle screams. Her arms flap wildly at her sides as spit flies from her mouth: she is losing control. "You did something – something she ate – it's all your fault!"

"There's no time!" Eleanor cries back. She forces the triumph into the pit of her stomach and summons up terror. "We need an ambulance – why hasn't anyone called one!" She pulls out her mobile phone and dials the emergency number. Nothing happens – it is the American phone, empty of SIM or any kind of mobile connection. Yet she tosses the phone down on the table as proof that she at least tried to help.

Raquelle is still on her, spitting obscenities. "The cake!" she says. "What was in the cake – you know she can't have nuts!"

Eleanor blanches. "I don't know!" Then, stumbling backwards, she lets the realisation dawn on her. "But we ordered celiac cupcakes – ones with almond flower – Raquelle, I'm so sorry..."

The tears begin to flow heavily now; Eleanor's knees give way. Raquelle turns from Eleanor with a sneer of disgust and begins searching for someone to help. In the chaos, Eleanor slinks backwards into the crowd, wipes away her tears, and sneaks away.

Gina will be alright. There is no real danger. The hotel keeps epi-pens behind the reception and the bar. A staff member will remember in time to save her. But Gina will be left with the fear, the paralysing realisation that, at that particular moment, Eleanor held complete control over her body and her life. And after all those years of Gina weaselling her way into Eleanor's life while Eleanor was powerless to stop her. What a lot of power little Eleanor Sanders has gained.

Besides, now Gina is out of the way – and with her Raquelle. It would have been best to leave Henry behind too, but Eleanor can't have everything within her control just yet.

As she slips towards the door, a hand grabs her from the shadows. Eleanor jumps as a shadowy face comes into view. "Eleanor?" Amy asks. A quiver of fear runs through her voice. "What's happening? I heard screams."

"Allergic reaction," Eleanor says. "Someone's hurt. You need to find an epi-pen."

"Is that where you're going? To get help?" Amy's eyes widen and her lip quivers, but her gaze is whole-hearted. She truly believes Eleanor wants to help.

"I – yes – I just–"

Eleanor can't face it. She isn't the girl Amy thinks her to be – she hasn't been that girl for a long time. Maybe she never was – perhaps her a vicious streak that yearned to poison young women and weep false tears was always in her.

But Amy believes in her. Someone thinks there's hope.

She looks out towards the street. Somewhere, the others are waiting. She has planned this for so long.

Amy's eyes are pools of hope.

"Call an ambulance," Eleanor orders. "I tried, but I don't think the call went through. Then get the epi-pens under the bar." She pauses. "You can save her. I know you can."

"And what about you?"

"I have friends that have gone out there," Eleanor says. "I need to find them."

It could ruin the whole plan, speaking to Amy like this. But as Amy disappears into the hotel, sneaking one last glance behind her, a warmth spreads through Eleanor's chest. At least a part of that bright-eyed little girl, who knew no hate or evil is still alive.

She steps out of the hotel into the cool night air. Cheyenne, George, and Henry are waiting for her, as promised. Perhaps they are too drunk to hear the screams, or perhaps they are just too drunk to care.

"Everything alright?" Cheyenne asks with a wave of her hand. "Heard there was some sort of commotion."

Eleanor shrugs. "Nothing much. Some minor medical scare. Now–" she grins and proffers them a drink – "What do you say we head to the castle?"

1st January. 00:00.

Five months before the party.

Jack kissed her right as the fireworks went off. Two bursts: one outside, one within her, each just as colourful as the other. She was a firebird among the firecrackers, drifting through the updrafts in the LA sky.

"You're so beautiful," he murmured as he leaned into her. "I'm so glad you're here."

Eleanor nodded as she fingered the pendent around her neck. A ring hung from it. A Christmas present from Jack. "No pressure to wear it on your finger," he'd said as soon as she unwrapped it. "Just a reminder."

He bought her other things too. Perfumes and clothing and books. A shower of gifts, as if to remind her of his presence, his generosity, his wealth. That he was working now, that his breath didn't stink of anything more than alcohol and e-cigarettes. That he loved her.

Eleanor's present was a bottle of Scottish whisky and the news that her dissertation was finished. Now she was back to scripts, and – a sly glance at Jack's parents, sitting across from them on the sofa – was working through an early draft of her memoir. Right now she was still on her childhood. "Boring stuff really."

"Not to us," Jack's mother chimed in. "It's all very exotic – being from England."

Eleanor waved her hand airily. "Oh, America is much more exciting. Especially since Jack's here."

That seemed to endear her to Jack's parents, who took them on a windy stroll through their small beach town. When they reached the sand, Eleanor peeled off her trousers and waded until the water reached the top of her thighs. She looked back and grinned manically.

"You'll catch your death out there," Jack's father warned.

Jack shook his head. "She loves the ocean. Loves it even more than she loves me."

The water was wonderfully cold: fresh in a way that the Scottish ocean could never manage. This was an ocean of possibilities, of new hopes; the past was washed from her skin with every step she took in.

Jack still didn't know about Kirstie. No one knew, as far as Eleanor was aware. Kirstie, beautiful, smiling Kirstie, who was everything other than being Cheyenne, has spoken of the affair to no one. Perhaps because she felt it was embarrassing, to be thrown out of Eleanor Sanders' bed like that. Or perhaps, just perhaps, Kirstie had a good heart.

Eleanor wouldn't know what that felt like.

On the drive back to Los Angeles, Jack wouldn't stop talking. About jobs, about her scripts, about how exciting her memoir was. Eleanor leaned against the window and watched the ocean speed by. How beautiful this country was. And how terrible it could be.

She'd found plastic bags of powder in Jack's boot and glove compartment when she arrived. She lectured him, told him how irresponsible he was, how easy it was to fall back into a habit, how the police would treat him if he were discovered, what the press would say. How he'd been lying to her.

They weren't all his, Jack reassured her. They were his friends'.

He was a very good actor. Eleanor wasn't sure what to believe.

The New Year's Eve party was a familiar venue: some famous actor's bash in their hilltop mansion. Eleanor kept her elbow firmly locked in Jack's all night. They sipped champagne and nothing else.

At five minutes to midnight, Eleanor's head was turned when she thought she saw a flash of blonde. She poked Jack, who was busy chatting up a colleague. "Jack."

He tuned. "What?"

"Do you know if the Leonsdales are here?"

He frowned. "Don't think so. It's a younger crowd, on the whole."

"What about their daughter?"

Jack blinked in confusion. "I thought you said she was spending the holidays in England with her boyfriend?"

"I thought she was!"

The actor friend leaned in. "Sorry: is this Cheyenne Leonsdale? The one who's gone off abroad?"

"I'm at university with her in Scotland. We were good friends in first year."

"Were?"

"We drifted apart," Eleanor lied. "And I thought I saw…"

Too late. The fireworks went off with a boom, and Jack leaned in and kissed her. It was a wonderful distraction. Jack was hard and steady, so unlike Cheyenne with her fickle moods and her supple curves and…

She loved Jack. Jack was wonderful. She pressed into him harder, setting him stumbling. Eventually they made their way into some guest bedroom where they undressed. Eleanor managed to smear her lipstick over seemingly every pillow.

"You were so worried," Jack said as the sun dusted the hilltops, "about that Leonsdale girl."

"I told you: we had a falling out, and I don't want her parents to know about it."

He frowned. "If it was that important to her, wouldn't her parents know already?"

"Oh, she cares," Eleanor insisted. "We fought about it the last time I saw her."

"Then how are you going to treat her in your book?" Jack propped himself up onto one elbow in thought. "You could just exclude her all together."

"I want to write about her. I just don't want her parents to go off me. And really, it's her friends that are awful, not her. They just say things about me, and she listens."

Jack tsked. "Well, maybe when the book comes out we'll be big enough that the Leonsdales can't touch us."

"The Leonsdales can touch everybody. And I'm not exactly big – no one cares about screenwriters. And I'm on a break."

"But we're a duo! You write the scripts, and I star in them!" He grinned. "Or you could just get into directing: people love directors. And they make more money."

"I'm not doing that."

"You're no fun."

Jack kept Eleanor occupied for the rest of her trip, though whether that was for her benefit or his, she couldn't tell. He took her hiking, swimming, surfing; they went to the art museums, the cinema, to see a play.

"You should text Penelope," he suggested one night. "Tell her you're in town. It's good for you to know someone that isn't me, and even better to know Penelope Hale."

Eleanor hadn't wanted to see the singer. She was too distracting, too irrevocably tied up with Cheyenne for Eleanor to be able to separate her into her own person. But Jack was right, she was lonely in Los Angeles. She messaged Penelope without expecting a response.

Surprisingly, one came within a few hours. Penelope was around that night; she invited Eleanor to dinner. Some exclusive steakhouse, remarkably private but remarkably expensive.

Penelope dressed for dinner the way Eleanor dressed for a film premiere. Her dress was gorgeous, full length and shimmering, but Eleanor couldn't help feel it was so elaborate to take attention off her body. She looked even frailer, if possible, than six months ago.

"You will eat, won't you?" Eleanor asked after they got through the opening pleasantries. Penelope didn't seem to mind the question. Instead she only nodded.

"There was another stint in hospital last month," she murmured. "Only three days, and thankfully I wasn't touring. But it's not good for Calypso, to suddenly be alone. I had to call my parents to get them to feed her, and that only caused more arguments." Her face went stony; she dropped her fork and a metallic clang rung out. In a lesser establishment heads would have turned, but this place was at least classy enough to grant its clients peace to display a modicum of emotion. "I have to get her a friend. There's a black kitten in the shelter I'm picking up tomorrow. Her name will be Sappho."

"More ancient Greek poems," Eleanor said.

"Songs," Penelope corrected. "You know they called her the Tenth Muse? Some stuck her on the same level as Homer. But she preferred the mundane topics: stuck to everyday life instead of war. It's just as beautiful though, and just as tragic."

"You would have liked university." It was too easy to picture Penelope in Scotland, sitting bolt upright in lectures as she furiously scribbled notes, eyes flashing inhumanely fast over pages of books, poring over essays late into the night. Yet as soon as the image left the classroom and began to creep into everyday life, the fantasy hit a sudden block. Penelope could never have lived like Cheyenne did, wearing tweed by day and sequined tops by night. What would the girl in front of Eleanor have done at such a school, other than hole up in her room and churn out song after song after song? Nothing but eke out a terribly lonely existence. "Or maybe only some parts," Eleanor admitted.

Penelope shrugged. "Before my career took off, I was going to enrol in UCLA. I can't really, not without causing a scene. And I have to go in for treatment three times a week, so I'd miss half my classes. But I have books." She tried to smile, but it ended up looking more like a grimace.

"You know you can always call Jack if you need a break," Eleanor suggested. "Not to talk – I know you don't know him – but he can feed the cat."

Penelope chuckled. "You're very sweet, Eleanor."

"Oh, not at all. Everyone in Scotland hates me."

"Maybe you only get along with people who don't get along with other people." Penelope took the tiniest bit of her steak, then took a full minute to chew and swallow it. She made a face as it went down, like it stabbed her throat with a thousand tiny knives. "And Cheyenne is difficult, especially since she's been hurt before."

"She still doesn't forgive you."

"Of course not. Why would she?"

It took her an hour and a half, but Penelope finally managed to eat the whole of her meal. "You should come back home with me," she told Eleanor. "I'm not meant to be alone after eating. In case I, you know." She mimed a gagging motion.

The house, while still larger than Jack's, didn't feel so cavernous when all the lights were on. Penelope flopped down on a sofa in the living room – comically huge for a house with only one person – and started scrolling through her laptop. "I want to show you something," she declared. "It's not very good at the moment – just a draft." She navigated to an audio file and pressed play.

The sound quality was poor and there was a lot of excess noise in the background, but Eleanor got the gist. It was a ballad about a friend: one long ago wronged and long ago gone. The song was one of regret for what had been lost, and a longing for what could have been. Penelope's vocals were more mournful than anything Eleanor had ever heard her sing.

"It's good," Eleanor remarked at last. "It's just – it hurts to listen to. It's hard to think of her right now – not when I have to see her again in a week." They didn't need to name the 'she': Cheyenne's name hovered in the air as a malignant presence.

Penelope nodded. "It won't come out until next November. My label wants a new album right in time for the holiday rush. By that time, she'll be long gone from your life."

"Do you think she'll ever hear it?" Despite herself, Eleanor was already picturing Cheyenne listening to it, crying, caving. But then the image turned to her running back to Penelope, leaving Eleanor behind. Longing turned sour in her throat.

Penelope shrugged. "Someone will tell her about it eventually. But it's not for Cheyenne; I don't care if she ever listens or not. It's just for me."

Just for her. Eleanor's scripts, her memoir, had been tied to the Leonsdales for so long it was hard to separate her art from Cheyenne. Everything Cheyenne would one day see, would know about. She wrote in a hyper-aware state, poised to please her.

She hadn't tried not caring. She wasn't sure she could.

Penelope played her a few more demos, and Eleanor tried to keep her mind in the moment. But her thoughts were lingering, and eventually she said her good-byes and returned home.

Jack had gotten sloppy. Eleanor walked straight into the kitchen to find him snorting lines.

"Jack." She wasn't angry, just disappointed.

He blushed. "It's not very much."

"You said it wasn't yours."

"Only because I knew you wouldn't approve!" He stood up but his voice wavered. "I am trying Eleanor. Trying so hard. But sometimes it's a lot, and you're leaving tomorrow, and I don't have work for another week…"

She enveloped him in a hug. Try as she might, she could not hate him. He was too pathetic. "Please don't lie to me," she whispered. "It's worse when I find out like this."

He swallowed. "You know I'll do more. When you're away."

"I know." She gulped. "But please try." Her fingers brushed his chin. "You'll act, and I'll write a memoir, and then I'll come back and we'll be rich and famous and you can go to rehab and no one will care. Or even if they do, it won't matter. We'll be untouchable."

"Untouchable," Jack echoed. There were tears in his eyes. "I'm sorry."

17 January.

Five months before the party.

She sent the text after a glass of wine, when her nerves were steeled enough not to second-guess it. *We should talk.* Then, as if an afterthought, *I'm sorry.*

Eleanor was certain Cheyenne wouldn't accept. Cheyenne had a marred face; her best friend had his livelihood destroyed. Their last meeting had been a tempest of anger.

But then again, Cheyenne liked to know about others. That was how she gathered power. Perhaps she'd agree to meet Eleanor; perhaps she'd be drawn irresistibly towards it like a fly to the sickly sweet mouth of a Venus flytrap.

Cheyenne's response came a few hours of later, in the wee hours of morning. Eleanor had been trying to work, but then gave up and scrolled through social media, desperately seeking out Jack's name.

We don't need to fucking talk. You slashed my face up.

Here came Eleanor's trump card. *I was on drugs that night. Tainted ones. And I know it doesn't make it any better, but I've regretted it ever since.*

I miss you.

My boyfriend does the same thing sometimes. He hurt me once, when he was on tampered shit.

For hours, there was nothing. Eleanor spent the night awake, pacing back and forth on a knife's edge, staring at her phone. Waiting for Cheyenne to notice her, to talk to her, to want her back in her life.

Notice me want me love me. She typed out the letters into the text box before deleting it. *Love me love me love me love me love.* For it had always been Cheyenne. A wild, radical part of her said it would leave Jack a thousand times to be with her. Another thought of the crushed look on his face when she told him. He would crumple, sink, fall back into a pit of which there would be no escaping. But Cheyenne, the fantasy of Cheyenne, bright and bold and brash, Californian confidence, desiring nothing more than to be worshipped by all: who wouldn't want her? Who could resist?

Cheyenne texted back at 8:34 am. *Meet me in the square at nine*.

She was wearing the same trench coat Eleanor had seen her in at the coffee shop. In fact, everything about her was unchanged, apart from her skin: she seemed to have become even paler. The Californian tan was long gone.

Eleanor wore her ring necklace from Jack around her neck. It burned with every step, but it kept her grounded. A reminder of what really mattered.

She stopped a few feet from Cheyenne. A respectable distance for acquaintances. "Hey."

Cheyenne's eyes flicked up. She had a fur muff on that made her look like an aristocratic Russian, about to be cut down by the revolution. "Hey."

"You look nice," Eleanor said blandly. Always good to start with a compliment: that was what Cheyenne had taught her, as she'd strolled into clubs and Eleanor had scurried behind.

She gave a polite nod. "So do you." Then the hint of a cold and wary smile – but is it mocking? Eleanor can't tell. "You finally learnt how to apply makeup."

"I learnt from the best."

Cheyenne nods. "You learn fast, down in LA." Of course this is what she thinks Eleanor means, that Hollywood has moulded her into a cover-ready mannequin devoid of passion and individuality. What she doesn't remember is that night, years ago in a cramped dorm room that stank of sweat and alcohol, when Cheyenne Leonsdale leaned over Eleanor Sanders and told her she looked like "an ugly duckling". Cheyenne pulled open her dresser and started touching up her own makeup, while Eleanor watched, half starstruck and half laser-focused on soaking this esoteric feminine knowledge in.

"You look nice," Eleanor said when she was done.

Cheynne sighed. "It's all in the contouring. Look, I'll show you." And when she leaned in, stroked Eleanor's face, it was closer to religion than anything Eleanor had ever experienced in stuffy old churches, more powerful and primal than the scriptures that bored her to death at primary school. This was ecstasy. This was life.

Eleanor never set foot in that dorm room again, at least not when there was only Cheyenne present. Sometimes there was a crush of people, assembling at the pulsing heart of their friend group that was Cheyenne's room, but never again was there to be a moment that intimate, that profound. Yet from that day on, before she went out, Eleanor would trace powder across her face the same way Cheyenne had done, desperate to imitate that fleeting touch.

"You want to walk somewhere?" Eleanor asked. They couldn't just stand here. "The sea?"

"We can go along the cliffs. Towards the castle."

"Remember when we went there for my birthday?" The words weighed heavy on Eleanor's throat. "Seems a long time ago."

"Plenty's changed." Cheyenne frowned. "Maybe it was inevitable. Maybe we were never cut out to be friends."

"You never know. In another life…" *In this life, if she would only kiss me, fuck me, love me.*

"Yeah." Cheyenne didn't sound convinced. "So you were high that night, then?"

"I was on everything. And plenty of it was sketchy. In America they're always going on about fentanyl in the opiate supply."

"How the fuck did you get your hands on those?"

"I was depressed and I needed an outlet. There are plenty in this town, if you know where to look." This entire farce was reliant on Cheyenne not knowing the ins and outs of the local dealers that well. But the likelihood was Eleanor was safe: Cheyenne wasn't the type to get her hands dirty herself. That was for her minions.

Cheyenne shrugged. "I have them sometimes. They've always been alright for me."

"You weren't taking the amounts I was."

"No," Cheyenne agreed. "I wasn't."

They had reached the castle. Silence reigned as they started out: the cliffs, the ruin, the all-encompassing, ever-beloved sea.

"I'm sorry I did that," Eleanor said again. "I'm sorry I did all of it. It was so stupid."

"You're lucky we didn't call the police." Cheyenne paused. "I was going to. But George talked me out of it. He said you were sick – like he was sick, back when he wouldn't leave his room. And that locking you up in a psych ward would only make you worse."

"And you agreed with him?"

"No. But then I remembered Penelope Hale." Cheyenne smirked as Eleanor looked up in surprise. "She once swung her book bag at me. Another time she overturned a desk and chucked a chair at my head. Bet she didn't tell you that when you had your little chit-chat in California."

Eleanor's skin prickled. "I'm sorry," she said, but carefully. She wasn't the only one who could bend the truth.

Cheyenne let out a sigh. "She was terrible to me. But sometimes I wish I could have helped her." She cast an appraising look at Eleanor. "Do you think you can do that?"

Eleanor shrugged. "I don't know. I hope so."

Cheyenne tutted. "Americans. Crazy right?"

"Your accent's coming along nicely," Eleanor admitted. "You can barely tell you walked out of Beverly Hills."

She scoffed. "Don't make me laugh. It needs another ten years."

"Do you have a job lined up? Or are you marrying Henry to get your hands on a visa?" Unconsciously, Eleanor's hand reached up to brush her ring. She pulled her fingers away as soon as she realized what she was doing.

"I've got a position at an investment banking firm. Very competitive, but I'm on track for a first." And Henry almost certainly had some relation to a member of senior management, but Eleanor was in no position to point this out.

For a moment, a picture of Cheyenne's entire life stretched before her: endless mornings spent sipping coffee and putting suits cropped to be just feminine enough, days in meetings spent typing mindlessly, a house in the suburbs with two and half children and a dog and Henry, his hair just beginning to go grey. Cheyenne would come home from the office on weekdays and tennis on the weekends, flash a smile she was just forced to pay a premium to her surgeon to maintain, and everything would be so nice. A perfect copy of the lives of Gina and Raquelle and George and every other university-educated upper-middle-class worker: terribly, banally, nice. Eleanor's stomach curled with something that wasn't quite hatred, or envy, but rather the sharp tang of regret.

"You were always good at economics," was the only thing Eleanor eventually said.

For a second, Cheyenne looked like she was about to smile. Instead she only sighed. "You know we're not going to be friends again?"

"Of course." But she had hoped it, wished it, dreamed it. Dreamed of being more than friends.

"That's good." Cheyenne looked out upon the castle, not meeting Eleanor's eye. "But thanks for telling me. And I'm sorry about your boyfriend. I hope he gets better soon."

"I think he is." Eleanor fingered her ring. "I really think he is." Then, on a whim, a thought burst into her mind. "You should tell Penelope that too. Her eating disorder's bad."

Cheyenne blinked. "Yeah, well. Maybe I'll message her."

"She's still very upset about the way it went down."

"It wasn't my fault."

"Wasn't hers either."

Cheyenne shrugged. "Then I guess we're at a stalemate."

For a moment there was silence. Then Cheyenne tutted and pulled her muff closer. "I have a lecture. See you around, Eleanor."

"See you around." She stayed where she stood as Cheyenne walked away. The castle suddenly seemed emptier and more desolate than ever.

What had she thought would happen? That Cheyenne would see into her heart and come running into her arms? That in Eleanor's absence, she had become the girl Eleanor had always dreamed about, the one who wanted her back? That they would become lovers and ride off into the sunset together?

Of course not. But she hadn't thought it would be so... cold.

She had smashed a glass in Cheyenne's face. Of course she would react like this. And she was Californian now, American, the very thing Cheyenne hated.

At home, she screamed into her pillow, then looked at pictures of Jack and screamed some more. She was just as English as Henry, and soon to be richer. Why did everyone hate her except some half-blossomed drug addict who had thrown away his career when it had barely started, and a singer who was starving to death?

It wasn't as if she was wholly in love with Cheyenne anyway. There was bitter hatred on Eleanor's end too, the sort you only felt for the people you truly cared for. Love and hate, twined around each other from beginning to end, with Eleanor stuck at their trembling, rotating core.

"Fuck Cheyenne," Eleanor whispered into the duvet. "Fuck George. Fuck Henry. Fuck Raquelle. Fuck Gina. Fuck Sam. Fuck Jack, for not getting his act together." *Fuck Jack, for making me need him too much to leave.*

Her script that night was some trashy slasher, where blonde-haired, blue-eyed girls with valley accents were systematically ripped apart by serial killers that emerged from the watery depths. It made Eleanor feel better for a few hours, then catapulted her into feeling worse.

Finally, when it was three in the morning and she had no tears left to cry, Eleanor stumbled to her feet and pulled open her closet. There, right at the back, under piles of clothing she hadn't bothered to fold – why bother, when the maid would do it for her within the week – was a tattered cardboard box. There was only one item left inside: a canvas, streaked with blue and gold, so vivid you could almost imagine yourself there.

Not that Eleanor had to imagine.

For a moment, she debated destroying it. Maybe that was what kept her so wrapped up in the life of a woman who hated her: she'd never finished the job of severing their ties on that horrible, bloody night. One trip to the kitchen, one swipe of the steak knife, and it would all be a distant memory.

But they had been so happy.

She couldn't do it. Deep in her heart, she knew she never would.

Eleanor hung the painting over one of the mantlepieces, next to a seating area she preferred not to use. It was perfectly pretty, from a distance. She need never approach closely enough to see the smiling girls, to remember the way Cheyenne's hand gripped her arm or the tinkle of her laugh.

It was stupid to keep it. All the painting did was foster wild fantasies and keep Eleanor's desperate hopes alive.

Yet it might torture Cheyenne and George too – had they worked out there was one missing? Did it eat away at them every night, wondering what Eleanor had done with it? It would all be worth it when they inevitably arrived in her apartment – for they would visit, and they would grovel – and realised how she lorded over them, how she hung her ill-gotten prize above her fireplace and shoved it in their faces.

When she finally fell asleep, her dreams were filled with fantasies of revenge.

1 May.

Six days before the party.

Eleanor spent the rest of term speaking to no one. She sat in her penthouse, swam in mornings, rejected half of Jack's calls claiming she was busy and worked on her manuscript.

It was essentially finished now – Jack's agent would be delighted. Her childhood was recoloured as charming, her early work remade to be meticulous, her relationship with Jack sketched out as wholly touching. There was, of course, still a gaping hole in the centre that Eleanor felt too nauseous to touch, so instead she avoided it. She spent her days wearing a groove into her floor as she paced like a caged tiger, or lying in bed drinking bottles of champagne as she tried to persuade herself inebriation was the way to inspiration.

Lately, Eleanor had been wondering how long it would take people to notice if she died. She spoke to no one except Jack, rarely left her room.

It would probably be some maid, who came in once a week to dust and make the bed. Or maybe the guest below her, complaining when their room began to stink.

What a thing wealth had bought her. Someone to discover her body.

If Cheyenne died, she'd be discovered in an instant. No, even better: someone would notice as she had her fit or stroke or heart attack and rush her to the hospital, and the princess of Alexandra Place would live another day. Her saviour would probably be Raquelle, who would stand simperingly at her side and smile. The thought made Eleanor want to throw up her very expensive champagne.

Cheyenne, Cheyenne, Cheyenne. What to do about Cheyenne? And really, hadn't that always been the question? The great obstacle she'd always face, whether discussing her personal life or her career? She was how Eleanor entered the industry, she was the girl Eleanor loved, Eleanor hated. There was hatred and there was love, fascination, obsession, anger that Eleanor would never be Cheyenne, never be wanted by her, all of it oscillating back and forth until Eleanor was forced to flee to the beach and swim until exhaustion shut down her brain.

She would never get Cheyenne back, so perhaps she should just be scathing about her in the book, burn the last scaffolds of the bridge that had hung tenuously on. But nor did she want the Leonsdales coming after her, ready to run her career into the ground. And yet, there must be a confrontation: for better or worse, Cheyenne Leonsdale couldn't get away without seeing Eleanor Sanders one last time.

When she grew tired of biting her nails to the quick as she thought, Eleanor scrolled through her phone. A graduation ball had just been held: some sunny thing where the men wore straw hats and the girls giggled in their floral dresses. Cheyenne was there, of course, arm wrapped around Henry. George was at her other side, smiling slightly at Raquelle. Gina and Sam were still together. As Eleanor stared at them, young and radiant and happy, having the time of their lives as the world seemed to spread out at their fingertips, the old anger returned. A pointed fury, burning red hot: the tip of the hammer poised to strike.

Anything to make Cheyenne see her, Eleanor decided. Anything at all to ensure that Cheyenne Leonsdale would never, ever forget Eleanor Sanders.

That afternoon, she rang down to the hotel reception and arranged to rent out the entire ground floor. That evening, weary students returning from their shifts at the hotel eagerly told their flatmates that Eleanor Sanders – the one with the fancy boyfriend who was going to be nominated for an Oscar – was having a birthday party. That night, out at the only nightclub in the whole town, drunk boys waxed lyrical into the ears of girls they were chatting up that they were going to the birthday bash of Eleanor Sanders, because her boyfriend might be there – the one who was in the news for the parties he attended and the drugs he took. The next morning, gaggles of society girls said they were going to Eleanor Sanders' event because they wanted to meet the girl who had stormed out of Cheyenne Leonsdale's house the night she was rushed to hospital. The next afternoon in a film studies seminar, someone mentioned that Eleanor Sanders, whose film was in production, was hosting an event and it would be good for students' aspiring careers to go and network. And the next evening, people stared at Cheyenne Leonsdale as she walked down the street, trying to read into the carefully blank expression plastered upon her face.

6th May. 22:37.

Three hours into the party.

The streets are deserted this time of night: everyone is either at the party or at the pub, drinking up the courage to make it to the party. Eleanor slows herself to the others' pace, she adds a few drunk stumbles for effect.

"Mind the bottles!" she calls when George grabs at her coat and sends them crashing against each other. They are hanging heavy in her pockets, weighing on her conscience. Hopefully they won't have to get so drunk they won't remember this in the morning.

Breaking into the castle is easy, the fence is only waist high. Henry yells at them to mind the security camera, but it's too late: Eleanor has already wandered into its vision. She shrugs as he glares at her. "It's not like they'll be checking it this late anyway."

It's been three years to the day since Eleanor last walked into the castle with this group of people. She supposes she should be sad, should reflect on the breakdown of their relationship, but Eleanor can't summon the right emotions. In truth, they were already ending three years ago.

Deep within her, the old hope curls. It's been beaten and bruised and dragged through hell, and yet it still has the strength to rise again. Cheyenne is drunk, her prejudices close to vanished. She could still stumble into a sudden drunken clarity and remember Eleanor. If Eleanor can just get her without the others...

It's a stupid idea. Too dangerous. For there's something else living within Eleanor as well, twisting its bitter tendrils around hope and hitching a ride on its back. It's too horrible for her to consciously entertain, but it's been there all along, buzzing expectantly under her skin like a parasite. Why else didn't she drink tonight? Why else did she bring them here?

She's being insane. Perhaps she has drunk too much, even though she's been so careful not to. Cheyenne and George will not take her back, but she will not harm them. Perhaps scare them a little – one final act of revenge – but no more.

Eleanor uncorks one of her bottles and holds it to her lips to make it look as if she's drinking. When she passes it to George, he's too drunk to notice anything's amiss. As the prosecco moves around the circle to Henry, Eleanor grabs Cheyenne's hand. "Can we talk? Just for a second?"

Cheyenne's eyes aren't quite focused, but she nods and lets Eleanor lead her away. It's a simple step over a crumbling wall to a ledge that hides them from the view of Henry and George, just big enough for the two to stand facing each other. This close, Eleanor sees, for the first time, brown streaks at the roots of Cheyenne's blonde locks. She forces herself not to cackle: so Cheyenne was never as flawless as Eleanor wanted to believe.

"So," Cheyenne slurs, "what's this about?"

"I'm writing a book," Eleanor blurts out. "A memoir. Something about my English life: my publicist said Americans love that. You would know, I suppose."

"That I do." Cheyenne's face opens into a lazy smile, displaying those artificially straightened American teeth. "Do you want to talk about the American market? We can do that in the morning, when I'm sober. Or if you have another script, we can go over pitches for that…"

For a moment, Eleanor's mind reels. She's being so nice. What's going on? Is it possible – really, truly possible, that hope has won out? That her wildest dreams are coming true?

She shakes it off, she has to press on. "That's not the point." Cheyenne isn't getting it – why isn't she getting it? "The memoir – you're in it."

"And?" She waves a hand. "What, are you just a bit mean about me? I know we had a falling out – it's okay. Write what sells."

"You're not angry?" This is inconceivable. All the time Eleanor has spent fretting over this, all the thought Cheyenne puts into her image, and she isn't worried about getting it smeared in a Hollywood tell-all? This was meant to rile her up, and the fact she doesn't care – could Cheyenne finally be coming back?

Cheyenne's teeth sparkle in the moonlight. "You know what they say. No publicity like bad publicity."

"Come back to Los Angeles with me," Eleanor blurts out. "We'll go together. Fuck Henry; fuck Jack: I don't need them. But me and you – we'd be unstoppable." For a moment, she imagines the life she could have: the fame, the adoration, the beauty, the wealth, all of it encapsulated in the girl in front of her. The girl who was the first to truly see her: to want Eleanor for what she was, and imagine what she could be.

Cheyenne's eyes have glazed over. She sways, cocks her head, and laughs. "You alright Eleanor? You don't sound all there."

"I am all there! Cheyenne, I love you–" she grabs Cheyenne's face and pulls the girl in close – "I've always loved you – listen to me!"

Eleanor isn't sure what she's expecting. A kiss perhaps, or even a heartfelt hug, some tears. She is baring herself to the world, begging for Cheyenne to see her, to acknowledge her, to understand her. To show Eleanor that she isn't alone. What she isn't prepared for is Cheyenne to throw her head back and drunkenly chortle into the night air.

"God, calm down! It's not news, you know. Everyone's been saying that since first year. You're not very subtle."

Eleanor goes very still. She can hear her heart pounding, her breath panting. There is blood in her mouth. She's bitten down so hard on her cheek it's started to bleed. "You knew the whole time?"

"Course. But it wouldn't work – I could never go steady with someone like you. It wouldn't fit the image. And Henry's just so wonderful – how was I supposed to know you'd go mental?" Her laugh is getting huskier with drink. "Come on Eleanor – you realised the same, didn't you? That's why you've got Jack."

Rage floods through Eleanor, burning icily hot. All that time she'd been nothing to Cheyenne but an entertaining toy to support her ego: another lover, another admirer, another adorer. How exotic, Cheyenne must have thought, to have an English girl mooning after her. And how simple she must have presumed it would be to drop her once she found a more suitable fit for her image.

But Cheyenne made one mistake. She didn't realise how dangerous the girl she'd used could be.

She'll show Cheyenne. She'll show her danger. She'll show her how 'mental' she could actually be.

Eleanor leans forward and kisses Cheyenne deeply on the lips.

It is nothing like her fantasies. Cheyenne doesn't want it: she screams for Eleanor to get off, and when that doesn't work, shoves her as hard as she can.

But Eleanor is pressed against a wall with nowhere to go.. And Cheyenne has her back to the sea.

She plummets with a scream.

One afternoon, back in Los Angeles, Jack took Eleanor to visit the tar pits. Tens of thousands of years ago, animals would lumber into these hidden hazards and become mired in the pitch: their companions would be forced to abandon them as they sank, slowly and inexorably to their death. In her dreams, when Eleanor stumbled to the castle and tumbled into the waves with Cheyenne, they fell like that: sickeningly slow.

But reality is nothing like dreams. Cheyenne was there and then she was gone, the echoes of her last scream snatched away by the wind. As if she never existed at all

Now is the time she needs to think, but it's as if Eleanor's mind has been drenched in the tar she dreamed of. In her fantasies, she would have been embracing Cheyenne by now. In her nightmares, she jerked awake after the girl was pushed off. Yet even as she tries to muster a plan, all she can feel is the dawning gulf of realisation.

Eleanor is in tears when Henry and George reach her. "She fell off!" she cries, pointing a trembling finger at the sea below. "She fell!"

Henry's eyes dart between the parts of the scene before him: Eleanor, tears leaking from her cheeks, screaming bloody murder, and the open void stretching out below. "Get off the ledge, Eleanor. George, go and look for a way down." He steps over the wall to where Cheyenne stood and peers down to see the waves crashing on the rocks. The tide is high this evening, and the darkness means it's impossible to see more than glimpses.

"Cheyenne!" he calls, inching closer to the edge. "Cheyenne, can you hear me?"

Eleanor peers over with him. He's too focused on Cheyenne to notice her, but Eleanor's mind is racing. Did he hear Cheyenne say "get off" all the way from the courtyard?

He heard her scream as she went over. Of course he heard what came before. But how long until he realises? He's a smart man: when he puts the pieces together, what will he do to Eleanor? She's almost as close to the cliff as he is.

Even if he doesn't hurt her, she'll be destroyed. They'll imprison her for murder, she can wave goodbye to Hollywood and Jack and making something meaningful out of her pathetic little life.

Henry is very near the edge now. He needs to be careful; in his frenzy he's becoming unbalanced.

There is no choice. The second Cheyenne went over there ceased to be a choice.

Henry realises a split second too late. He turns, but Eleanor's hands are already on him. She shoves, and for a second she is afraid that she is going over too, but she is further back than Henry, and her stumble forward doesn't take her off. She hears his furious yell as he falls, hears the crack of a body on the rocks, but any further sound is drowned out by the crash of the waves.

For a moment, Eleanor stands breathless. Both down the cliff. Both by her hand. She really did it.

It was so easy. That is what sticks out to her, even now: in the coming days and months, and, if she survives this, years, it will stand even more starkly against the nebulous background of the case. A few steps. One push. Barely any effort. And a human life is gone.

Then a scuff echoes from further down the cliff, and she remembers George. Eleanor climbs back into the castle. But instead of waiting in the main courtyard, she ducks into one of the side passages: the one that led to the dungeon. She lingers in the shadows as George stumbles around the castle, growing ever closer.

Malice – a twisted, serpentine creature that is now finally rearing its head and hissing in pleasure – whispers to get rid of George too. He's just as bad as Cheyenne, maybe even worse: whispering in Cheyenne's ear, laughing at Eleanor behind her back, slipping away with Gina and Raquelle. Always upset with Eleanor, always causing friction. It would be easier, simpler, just to–

But George. Something within Eleanor kicks back against the snake, and suddenly the last three years wrap around Eleanor, smothering her with memories she long ago buried. Her, Cheyenne, and George on the beach, George calling out to stop the girls from getting swept away. The trio on the quad, their moods as bright and sunny as the weather. Eleanor wrapped between George and Cheyenne's arms on a bleak October night, feeling as if her heart might burst from happiness. All those scenes memorialised in George's paintings, that preserved the light and joy of those moments forever.

And Eleanor tore them to pieces.

He ripped them first, she reminds herself. The same words she's repeated night after night when she can't sleep. In destroying my trust, he destroyed his art. The images were no longer beautiful.

But she'd kept a painting all the same.

"Henry?" he calls out. "Eleanor? We can use the steps to get down, but we'd have to go back over the fence and the tide's very high. I think we need to call the police."

What will become of George now? Could they leave together, safe and sound? George might not be as great a prize as Cheyenne, but he's a solid second place. He's still Eleanor's. She could still win him back. The trauma of the night, and the horrible accident that unfolded after they got too drunk, serving as a bonding moment. Jack won't like it, but Jack will have a traumatized girlfriend he needs to please. Maybe Eleanor can even bring George to Los Angeles? He can go out with Penelope Hale.

George's voice grows wearier, his footing more precarious. Eleanor's fantasy is shattered as reality sweeps around her like a flash flood. "Henry? Eleanor?" Desperately: "Cheyenne?"

Eleanor lets him approach the edge before she creeps up. But she's approaching from far away, and he turns to see her silhouetted against the moonlight. "Eleanor? Is that you?"

"George?" she forces her voice to sound quivering and breathless. "George, Henry fell too!"

"He did?" George frowns with despair and confusion. "I heard him yell – we need to call someone!"

She can't allow the police to come here: not when she can't control the narrative. Instead, she blurts out the only thing she can think of that will catch George's attention. "I kissed Cheyenne," she admits.

George throws his arms up in desperation, and Eleanor's fantasy vanishes. "Are you insane? She never wanted you; is never going to want you! She won't forget about you hanging onto her for clout and destroying people's property and shoving your nose in where you don't belong! You bringing us up to the castle for some stupid grand gesture wasn't going to change that!"

Eleanor bites her lip. They could still be in there – their younger selves, a fresh and innocent George and Eleanor from before the world tore them apart. She can still fix this: George can apologise, can fall to her feet in tears, and she, graciously, will find it in her heart to forgive him. "She told me you all knew. You could see I was in love with her all along."

"What does that matter? She didn't want you back!"

"You could have been kinder. You didn't need to shut me out!"

"Shut you out!" His face is warped with fury as he takes a step towards her. "Or perhaps we were being normal fucking people who thought you were too much with your stupid, obsessive, suffocating, manipulative little act. Everyone always thought it was mental that you couldn't bear to be left the fuck alone! And we were right, weren't we, because you turned out to be a complete maniac! And a killer too – because who put her in the sea, Eleanor Sanders? Who lured us here just to pick us off one by one? They'll love you in the criminology classes for this!"

"George…" Her plan is crumbling

"You killed them, Eleanor! Killed our friends!"

"You just said they weren't my friends."

"And whose fault is that? Who fucked it up? Because it sure as hell wasn't–"

He doesn't get to finish. Eleanor rushes towards him at full speed and pummels his chest, screaming as she pushes one thumb into the corner of his eye. He screams and pushes her off him, sending Eleanor dangerously close to the cliff's edge. As George prepares to charge, Eleanor lingers, then ducks out of the way as he gets close. He trips on a wall of stones barely visible through the grass, and as he loses his balance Eleanor sees her chance. She runs forward and shoves him over the cliff, sending him plummeting into the sea.

This time she watches him fall. She sees the body contort as it hits the rocks, sees it twist and turn as the waves buffet it, watches the corpse being dragged under as it's carried out to sea. And it must be a corpse, mustn't it? No one could survive that.

The darkness lurking within her hisses with pleasure. Then it sinks down to rest, leaving nothing but a gaping maw of horror.

What was she thinking? Why did she let it take over? That twisted fantasy that has now revealed its full savagery. They were supposed to be enjoying drinks now, with Cheyenne a little angry, or better yet madly in love with Eleanor and about to dump Henry. Even in the worst-case scenario, she could have escaped with George – maybe even Henry, he could have survived this too – and wept over the terrible accident that drew them back together. Hope was meant to win the day.

Instead, she left only murder in her wake.

Not murder, the dark thing reminds her. An accident.

An accident that looked very much like murder. The horrible serpent slithers up and whispers: it knows what to do. It can guide her now, and then she will never have to listen to it again.

First thing's first: Eleanor starts pacing up and down, over the spots that she had run and fought and shoved. Now there are only the footsteps of a distraught girl searching for her friends – a distraught girl who is probably too drunk to call for help in her state (but just in case, Eleanor takes out her phone and drops it down the cliff face into the sea). She waits a few more minutes, just to delay things further, then rushes out the castle doors, stumbling every so often as if she were really drunk.

The entry post is little more than a shack, but the security camera has an excellent view of the ticket window. Eleanor runs up and bangs her fists on the empty door, wailing as she tries to call for non-existent help. She goes at it for a full minute, then wipes at her face and starts making her slow way down the street towards the town.

Now comes the difficult part. As soon as the security camera is out of sight, Eleanor pulls out the remained bottle from her coat and starts to chug it. This must be done in moderation: she must be drunk out of her mind so she is authentically haggard and frazzled, but sober enough to not say something incriminating.

Her stumbles are becoming authentic now. When she begins to pass people on the street – she's getting to the busier part of town now – they ignore her: just another drunk in a trench coat. She needs to get home – yes, that home, the hotel, not her old halls or Cheyenne's townhouse or the swimming flat near the pool. The home that comes from Jack – and herself, it comes from herself, she made the money too – she should think of selling it, no use keeping an empty flat to lord over a town Eleanor has come to hate, even if it's an investment – they'll strip her of everything after this, if they find out – no they won't because she didn't kill them – it's so cold why is it cold it's May for God's sake–

And she's there, stumbling up the steps of the Radcliffe, some blurry-eyed third year groping at her coat as she walks in. There is carnage everywhere, but whether the bowls were turned over during revelry or the frantic search for an epi-pen, who can tell? Her mind is spinning – she needs to sit down – she needs to call, now –

"Phone," she chokes out, and then, when no one responds, repeats it louder. "Phone! Police! Help!"

Someone is there – it's Molly. Eleanor would recognise her red curls anywhere – pressing the phone against Eleanor's ear, and then, when Eleanor is unresponsive, talking to the operator herself. "Emergency? My friend just walked in, drunk out of her mind, saying she needs help... No, I'm not sure what happened... She wanted the police, but I don't know..."

"They fell off!" Eleanor screams, loud enough that Molly nearly drops the phone in shock. "They fell off – George and Henry and Cheyenne – God, Cheyenne..." She is sobbing now, loud enough that everyone around her in the lobby is staring, and it's all gone wrong, or perhaps it's all gone right, and she is so, so, drunk...

The sirens of the police car scatter all but the most dedicated revellers into the night. A tired-looking policewoman with a deadly serious expression on her face coaxes water into Eleanor while listening to her relate her story. Eleanor can't – or won't – say much: it's mostly a frenzied repeat of: "they fell". Eventually, she mentions "the castle", and a group of stony-faced officers discuss in hushed tones and begin to coordinate their next steps. They won't find anyone until dawn – but this is Scotland in the summer, and daylight is never far away.

She's too hysterical to have her statement taken now, so the police let her return to her room. She drifts in and out of sleep, trying to forget – or maybe to remember, so she can keep her wits about her. Her head hurts; her limbs are leaden: but those are just symptoms of a hangover, not guilt.

When she wakes from her last nap the police are almost all gone. The one hold back is an elderly officer in the corner, who occasionally looks up at his charge as he frowns at messages popping up on his phone.

"I'm going outside," Eleanor announces. "I need some fresh air."

The officer grunts. "Mind the cameras. The press are out there."

The words are meant to warn, but they send a warm flush through Eleanor's body. Paparazzi. Public image. This she knows how to do.

So, when she makes her way downstairs and collapses on the steps, her position is chosen carefully: a sobbing girl on the steps of a grand hotel, sobbing as she awaits the news of her beloved friends' demise.

7th May, 12:00.

17 hours after the party.

She was meant to be packed by now. Instead, everything is a haze: the police are in and out of her apartment, the frenzy below, the incessant pounding in her brain.

She didn't mean to push them. Or did she? She had thought about it, occasionally turned the idea over in the back of the mind, but that had been a sick fantasy, not actual intent. It happened in one moment: the heat of betrayal, the adrenaline rush, the threat of losing everything, the incessant craving for power. And they had been angry with her too. It wasn't as if it was unprovoked.

But for three people to be gone – to have left the world completely because of Eleanor – that sends Eleanor reeling. Yes, she'd had a thousand fantasies – ripping Cheyenne's throat out, laughing over George's grave – but they were only that. Most of the time she'd only felt regret whenever she thought of them.

You wanted this, her inner serpent whispered. *Now she's gone, she cannot mock you: can't parade her perfect friends and perfect family and perfect life. You've outshone her forever.* And isn't that what Eleanor wanted: for Cheyenne Leonsdale to forever be mentioned in the same breath as Eleanor Sanders?

A knock at the door breaks through the haze. Eleanor groans and shuffles to the door. She isn't sure if she can take more questioning: her mind is likely to melt.

It isn't the police. A young man stands in a navy-blue uniform, looking apologetic. He can't be much older than Eleanor, and her first thought is one of revulsion at herself. Here he is trying to save people, and she's pushing them into the sea. Then comes the nausea as she braces herself for what he's here for.

He introduces himself as Officer Rogers, calls her 'madam', and waits for Eleanor to invite him in. For a second, she stands frozen, before she forces her hands to usher him into the living room. His initial gaze around can't help but be tinged with awe, and despite herself she feels a rush of pride. Look at what she's built for herself. His little search and rescue can't come close.

For half a second, Eleanor's eyes flick to the painting on the mantelpiece. Cheyenne's shining eyes seem to stare at her accusingly. She swallows for courage.

"Well," he says, settling down on the sofa, "I'm sure you know why I'm here."

There are two options, one significantly worse for Eleanor than the other. If any of them are alive, Eleanor has to change her story fast, get her version in before the others destroy everything. But based on the solemn mood, the way Rogers rocks back and forth uneasily, Eleanor thinks she might be safe.

"We got the aerial search out as soon as it was light enough," he goes on, "and an hour ago we found something."

Something, not someone. She is alright.

"Who was it?" she breaks in, careful to let her voice waver.

He sighs. "Based on the descriptions given to us, we have reason to believe the body belongs to Henry Alcott. But in order to confirm, we need someone to identify..."

"Did it – he – have blonde hair?" Rogers nods an affirmative. "It's Henry."

"Miss Sanders, protocol demands an in-person identification..."

"Ask someone else!" It's not an act when her voice breaks and tears well in her eyes. "I don't want to see him. Not after I watched him fall." To face the corpse, its blank eyes staring accusingly at her: she is certain what remains of her brain would snap.

He swallows awkwardly, but eventually the pressure of a crying woman whose nails are still torn and dirty and who hasn't yet changed out of her party dress overwhelms him. "Do you know who would be able to step in?"

"Gina Daniels would do. Or Raquelle Gyan." Let them see that hated face one last time instead.

He excuses himself quickly after that. Eleanor slumps on the sofa until she is satisfied he is really gone, then steps up and strolls towards the window. The sea lies beneath her, as strong and steadfast as ever. It is Eleanor's. She is its own. That she ever thought it wouldn't protect her seems absurd.

She doesn't realise how long she's been standing there until she hears a cough behind her. Amy is standing in the doorway, a mop in her hand and her uniform wrinkled. "Room service," she announces. There is a trace of quiet sarcasm in her voice.

Eleanor slumps down over the railings. "I thought the staff were off today. After... all this." She gestures downwards at the street, clogged with police cars and news vans.

She shrugs. "This got me past the reporters and the caution tape," she says, gesturing to her uniform and name badge.

"Are you coming for Liz and Molly, or for yourself?" There's no malice in the question: Eleanor is too tired to even consider being bothered.

"They didn't think you'd want them."

"But you think you're different?"

"I just didn't think you'd have anyone at all." If anyone else – with the exception of Jack – had said that, Eleanor would have bristled. But here, with this girl she's known for less than a day, a strange calm overtakes her. Perhaps it doesn't matter, not after last night.

"Besides," Amy goes on, "if you don't want me, I'll just do the cleaning."

Eleanor's voice is hard and dry. "You know I don't want to talk about it."

Amy shrugs again. "Then I can just be here. It's not good for you, to be alone."

For half an hour, there is nothing but quiet. Just the sounds of Amy going around in a slow, methodical sweep of the room. Finally, she collapses down on the sofa next to Eleanor. "I never knew Cheyenne or Henry or George," she says at last. "But I know you were friends."

"Used to be friends." Dangerous, to profess this to this strange girl, but it's a story Gina and Raquelle are sure to tell anyway. "We had our fallouts. But this… we were getting back together. For a second, it all felt perfect. Like a fairy tale, or the end of a film."

"I'm sorry," Amy says. Hesitating, she adds, "it's not the same, not really, but there was a boy at my school who was killed in a road accident. Drunk driver. It was so awful afterwards. There was the funeral of course, and the memorial surface, but afterwards there was only a horrible empty space where he should have been. It played with your mind, seeing it every day."

She is so innocent, so bright-eyed and well-meaning. Eleanor might as well be back in California for all the ability she has to close the gulf between them.

"I could have fallen instead." It's a lame excuse, but it will help her if Amy is questioned. "We were all so close together, all of us so drunk… I could so easily have gone over the edge."

"You don't deserve it," Amy says definitely. "I mean, no one ever does, but Liz always liked you. I remember hearing her gasp when she saw that her roommate who'd gone on a study abroad had made it big."

"Don't flatter me. You don't need to."

"It's not flattery." Amy gives her a sad smile. "It gets better, Eleanor. I promise."

Eleanor tries not to take the words to heart. Amy doesn't know her, doesn't know what she's done. But when the other girl finally leaves, the emptiness of the flat becomes cloying and Eleanor can't shake the feeling a hole has been punched straight through her heart.

7th May, 13:21.

Eighteen hours after the party.

It is hunger that drives her out. She is nothing more than an animal anymore, reliant on base instincts for survival. Food. Water. Shelter. Safety.

Except she's not safe. Is she safe? If they find the bodies...

But her fridge is empty – she was meant to have been gone by now – and she cannot stomach another nut. She could call room service, but then she would risk seeing Amy. The police might deliver something, but she doesn't want their shuffling boots around her flat any more than necessary. Of course, there is nothing to find. Still, she won't take the risk.

The corner shop lies in the opposite direction of the sea – dangerous, for Eleanor to be leaving her protector, but mercifully away from bloated, battered bodies. It is five streets away, and almost immediately the cameras start. First are the reporters, still camped outside the hotel. The flash of their lenses is almost a comfort, it reminds her of Jack. Jack, who used to blush when he called them and try to shield her face; Jack, who loves the sea almost as much as she does, but loves the mountains more; Jack, whose face will twist up in horror when he hears what she has done.

Except she hasn't done anything. It was all an accident.

The reporters, mercifully, do not follow her. Unfortunately, they're replaced by the stares, the points, the phones. These people have faces, not mechanical lenses; these people have walked past her every day. Then she was the mysterious Eleanor Sanders, the glamorous Eleanor Sanders; before that she was the withdrawn Eleanor Sanders, the always-moping Eleanor Sanders; and before that she was Cheyenne Leonsdale's Eleanor Sanders. Now she is Eleanor Sanders, who might have killed someone. Eleanor Sanders, who lost her mind.

Let them talk, thinks Eleanor furiously. *Let them hide behind my back like the cowards they are.*

Unfortunately, they don't stay that way for long.

Eleanor has just walked out of the shop, clutching her groceries, when a fist collides with her face. She drops the bag in shock, kicks as she feels someone pushing her against a wall, winces as her arms are twisted painfully above her.

It's Cheyenne, she thinks. Cheyenne and George, who have survived and are taking their vengeance. There are three: even Henry then, miraculously reincarnated.

But the girl at her side has dark curls that corkscrew past her shoulders, and the girl glaring at her face wears a schoolgirl's bow.

"You little freak!" Raquelle's face is inches from Eleanor's; her teeth bared. If Eleanor had the strength to lean forward, she could rip her throat out, but she's still reeling from the shock. "You lured them to the castle on purpose, didn't you? You killed them! You hear me? You killed them!"

She hits Eleanor again, right in the nose. Eleanor hears a hideous crunch. She tries to cry out, but blood fills her mouth, choking her. This is what Cheyenne felt, she realises, and George and Henry, all of them drowning together as their faces were bashed in, the ocean a sea of blood around them–

Her hands are released. She drops to the ground, panting. It's only a moment before another hit comes, then a kick, and a series of stamps and slaps and screams. Now Sam towering above her. "Did you poison Gina?" he demands. "Did you try and kill her, too?"

It hurts so much she just wants to die – why isn't she dead yet? Is this her punishment, to wait life out through wave after wave of pain? Her fingers touch something damp, which could be anything from rain to saliva to her own blood, and Eleanor is content to die in a gutter, it's what she deserves anyway, if only it would come sooner.

Just as suddenly as it began, the assault stops. Eleanor briefly considers that she might be dead, but the pain is just as strong, if not stronger, than it was before. Are they going to draw it out further? Let her gain just enough strength for it all to be beaten out of her again?

"That's enough," a gruff voice demands. "What is the meaning of this?"

"She killed them!" Gina's voice has gone pitchy with rage and fear. "She killed our friends, and she tried to kill me! She's a psychopath, she always has been."

"That is a serious accusation. And even if it were true, you cannot just go around beating people up for revenge. These matters involve a court of law."

"She won't get done for shit in a court of law! She'll bat her eyelashes at you, and shed a few tears, and talk about how she's such a prosecuted little thing, and you'll let her go!"

"Miss, I'm afraid I'll have to take you in. You and your friends. This is unprovoked assault on a citizen."

"I'm telling you; she's guilty!"

"It's easier for all of us if you cooperate."

"I can't…"

That's the last thing Eleanor hears before more hands are touching her, lifting her even as she twists away with what little strength remains.

?????

Eleanor wakes in an empty white room. This could be death, she supposes. It isn't that bad. Almost comfortable, in its own strange way. Certainly peaceful, before she loses her mind.

A harsh beeping cuts through the silence, and she groans. Still alive.

A woman in a white uniform wanders in and smiles when she sees Eleanor awake, if not fully alert. "Eleanor Sanders?" she asks as she leans over her.

Eleanor nods.

"Can you speak for me?"

"A little."

"Try to drink some water." The nurse watches while she downs a whole glass. It tastes of blood. "Do you remember why you're here, Eleanor?"

She remembers plenty. She remembers the party, and the castle, and the sounds they made as they fell. She remembers the cameras, and the trip, and the impact of a fist–

"I bought tomatoes." She loves tomatoes: one of the few fruits that taste better in this country. "Did someone pick them up? And my bag – I love that bag. It's from LA…"

"The police returned your shopping to your flat." She consults her clipboard. "The penthouse at the Radcliffe, correct?"

"Not mine. Jack's really." She misses Jack. But he will be disgusted with her now.

"Jack Flannigan?" Even the nurse reads the news. Of course she does: that's what common people do. Eleanor nods and tries to look haughty, like someone famous and important. Her ribs hurt so much she doesn't suppose she manages it.

The nurse pauses, taps her pencil against her clipboard. "Do you remember what they said to you? The assailants: Raquelle Gyan, Gina Daniels, Sam Kissinger?"

"It was an accident!" Her breath is coming in short bursts. Perhaps she's already imprisoned. "Cheyenne pushed me; I didn't mean…" She stops herself. Already she has said too much.

The nurse raises an eyebrow. "They have been taken into custody for questioning."

"You can't believe them! They think I'm a psychopath. They say–"

She puts her palm up to stop Eleanor's rambling. "My job isn't to believe them or not. It's to assess you. And whether they're causing you enough distress that you need to remain here…"

"I saw three people die. If I need psychological assessment, it's for that."

Another scribble on the clipboard. "On the physical side, Miss Sanders, it looks bad, but it should heal without too much trouble. The broken nose was the worst of it, but there's also heavy bruising, especially on your face and ribs. You're not to touch it," she says quickly as Eleanor's hands drift towards her throbbing face. "When you can stand up, you're free to go home."

* * *

By the time Eleanor gets back onto the street it's seven in the evening, but the streets of Scotland are still light with summer sun. Her coat is bloody but otherwise unscathed: she wraps it around herself and tries to cover her face. It's not much use. Her infamy has only increased. The streets fall quiet when she passes and burst into conversation in her wake.

She has no desire to go back to the flat – not home, as the nurse said, not with its packed-up boxes and stain of guilt. Perhaps it never was home, but if so, neither was her flat with Molly and Liz, or her dorm room, or even her parents' house. Was Jack's house home? Not anymore.

So she goes to the sea, the one place that has always welcomed her. Her feet are one of the only parts of her unscathed, so she takes her shoes off and lets her toes sink into the sand. It's cold; it always is in Scotland. Her feet throb with the chill until they hurt along with the rest of her.

She walks the whole lengths of the beach, eyes fixed to the sand. She doesn't dare articulate what she is hoping to see, even as desire throbs within her heart. But every time a dark shape materialises on the horizon she gasps, and every time it reveals itself to be nothing more than a log she lets out a sigh of relief, and another of frustration.

She doesn't want to see their faces. But she wants to know they're dead.

She walks for hours, until the sun sinks beyond the hills to the west. In California the sun sets over the sea, turning it into a coral reef, all rosy pinks and delicate purples. Here the ocean is to the east, so as the sun sinks the ocean simply metamorphosises into a menacing black abyss. Anything could be hiding in there: millions of corpses, fish and whales and unfortunate humans, drowned or disposed of. It is a sinkhole, and it will relinquish nothing.

That night, as she tosses and turns and tries to sleep, Eleanor listens to the waves, trying in vain to work out what they're carrying.

8th May, 10.32.

Thirty-five hours after the party.

The ringing of the buzzer startles Eleanor awake. The doorman stopped letting the police just waltz on up yesterday afternoon, saying they had a reputation to maintain, and Eleanor has been mercifully free of visitors since then. She has yet to leave the building again. She hasn't yet figured out the story she wants to tell. She will wait, and watch, and make a splash when the time comes. And bring Gina, Raquelle, and Sam down at the same time.

As long as Cheyenne, George and Henry haven't been found alive, Eleanor tells herself, she is fine. And out of the two left, George is the only dangerous one: as far as Cheyenne is – was – concerned, her fall was accidental.

She paints the perfect look on her face – tired, perturbed, slightly shocked – only for it to fall away as soon as she opens the door. Her replacement expression is one of genuine confusion. "What are you doing here?"

Jack shrugs. "I came to see you. I'm just sorry it took so long – it's twelve hours from LA, and the planes leave at night–"

She pulls him inside.

It is odd to see him here: Jack and Scotland exist in such wholly different spheres in her mind that to witness them cross is disturbing. Here is a setting so removed from the sun-drenched slopes of LA: the bathroom where she cried tears of agony, the living room where she plotted revenge, the bedroom she fucked another girl in, the balcony where she paced in self-loathing. So many things he doesn't know about her. So many things she doesn't know about him.

"Eleanor." Jack brushes her face and sets off the throbbing in her nose. She winces away. "What happened?"

"Someone attacked me – Cheyenne's friends, but not mine. They've always hated me and they blame me and..."

Her hands are shaking. Jack notices, steps towards her, twines her fingers in his. "It's alright Eleanor," he whispers. "I'm here now."

"It's not alright." The quiver in her voice is real. "People are dead, Jack. People are dead, and everyone thinks I killed them!"

"Well, did you?"

His frankness stuns her. Out of all his reactions, she has not accounted for this. But Jack must have seen all sorts of things while she's been away. Has been to the seediest of places, been involved in the darkest of deals. But this is far greater than backroom drug dealing.

Cheyenne might have sent Eleanor running to California, but Jack has kept her there. He built a life for her, gave her a home, bestowed upon her fame and a reputation. If she scares him away – if she trusts him with the truth and he turns on her – then everything is ruined.

But if she tells him, and he doesn't run... If he understands...

"It was an accident," she says. "At least at first. But then they were all going to turn on me, so I..."

"And you haven't told anyone?" There's nothing accusatory in his gaze, only cold calculation.

Eleanor begins to soften. He doesn't hate her. It will be all right. Then, as she takes in the determination set across his face, she realises what she has done. Now she has confessed, she cannot take it back. Thick or thin, rain or shine, pain or joy, she is tied to Jack, or he could destroy her life as easily as he handed it to her.

She pulls him into the room as she bristles. "I'm not an idiot."

"Of course you're not." He fixes her with a scrutinising stare. "You know if you're caught, we're ruined. You of course, and me by association. Not to mention I'll be back on those fucking drugs within a month."

"I won't get caught. And you were never off the drugs"

"Of course you won't. And I will get off them, because we're getting married, Eleanor. Married. And then you'll write a string of blockbusters with lead roles tailor-made to me, and we'll live in perfect harmony with a clutch of adorable children."

"You've really thought this through."

"Because I need you!" His fists clench, and for a second Eleanor expects him to start tossing her furniture around the room. "I need you to write for me Eleanor! And to keep me clean! And I need you to love me!"

For all his flaws, he knows emotions. He's an actor, it's his trade. And he has always – with the exception of that one terrifying moment when he was high – been able to wrap Eleanor around his little finger.

He needs her. Doesn't it sound wonderful. *He* needs *her*. Power at last. Exchanged for a sword for him to dangle over her, a threat that if she ever leaves him, he will spill her confession. But why would she leave him? She is nothing without him; he is nothing without her. They have, in their twisting, tangled confusion, become one, bound together with the stains of blood under Jack's fingernails when he grabbed her, the mud on Eleanor after she returned from the castle.

If there is no Cheyenne, she needs someone else to fill her obsession. Jack has stepped in at the perfect time.

"Do you want some tea?" she finally offers. Calm, restful, English. Exactly the sort of thing he needs.

He blinks, seemingly shocked by the normalcy, but accepts. "Christ," he says after a while. "I need a hit."

"Well, you can't have one," snaps Eleanor. It is such a strange thing to say, a mirror of their previous, half-mundane life, so removed from the present, that Eleanor suddenly bursts into laughter. Jack follows a second later, and the crescendo of hilarity only swells to greater and greater heights.

Two people cackling after three have been killed. They're acting like typical movie-style murderers.

If Jack is to be a murderer, Eleanor reasoned, he needs the whole story. So she sits him down and tells him, in cold, clinical detail, the tale. There is no use getting wrapped up in emotion now and she doesn't share quite how deeply she felt for Cheyenne. Now is the time to plan.

"There's no concrete evidence," she says at last. "All three of them are certainly dead, and the scene of the... *incident* is too muddied for them to get any footage. Besides, I'm on camera and in front of a crowd of witnesses looking distraught. The most incriminating thing is the nuts, and even that can be played as a drunken mistake. After all, they were in my room, not at the party." It all sounds very cold when she says it out loud.

"But of course," she adds "I can't put anything about all this in my book."

"But it'll sell." Jack leans forward, eyes twinkling. "It'll sell like hotcakes, now you're at the centre of an investigation."

"And when it sells, it needs a good story..." Eleanor says, her thoughts whirring.

Jack blinks. "Well, stories are your forte."

"So it can't just be an accident." Eleanor sips her tea. "The narrative can't stay as it is. People will get suspicious; they'll say that Raquelle, Gina and Sam have a point. There's got to be something else."

Jack raises his teacup to his lips. "And what are you going to do about that?"

The gaze she fixes with him is as cold and solid as the rocks that buttress the bottoms of the sea cliffs. "You're an actor. I need to practice with you. Only then can we make it public."

The moratorium on police presence also means the crowd of reporters outside has fizzled out, so Eleanor has a little time before people start pointing and whispering. She grips Jack's hand, even though she isn't sure she needs it. What matters most is that people believe she is crumbling and he is there to support her. Nothing sells like a love story.

They are made to sit in a police station waiting room, cold and dreary. Eleanor isn't acting when her hands shake uncontrollably as she sips a paper cup of water. Now or never. There is no turning back. She chews the edge of the cup hard enough the paper starts to disintegrate.

"Miss Sanders?" An officer pokes her head out of a door and leads Eleanor to a windowless back room. She fidgets, shakes her leg, pictures Jack's face in her mind. His final promise of a life together, in a place where no one can touch them. Success and fame, made stronger by her soon-to-be bestselling memoir.

The officer returns, accompanied by a balding colleague. "Now, Miss Sanders," she says, settling down, "why did you want to come in today?"

Eleanor takes a breath. Now or never. "I came to tell the police I'm leaving for the USA. I can't stay here any longer, not after what's happened."

The officer raises an eyebrow. "Miss Sanders, you are aware the criminal investigation into the deaths of your friends is ongoing?"

"I was getting to that." She gulps, summons a few sobs. "I think I remembered something else that happened that night – only I'm not quite sure if it was real. We were so drunk, and it's all so confusing...'

"There, there love," the other officer says in a thick Scottish accent. He's fallen for it hook, line, and sinker. "Just do your best to remember."

Eleanor sniffs. "Well, it all started because I'm writing a book – a memoir, you see, about my life in the UK. My publicist told me to, you know – Americans think this place is just so interesting–"

"The other night, Miss Sanders?" the female officer butts in.

"Right. Well, George and Cheyenne and I: we were tight in our first year, but then we had a falling out. A terrible one, hurt me so much. And to tell you the truth, they don't come out of it looking very nice. But it's terribly important to my experience at university, so I thought I had to include it.

"So that night, I decide I have to tell them about it. Nothing too detailed, just a warning that I'm writing a memoir and at times there might be unflattering descriptions of them. I was a nervous wreck, but I got them alone and told them. They all seemed to take it well, so I didn't think anything of it. Then Cheyenne suggested we all go to the castle – she loves that place – so we decided to head there to get some fresh air, away from my party. I made sure everything was set before I left – restocking the food, checking the guests – but Gina must have eaten something with an allergen in it and collapsed on the floor. I found help and ran to catch George, Henry, and Cheyenne up, but they were almost at the castle.

"I had to admit, I was getting nervous. I wanted to turn back, to help Gina. But when Cheyenne found out that Gina was recovered, she wanted continue inside. There was alcohol, and we sat by the cliff edge and laughed, and for a second it was just like it used to be, and I was on top of the world.

"Cheyenne asked me if we could have a word over by the cliff edge, so I went with her: I thought she was going to apologise, and we would have a real heart-to-heart. But then something changed in her eyes. They went dark, and she grabbed my dress and started pulling me towards the cliff.

"I screamed. Henry came running right away. When he saw what had happened he was horrified. He screamed at Cheyenne to let me go and demanded to know what she was thinking. In the chaos she loosened her grip on me, and I shoved her to get away." Eleanor paused for dramatic effect. "She lost her balance and went over.

"Henry was in shock, and while he stood there George came running over. He started screaming at Henry about how stupid he was, that they needed to kill me or I was going to ruin his reputation. Henry didn't believe him. They argued, and there was a tussle – and I was drunk; I couldn't really follow – but in the end, George went over too.

"I was left, shell-shocked as you can imagine, and Henry, who just sent George plummeting to his death. He was in shock too, he clearly couldn't believe it, and kept wandering over to the edge, calling for Cheyenne. He kept getting closer, desperate for an answer, and then he was gone." Eleanor gulps. "I don't know whether he slipped or jumped.

"The rest happened as I said earlier. I dropped my phone, so I stumbled back home to call for help. But I was so drunk: no one was listening on the street. By the time I finally got the police on the phone, I was so shocked, so confused, that I wasn't sure if what I had seen was right or if I'd only imagined it. But now, when I'm sober – I think that must have been the truth."

For a moment, silence reigns in the interrogation room. Then the officer sighs. "You realise," she says, "this is a serious accusation."

"I know." Eleanor allows her voice to waver. "But I can't spend my life keeping this to myself. People – people need to know." A few sobs, and then she fully breaks down, head in her hands, tear-stained cheeks, even all-out wailing. The officers sit awkwardly until Eleanor finally turns her head up to expose her puffy eyes. "I want to go home."

"We'll get you home," the older officer coos. He turns to his colleague. "We've got her testimony on tape. Surely she's free to go?"

The woman frowns, but nods. "If there's a court case, you will have to return. Even if you're in the US."

"But there won't be." The officer pats Eleanor on the arm the way you would comfort a distraught cat. "It was an accidental death: involuntary manslaughter and self-defence at best. There's no proof but her testimony, and she just admitted that she accidentally shoved one over, which is more guilt than she had before. The friends that think she was guilty assaulted her on the street: they're unstable at best. The families might press for an prosecution, but they won't get a verdict."

"My boyfriend has a team of lawyers," Eleanor brakes in. "From LA. Could they represent me remotely, if it came to that?" She is still sniffling, but the mention of American money gives the officers additional pause.

"I'm sure you won't need it pet," the man assures. "But We can make a foreign lawyer work. No problem at all."

Eleanor continues to sniff beautifully as they escort her out; sheds a few pretty tears as she and Jack walk past the cameras down the street. If anyone notices the squeeze between palms, they will think of it as nothing more than a comforting gesture. But to Jack, it communicates everything. Success. They will be alright.

10th May. 11:00.

Four days after the party.

The memorial service is held in the town church, somewhere Eleanor has never set foot before. It's a grand place, with towering stained-glass windows, but centuries of candle-lit sermons have rendered the walls soot-stained and dreary. Seagulls squawk outside as mourners shuffle in. If Eleanor focuses, she can hear the crash of waves. The sea is never far away from the dead.

She had no desire to go. Henry's body may not be here – still in the morgue under investigation – but the granite plaques surrounded by flowers she's staring at now feel no less accusing. But she has to be seen, and be seen crying. Must look the part of the distressed, innocent girl.

On her right, Mrs Leonsdale gives Eleanor's arm what is meant to be a comforting squeeze, but comes off like the steady constriction of a vice. Cheyenne's parents flew in yesterday and met Eleanor earlier this morning, where Mrs Leonsdale spent the whole time sobbing gently and hugging Eleanor.

Mr Leonsdale was more stoic. "You were always such a good friend," he said, but his voice was icy.

"Don't mind him," Mrs Leonsdale murmured when he left the room. "He's looking for someone to blame. He still hasn't accepted that she's... you know." Eleanor wasn't sure she'd accepted it either.

Back in the church, every fibre of Eleanor's body is afire with anguish. It might have been an accident, but the guilt clings to her all the same. *I killed your daughter!* she wants to scream. *I pushed her over the edge!* Instead she only bursts into tears, and Jack, apologetic, lets her bury her face in his jacket.

It's good, Eleanor reminds herself. Looking distraught is exactly what the police, the students, the cameras are looking for.

On the other side of the aisle, in the row behind Eleanor, Raquelle, Gina, and Sam sit. Gina is sobbing fetchingly, Sam looks stony, and Raquelle is glaring daggers in Eleanor's direction when she thinks no one is looking. Raquelle went to the police station the night before to argue Eleanor's guilt, but was shooed away. The whole town saw her storming out, red-faced.

The priest drones on and on.

Seagulls again, outside the window. Seagulls and sea lions and waves, one great thunder, the inevitable ushering of life and death and rebirth.

Cheyenne is out there somewhere. George too. Floating along the briny depths, their eyes loose from their sockets, fish nibbling at flakes of their skin. Soon they'll sink, and eels will pick at their bones.

George's paintings looked like butterflies. None of those, under the sea. A seahorse, if he's lucky, but it isn't the same. No air for him to float through. His only work sits on her wall, screaming accusations of guilt at her every time she looks at it. Already her eyes glaze over when she looks in its direction. There'll be nothing left of him soon.

Cheyenne on her bed, sprawled out and laughing. She will never crack a joke again, never fall back overcome with mirth. Never look at Eleanor and smile softly like she did at the beach, on the hill, down in Nice, all those magical, wonderful hours. Now that blonde hair fans out around her as she floats like a mermaid, a siren, the beautiful thing that lures sailors to their doom.

No, not blonde: her final revelation was that she dyed it. Perhaps the colour has leeched out by now, transforming that lively face into something dark and wan. The bones jutting like Penelope, the eyes vicious like Eleanor's.

She is dead and gone, lady, dead and gone. Hamlet, Act 4, Scene 5. Now there was a good script: something weighty, about death. Water in it too: beautiful, drowned girls. So much accidental death: how fitting. And at the end, all the actors strewn over the stage as corpses.

The crowd is moving now, the whole affair finally over. Eleanor grips Jack's hand as if her life depends on it, lets him usher her out into the light. It is so crowded, a frenzy she hasn't seen since her party. And here are all the same people. There's Kevin Mills, pushed into the punch bowl after she kissed him. Emily Usher, who got into a fight with a first year over alcohol. Over there is Molly, to her right is Noelle. And in the distance, rounding the corner, a flash of blonde hair.

Eleanor's heart jumps to her throat. What a trick to play! Attending your own memorial, hearing all the nice things people had to pretend to believe about you. Seeing the sobbing Eleanor and getting ready to burst her charade moments later. Why hasn't she come forward yet?

Maybe, she thinks, just maybe, because she still loves Eleanor too much. Because a plunge in the sea had awakened the memory of that morning in Nice.

Oh, Cheyenne.

With surprising strength, Eleanor wrests herself free of Jack's grip. She plunges into the crowd, pushing past that group, tripping over him, knocking over her. She cannot lose sight of that hair.

"Cheyenne!" she calls. "Cheyenne! I'm here!"

Down the side streets, the crowd parting like the Red Sea. Around the corner to the central street, where a relief of St Andrew on the cross lies preserved from the Middle Ages. All the way down, until she careens to a stop before the girl who is standing, shell-shocked, in the middle of the square.

Eleanor knows her. Or recognises her, at least. It is some girl who studies English, who she used to see at nightclubs. Pretty enough, but nothing remarkable. Her best feature is that lovely, blonde hair.

"I'm sorry," Eleanor croaks out. "I thought you were someone else."

The girl says nothing, only gives Eleanor a look that could be fear, disgust, or pity. Eleanor can't decide which option she loathes more.

"Eleanor!" This is Jack, running breathless up the street towards her. "Eleanor, are you alright?"

"I just thought I saw her," Eleanor replies. "You know what it's like."

Of course he doesn't know. How could he be expected to? He knows what it is like to kill the girl you loved no more than she knows how it feels to pump a toxic cocktail into your body surrounded by the stars of the day, to stumble home to empty bottle after empty bottle. How ridiculous, to ask if she's alright. As if she will ever be again.

Jack looks around nervously at the growing crowd of onlookers. "Let's go."

They say little to each other all evening. Eleanor stands by the window and looks out, watching the sea, the stars, the people. Most of all the young ones, the students, the same ones who were at the memorial this morning, now out and frolicking once again. Is this what she once was? Before things had soured, when she could still pretend Cheyenne was hers?

They are very high, up here. So far removed, physically and mentally.

Once, in the forties, a woman had jumped off the Empire State Building. She landed in a car, face up, her hair still perfect, her makeup intact. The beautiful suicide. But there was no helpful car to wait for Eleanor below, no artful backdrop to hide her crumpled body. To fall here would be to break herself beyond recognition, to expose her flesh for everyone to see. How sordid it all seems.

In contrast, there is the sea. From this distance, calm and unyielding as ever. That's where Cheyenne is, existing in a state of flux. Schrodinger's cat, though Schrodinger himself had hated that philosophy, said it was impossible. Eleanor hates the idea too, when it describes someone else. But she has to admit there is a certain romance to not knowing. As long as the cat is sealed in the box, people can wonder. People don't have to view the cat's desiccated corpse.

She turns trancelike, as if this whole thing has been a dream. "Eleanor?" Jack calls from the other room, but she doesn't seem to hear him.

"Going swimming," she mutters at last, when he doesn't let up.

It's a journey she's made so many times she might as well be unconscious. Down the stairs, the carpet still salt-stained from her endless trips. Across the road, where hordes of revellers are enjoying the late evening sunlight. Down to the beach, where she strips off her shoes, then closer to the water, where she discards her top and trousers. Not quite naked: that would be unseemly.

She is too acclimatised to the shock of the cold to gasp. Instead she simply wades, unseeing, unfeeling, into the depths. It feels like a sinister hug, a welcome back, welcome home. Her stride is sure and steady as she wades deeper and deeper, until her feet leave the ground.

Human instinct is to swim, not sink. How did Cheyenne feel, she wonders, how did George react, when they were pulled under? She supposes the shock of the impact must have hurt them, as would the waves. Now all is still, calm, innocent. What a lovely place to die.

But try as she might, she cannot stop paddling. Now there is rage in her, a kind of defiant strength. Let them see how Eleanor Sanders fought. Let her paddle herself to exhaustion before finally sinking into the murky depths.

She is breathing heavily when she feels the tendrils wrap around her leg. Cold, slender, creeping: the fingers of a long-dead hand. Here they are at last, coming to force her to join them. Are they angry, she wonders? Will they rip her to shreds? Or will it simply be another calm embrace, as Cheyenne wraps her in a kiss and forces water into her lungs?

Oh Cheyenne. Cheyenne, Cheyenne, Cheyenne.

It's lovely and cool here. This is a good spot, a good moment.

She wonders what Jack will say about her. What Raquelle will.

Poor Jack. He's already so fragile. This will send him spiralling. But there will be another girl, Eleanor tells herself. Another aspiring writer, or better yet, an actress just like him, someone who can sparkle.

Eleanor's here. She's coming for Cheyenne. She's ready.

Hands on her shoulders, heaving her – but from the wrong direction. Eleanor freezes in shock, then starts to thrash, push, hack – that's the water, being coughed out of her lungs. She lies on something firm yet rocky, soothing her with the motion of the waves.

"Eleanor!" says a familiar voice. "Eleanor, can you hear me?"

Her first thought is that Jack had followed her, he is on his surfboard and they are back in Los Angeles, and there are jobs and fame and opportunities and Cheyenne is an ocean away. Then the voice calls her name again, and she is snapped from her delirium. "Kirstie?"

"Are you okay?" Kirsty is the picture of concern, straddling the surfboard as she lays a hand on Eleanor's forehead. "You're shaking."

"Cheyenne, George – they were dragging me. I need to go – Cheyenne – it was their fingers!"

"Piece of seaweed," Kirstie says matter-of-factly. "You need to watch out for those."

"I don't..."

"You shouldn't be out here. Not in your state."

"But..."

Kirstie listens to no protests as she paddles back to shore. After a while, Eleanor relents, content to lie there and watch the waves lap against her feet, letting Kirstie carry her up the sand and help her back into her clothes. She walks her all the way to the back door of the Radcliffe, where she hesitates. "Is your boyfriend up there?" Eleanor flinches at the word.

"He should be."

Kirstie stares up at the penthouse with an unreadable expression. "You be careful, Eleanor Sanders. Make sure he's watching out for you."

The stumble up the stairs is slow. When Eleanor finally enters the room, Jack is at her side in a heartbeat, propping her up, offering her a glass of water. She shrugs it all off and staggers forward mutely. It is only when she collapses on her bed that Eleanor begins to sob.

Jack says nothing. What is it that can be said? Instead he lies next to her and envelops his body in hers. It is somehow more intimate than anything they have ever done before, more radical than the endless nights she traced every contour of Jack's body. In the connection, the musky smell of sweat and fear and pain and love, there is the assurance that they are together. That they will be alright.

January.

Eight months after the party

Eleanor Flannigan stares out across the Pacific Ocean as the waves lick at her toes. What a privilege, she thinks, to be able to watch the sun set over the sea. Back in Scotland, she could only see it rise: just the beginning of another hateful day in that hateful town.

She saw it for the last time only two months ago, when the final court proceedings cleared. Eleanor stood in the dock and sobbed as she delivered her statement. "Cheyenne and I... we were the best of friends as soon as we first laid eyes upon each other. We had our differences, our fights, but it was the sort of passion that only love could produce. We had finally started to make up, and that night was to be our final hurrah in the town, a place to reclaim those lost years. Instead, she, as well as her loving boyfriend and our other friend, were cruelly snatched from us through a terrible accident. It is the most unjust of circumstances." Even though there were no cameras, she cried very prettily. Thankfully the courtroom artist managed to get a good side profile that showcased the tears flowing down her cheeks.

She flew back to LA as soon as she testified at the inquest: a brief, no-nonsense affair that was nothing more than the routine investigation into a terrible tragedy. Eleanor was young, pretty, and innocent-looking; she had covered up the evidence well; and, true to his word, Jack's American lawyers were very good. Plus, when he showed up to escort her to and from the courthouse, his very appearance garnered interest, which created images of the crying girl on his arm, which invoked sympathy. Now she spends her days writing, watching Jack work, and heading to parties.

And what parties she is going to. Tonight, the premiere of her film at Sundance. A week tonight, the Oscars. Eleanor's script isn't eligible to be nominated this year, but Jack's acting is. Just as Eleanor predicted, he isn't enough of a heavy-weight to be up for best actor, but he is in the running for best supporting.

Someone will take her film there. She wonders if Molly will see it, if she will remember her as the girl from swimming she lived with once, the one who wanted to be a writer. Or if she will see some broken shell, witness of too much horror for any one person to handle, redeemed only by being Jack Flannigan's wife.

They married last month, as soon as the inquest was completely wrapped up. Why wait? It's not as if they will ever split up now: not after what Jack knows. She will stay or he will destroy her. And if he is ever tempted to stray, he will remember that Eleanor has already committed murder once. Or thrice, depending on how you count. So, there is nothing for them but days spent pressed together on the bed, minds on different sides of the world. Afternoons typing in the living room while the Los Angeles sun highlights the dust motes twirling around her head like an angel. Dinner and drinks with friends who won't think twice about covering the bill. One day, there will be the children, and the pets – not a dog though. Maybe a cat, like Calypso and Sappho. They can call theirs Circe and the cats will be sisters – and life will be perfectly, horribly nice. Just like Cheyenne's would be, if she weren't dead.

She thinks of Cheyenne often. Mostly while staring at the sea, either from the sand or the balcony of the beach bungalow in Malibu Jack bought her. There's barely any furniture in this one either – Jack claims he would only destroy it while high. Eleanor isn't so sure – he's been doped up less frequently since Scotland. Perhaps having death so close shook some sense into him. Or perhaps he just feels the need to be there for her.

There is no one there for Cheyenne. George, perhaps, but he isn't there in the same way Henry would have been. But they pulled Henry out, lay his battered body on a slab, and shoved him into the ground. How cruel not to let them sink into oblivion forever.

Eleanor wrote his parents a letter, after the funeral. She didn't go to the thing, of course. She had no desire to see his polo friends and weeping sister, let alone Raquelle, Sam, and Gina. So she wrote a real letter, on scented paper Jack said some actress always used, saying Henry had been extremely daring in trying to rescue Cheyenne. "A tragic accident," the letter read, "that displayed the passion and integrity of young love."

If Cheyenne is alone, does that mean she's lonely? Is she vengeful, out there still and waiting for Eleanor? Has she floated all across the globe and returned to her hometown because she knows that's where she'll find her?

If only there was a body. If only Eleanor knew. But she doesn't want Cheyenne pulled out: something within her feels Cheyenne deserves the sea. One last gift from Eleanor, a fatal token of her love.

Sometimes Eleanor thinks of walking in again, of holding her breath and simply refusing to surface. There is no Kirstie around to save her this time. Even Raquelle's done it, or something close enough: Eleanor got the news two weeks ago; a message from Liz on the old social media accounts she can't bring herself to delete. They had to pump her stomach. Now she's back at her parents' house, floundering like a toddler. Gina's on her way out too, starving away somewhere until she's skin and bones. The Penelope Hale style is very chic, but it's a long, difficult way to go. Drowning is easier. Should be easier.

It's the thought of Jack that stops her. If he can't find purpose in quelling her nightmares, who's to say he won't fall into the abyss again too? He claims there aren't any drugs in the house other than alcohol – and even then, just one bottle of champagne. Eleanor still isn't sure if she should believe him. In a perfect world, he would act only for the cameras, but their lives are far from that idyll.

Instead, when she gets that horrible feeling, she stares at the painting she hung on the wall: a beach scene, with two girls wading further into the sea. A viewer in the right mindset could imagine they'll never stop – they'll simply let the water close over their heads and vanish into the abyss together. A viewer with context of the painting's creation would tell you that one of the girls has already made the journey, she's merely waiting for her companion to join her.

"Are you sure you don't want to get rid of it?" Jack asked one afternoon. He had come across Eleanor standing by the wall, head tilted in contemplation as she stared at the strokes of paint. "It can't be good for you to remember."

"It's even worse for me to forget," Eleanor replies.

Everyone in LA says she should go to therapy. "It's good for you," says some singer over the bar once when pressing Eleanor about the inquest ("totally sick," according to her). "Really helped me work through my shit."

"Or you could just explore it, you know, within you," advises a comedian. "Always works for me." But they get all their self-deprecation out onstage, while Eleanor isn't eager to confess to murder in front of a crowd of people.

Her book, which sold well, admits only to the official story. There are few juicy secrets about her time at uni – other than some gripes about the budget of the swim team – and all the snide comments about Cheyenne were thrown out in favour of a sappy tale of friendship. Which it was, from one angle.

Besides, Penelope's already beaten her to the really dramatic stuff. Her album came out before Christmas, packed with heartfelt anthems about losing friends. The song Eleanor heard that night at her house is there, though now the girl she's singing about actually dies at the end. There's also a haunting cover of *My Darling Clementine*, with Penelope lingering and luxuriating in the descriptions of the drowning girl. It comes on the radio often, and Eleanor can't bear to listen to it. She bought a copy of the vinyl though, to show Penelope when she comes over. This is happening more and more, since Penelope can't be alone too much in case she starts to relapse. She's supposed to have supervision for every meal. Eleanor's around enough that Penelope wants her to help write something for her next album.

"You can even sing backing vocals," she says with a smile one evening. They are lying on Penelope's patio, playing with Sappho and Calypso; the kitten mews in seeming agreement. "You don't have to sing that well: God knows I don't."

"Don't say that about yourself," Eleanor says without thinking.

"Why not? It's true." Penelope shrugs. "I've just managed to convince everyone to overlook that fact because they like my words enough."

"Why didn't you become a poet?"

"Same reason you didn't become an author. I like money." Something hard lurks beneath the surface of her voice, a steely determination, and Eleanor wonders, not for the first time, if what Cheyenne said about Penelope tossing books and desks at her is true. Penelope has never let on one way or another, but since that first drunken meeting everything about Cheyenne is kept deeply under wraps. On the other hand, that means Penelope never asks about what happened that night in the castle.

Not that Eleanor doubts for a second Penelope has guessed. She's clever enough, but more importantly, in another life it could have been Penelope over that cliff, with Cheyenne at the other end. Or wait twenty years and Cheyenne might still have ended up dead, but it would have been Penelope who'd been desperate to kiss her. Strange, how these things cycle around through the years.

Spurred by Penelope's suggestion, Eleanor has started to sing. She practices in the lazy afternoons, when heat bakes the pavements and sends people scurrying inside to turn on their fans and shut the windows. She practices simple tunes: nursery rhymes, really. Jack finds them delightful, especially the ones they don't have in America. Yet when she moves on to funeral dirges, his brow begins to furrow.

"It's for Penelope," she protests, when he comes up behind her and squeezes her wrist: a silent command to stop filling the house with sorrow.

"No, it's not." His eyes are a dark pool of concern. "It's for *her*. Surely you don't need to remember that?"

But she does. She has to remember.

Maybe Eleanor *will* write a film about it. Something twisty, with deep explorations of the human psyche. A measured view of the situation, through a distant, detached lens. She will have to give it fifty years, let everything settle, but as her life winds down maybe no one would have the heart to think about it too closely. She can even write some part for an aged Jack, maybe a kind-hearted lecturer, or a wise grandparent. He'll like that.

Speaking of Jack, here he comes. Swim trunks on and board slung over his shoulder. He flashes Eleanor a smile as he fastens the tether around his ankle. "You want a go?" British slang; he is so like Cheyenne in some ways. So different in the important ones though – he has chosen California.

She rarely surfs. It reminds her too much of Kirstie: both sleeping with her and being rescued. But he looks so happy, and she is suddenly reminded of the first day they spent together, when he took her to the beach.

Eleanor reaches out a hand. "Only if you take me."

He laughs, and they paddle out together: Jack on the board and Eleanor hanging onto the side. It is only when they've reached the break that they finally switch. Jack helps Eleanor on the board and holds her tight. "Are you ready?"

She nods. "Alright."

And they are flying, Jack's arms around Eleanor, guiding her over the sea. The waves lead them to shore and the board keeps them afloat, a bubble of safety, separating the living from the dead lost down below. Two sides of a life, below and forgotten, and above and waiting to be seized.

Eleanor can't bring herself to forgive the blood on her hands. But if a murderer wants to live freely, then forget the murder they must.

That night, when she watches her film, Eleanor doesn't think of Cheyenne once. Her parents have put a memoriam in the credits, and she sheds a picture-perfect tear, but as the drinks flow and the praise comes in, Eleanor lets the blonde fall from her mind. The world is hers to seize. Let the dead sink deep below.

George, at least, is easy to forget. There was nothing for him: a funeral yes, but no grand show, no final exhibition. All those paintings vanished, a thousand butterfly wings shredded. Eleanor asked his parents, haltingly, about him at the wake. The parents said nothing, too lost in their grief and anger: just as George had been, Eleanor thought bitterly. It was his sobbing sister who told her he had never worked again since that awful accident destroyed his paintings.

Yes, Eleanor agreed. Such a terrible flood they had that winter.

They sold the penthouse the same day as the funeral: it went for at least thrice its value. Who wouldn't want the house where Eleanor Sanders, screenwriter, trophy wife extraordinaire, and possible murderess, lured Cheyenne Leonsdale, heir to her parents' Hollywood empire, for her sinister wiles? Eleanor has read the theories, seen the articles. There are rumours she had a torture chamber up there, others say the whips and chains were for more salacious purposes. At least the managers will get money. Plus, Amy quit, so she won't have to clean it.

Eleanor saw a photo of Amy when she lay awake one night, stalking Liz's social media. They were on a beach together with another girl Eleanor had never seen before, whose arms were wrapped around Amy. She leaned in for a kiss while Amy laughed. A dog ran around their feet. A wave crashed behind them. The sun shone.

The post had 65 likes. The video of Eleanor walking to the courthouse has been viewed more than half a million times. A picture of her tonight, on the red carpet, will surely rack up even more.

She and Jack don't return home until the early hours of morning. He is all over her, unusually aggressive: perhaps it's the rub of, for once, being stuck on the sidelines while his spouse gets all the attention. He is on top of her when he leans in. "Do you still love her?"

Eleanor flinches. "What?"

"You killed her. But you loved her too. Do you still love her?"

For a moment, she isn't sure what to say. When she finally speaks it is slow, cautious, a strenuous shift through the muddy silt of her mind. "I loved her. And I hated her. And I want to remember the emotions of her, but not the act. It's the latter that makes me so guilty."

"Then forget the act," Jack implores. "Put the emotions in the work, but the rest? Forget it. And–" he leans in closer – "love me."

It is the only direct command he has ever given her. Cheyenne spat out dozens. Who is Eleanor to deny him?

So she loves Jack, and she loves her siren bride gone down below. And Eleanor forgets there was ever a castle, or a smashed glass, or a kiss, and remembers only the heady joy of Nice, the thrill of LA, the soft caress of grass atop a hill, the grip of a hand on her arm as she waded into the sea.

If anyone asks, Cheyenne Leonsdale died tragically but peacefully in the ocean. If Eleanor looks out, she can still see her there, beckoning. But Cheyenne is a patient creature: she can wait for Eleanor. And Eleanor still has a whole life ahead of her to seize.

ACKNOWLEDGEMENTS

Writing a book is a long process. Looking back, even the author can take for granted the months and years of drafts, edits, revision, first passes, second passes, and last-minute tweaks, and just see the final book on the shelves. But there are a few people who have made all of this a lot easier.

First of all, thank you to my family: to Zeph and Athena-Tyche, and to Mum and Dad. You've made me smile since day one.

Thank you to Natalie Barracliffe, my amazing agent, who's been with this book since the very beginning. You can't imagine how much I screamed with happiness after I hung up the phone on our first call. Thank you for taking a chance on me.

To my not one, but two, amazing editors, Desola Coker and Gemma Creffield. Thank you for believing in this novel and giving it your time and attention. Thank you also to Ella Chappell, Raeesa Saint, Gemma Barder, Caroline Lambe, Christiana Spens, April Northall, Hayley Moss, and the rest of the team and Datura Books.

Thank you to the teaching staff at the University of St Andrews: this book wouldn't have come about without all the support and friendship you have given me. Thank you also to my teachers in grade school, who never gave up on me even when I was a nightmare.

Thank you also to the wonderful bookshops near St Andrews for supporting me and Siren, especially Topping and Company and Waterstones. A huge thanks to Murray and Jack, my faithless advocates on the inside.

And thanks most of all to the students at St Andrews: to the ones who hosted weddings at Castle Sands and stayed out far too late at Aikman's. This book quite simply would not exist without you. Though (I hope) none of you have murdered anyone yet, nor have relationships quite as dysfunctional as the ones in Siren, I hope you have found something of the spirit of the town you love in this book. Thank you especially to Murray, Sam, Delara, Olivia, Jonah, Mathilda, Nathaniel, Issy, Laura, Arielle, Ben, Amelia, Amber, Mara, Indiana, Evelyn, and all the rest of you.

DATURA BOOKS
catering to the armchair detective, budding codebreakers, the repeat offender and an emerging younger readership.

Check out our website at www.daturabooks.com to see our entire catalogue.

Follow us on social media:
X (formerly Twitter) @daturabooks
Instagram @daturabooks
TikTok @daturabooks